1

METRONOME

METRONOME

TOM WATSON

BLOOMSBURY PUBLISHING
LONDON • OXFORD • NEW YORK • NEW DELHI • SYDNEY

BLOOMSBURY PUBLISHING
Bloomsbury Publishing Plc
50 Bedford Square, London, WC1B 3DP, UK
29 Earlsfort Terrace, Dublin 2, Ireland

BLOOMSBURY, BLOOMSBURY PUBLISHING and the Diana logo
are trademarks of Bloomsbury Publishing Plc

First published in Great Britain 2022

A catalogue record for this book is available from the British Library

ISBN: HB: 978-1-5266-3954-7; TPB: 978-1-5266-3955-4;
GOLDSBORO SPECIAL EDITION: 978-1-5266-5445-8;
EBOOK: 978-1-5266-3957-8; EPDF: 978-1-5266-3959-2

2 4 6 8 10 9 7 5 3

Typeset by Integra Software Services Pvt. Ltd.
Printed and bound in Great Britain by CPI Group (UK) Ltd, Croydon CR0 4YY

To find out more about our authors and books visit www.bloomsbury.com
and sign up for our newsletters

For Jen

Sheep

A INA STANDS AT THE sink, drying the dishes from lunch. It is a bright day, warm for March, and shadows of cloud dapple the headland. The back door is open. On the step, Whitney's boots are thick with mud; he has been up in the field this morning, but for the last hour he has been clanging about in his studio. There is a sculpture he is hoping to finish, a series of figurines composed of things that have washed up on the beach through the years.

She inhales slowly and the clanging halts. The undulation of the waves becomes a soft unhurried rush, and the lull between each grows longer. When she looks up, she sees a large cloud passing over the croft, blocking out the sun.

Whitney whispers to her from outside. 'Aina. Come quick.'

From the back door, she sees him standing by the out-house, slowly wiping his hands on a grease-ridden cloth. He is looking up the path, towards the gate. Something moves. She did not see it before: a wobbling tangle of fleece with dried clumps of green stuck to its rear.

'What the Jesus is that?' she says.

'A sheep is what it is.'

'I can see that.'

The sheep stares at her and chews, moving its mouth slowly from side to side.

'Distract it,' says Whitney. 'I'll get the gate.'

She waves her arms and approaches. The sheep stops chewing. The stringy end of a carrot droops from its mouth. She takes another step, and the sheep lopes off down the side of the croft.

While Whitney goes to secure the gate, she hurries inside, rummaging in the cupboard for the speargun. When she steps back into the garden, the sun is shining once more.

He stops short when he sees her.

'You can't,' he says.

She slides the harpoon down the barrel and twists it into place. 'Can't what?'

'You can't shoot it.'

She thinks he must be joking, but he moves to intercept her.

'It might belong to someone,' he says.

She looks from the beach to the headland and up across the moor. 'And who might that be?'

'Aina—'

She pulls the stock tight to her ribs and lines up a shot over Whitney's shoulder. 'It's only a sheep,' she says.

He steps forward, palms outstretched, fingers splayed. The wind whips strands of his greying hair about his face.

'Think about it, Aina.'

'I am thinking.' She takes a step towards him. 'I'm thinking roast mutton with mint and potatoes. Barley broth. Mutton with oatcakes.'

Her words do not seem to have any effect.

'Think long term,' he says.

She stops. 'Long term? Parole's in a week, what does it matter?'

'For whoever comes next. The garden could use some manure.'

She looks about at the detritus of old projects and innovations; his failed attempts to make things grow.

'Manure?' she says.

'It's a more sustainable approach.'

'And what do you suppose it'll eat?'

'Gorse. Heather. Grass if need be. Come on, where's the harm?' He clasps his hands together and when he smiles he looks just like Maxime.

'I suppose it is only a week.'

'Right.'

'Until the Warden comes.'

'Right.'

'Then it's someone else's problem ...'

He nods.

She thinks for a moment and lowers the gun. 'You're feeding it. You're cleaning it. That's on you.'

'Of course,' he says.

She crouches beside the animal, placing her hand on its heaving flank. The sun glints off the hard sea. 'Where do you think it came from?'

'I don't know,' he says. 'Maybe it swam.'

'Maybe,' she says, unconvinced. 'Do sheep swim?'

2

Croft

THE FRONT DOOR is so warped that it takes all of Aina's strength to open. Both hands on the handle, she hears the jamb crack and something gives. She heaves, stumbles backwards, and the door swings in, rebounding off the wall. Everything beyond is a rectangle of white. Her eyes adjust. The corrosive sea air has left the door faded, blue paint peeling. In the distance, down on the beach, the waves break calmly in thin, orderly strips. The wind, the very reason she prefers the door closed, is barely a breeze, and the croft needs airing. She wedges the door open, returns to the kitchen and sips a cup of water. She will knock up some plaster for the dented wall in a minute; it shouldn't take long.

The layout of the croft is simple. Three rooms downstairs: a bathroom, a kitchen and a small living room that they call 'the nook'. Off the kitchen is a larder, where she keeps a small store of supplies – scratchings, really. A thinning selection of wares sit neatly on upcycled shelves. Pickles, a tub of oats and a prized tin of tuna, which she has set aside as a welcome gift for whoever is sent next to Long Sky Croft. In the floor of the larder, there is a trapdoor which leads downstairs to a cellar. A second flight of stairs leads up, via a tall cupboard door in the kitchen, to a long narrow attic with bare floorboards and two single beds.

They spend most of their time in the kitchen, since it is the easiest of the rooms to heat. And though the rooms are compact and few in number, they have taken her all afternoon to clean. She has gone top to bottom, beating curtains, dusting sills, sweeping the stairs and the brickwork behind the fire. She has mopped the flagstones, polished the sinks and the taps, and, in an attempt to get a shine out of things that do not ordinarily shine, she has worn the cloth so thin that it could pass for a veil.

It is only fair that they leave the croft in a manageable state. Whitney is right on that front.

Her hands are raw from scrubbing. Knuckles bruised. Even the pill clock gleams. Its casing, some kind of composite, resistant to heat, is criss-crossed with scratches from their attempts to force it open. Years of pointless endeavour, blunting claw hammers as they excavated parts of the cellar, trying to work out the exact dimensions of the clock. All without success. They will leave not knowing how deep it sits within the croft's foundations, or for how long it might keep releasing pills, every eight hours on the hour: 6 a.m., 2 p.m. and 10 p.m.

Their tether. Their leash. A constant metronome, ticking away, keeping them in check.

Whitney has left a book open on the table, the gardener's manual, brought to the croft by a predecessor. It is well used, a dog-eared paperback. The spine arches, near cylindrical, and there is an inscription on the inside flap, which she has read many times. A simple hand:

Forgive me, Lionel. If I could go in your place, I would. But I'll be here still when you return. 'Sky above. Earth below. Heaven within.'

K—

The name of the signee has been defaced and she wonders what K— might have done to consign Lionel to this fate. She pictures a middle-aged man, a few years younger than Whitney, tending the croft. Perhaps he died here, drowned among the kelp, or he keeled over and is buried in the barley field. Or, maybe Lionel paid his dues, one of the lucky ones who the Warden allowed home. Maybe he is cosied up with K— this minute. Maybe … but given the state of the place when they arrived, that does not seem likely.

Those cold uncertain days are ones she will never forget. The Warden had collected them on the mainland and taken them for processing. He did not tell them any more than he had to, just the minimum about the melting ice and how it had affected the permafrost, releasing spumes of toxic bacteria, which is why they needed the pills. *The Limits*, that is what he called this place.

'Says here, you'll be up for parole in twelve years.'

'Parole?' Whitney asked. 'You mean we can come back?'

'Didn't they tell you this already?'

'Tell us what?'

'Mind you, twelve years won't be easy …' The Warden nodded, crafty-eyed. 'But if you make it that long, there'll be an assessment.'

'Like an interview?'

'More like a test. You'll be given a choice, an opportunity to show you're loyal. It's different for everyone. I've known a few who have passed.'

He escorted them by boat, keeping them blindfolded in the hold throughout, who knows how many days. It had almost been a relief to get off that boat. To feel land, to see sky. All that space. And the croft, it was not what it is now. They have spruced it up, invested their time. You'd hardly know it was a prison.

She looks at the sideboard. Maybe the jigsaw belonged to Lionel as well. Or maybe it was brought by the detainee before him. There are other books too, besides the gardening manual. A couple of paperbacks, police procedurals set in Tromsø that they found aboard the freighter. They had provided a welcome distraction at first, but re-reading them down the years, they have become repetitive, diatonic, like the scales she was taught as a child. She revisits the non-fiction with greater regularity: the Japanese dictionary, and a Taschen book on early post-machine sculpture with essays by Gormley and Giacometti. She scans the shelves in the alcove, but the glossy, unmistakable hardback is missing. She does not remember when she saw it last. Probably Whitney has it in his studio. Although he practically knows the thing by heart.

What was K— asking forgiveness for? Presumably Lionel had gone in her place, willingly, by choice. That was it. It always came down to choice in the end, in The Limits … Their punishment was not simply about physical constraint. It has been carefully designed to accentuate guilt, resentment, feelings of complicity. And there is always a choice to make, at the end of things. It is inescapable.

And what of Maxime …

She remembers those last moments. The old man, a neighbour, had cornered her in the lobby. He shook his head. *So much commotion.* And she had expected a complaint to follow about the noise. About footfalls at all hours of the night. And she had her little speech prepared, about how they are very sorry and how they are looking for another apartment, somewhere on the ground floor, where they won't make as much noise. She reaches for her key, the one about her neck, but the key is not there. And the old man says, 'Is that your nephew back again?' Across the lobby, a bell pings, the elevator doors part, and she glimpses the uniforms inside. Police. She backs away. And she starts up the stairs. Starts running. Nine flights. Bodies line the hallway. There are people crowding the door. White shirts. Black ties. They talk into Dictaphones as afternoon light fills the room. She pushes her way inside, sees piano keys. Sleek lacquer. A blanket on the floor beside the stool. The sprinklers drip, water runs down the walls. The door to the cubby is open. Spent matches ground into the carpet.

Can it really be twelve years?

From the bookcase, she retrieves her music book; a thick tome in faded leather with a silver pen clasped to the fastener. She had intended to make a record of compositions throughout her time in exile. Melodies, short arrangements, a chromatic library of emotion.

She skims the pages. There are a few brief compositions in the early portion of the book, restless dissonant works, and the experimental Timepiece, a long-abandoned project to which she was adding one note per day. It seems naïve now, that she ever believed her devotion to music might outlast her guilt.

Instead, most of the staff lines have been overwritten with various entries in her neat and tidy shorthand. These began as detailed accounts, records of temperature, rainfall, wind speed, but she soon accepted the need for economy. Rationing the pages, condensing her thoughts, she marked the days with simple tally lines: four vertical sticks crossed by a diagonal – the geometry of gates – until she replaced the tally lines with the Japanese character for the number five, 五, which she draws using five strokes instead of the customary four. It is less visually suggestive than a gate, at least to her eye.

Time was the only thing that bore recording.

Of the notebook's 192 pages, as many as thirty remain unused, including ten blank pages at the back of the book. She can afford to be a little more expansive now. Uncapping the pen, she marks the previous day with a word: Sheep.

In the corner, the pill clock casts its pinkish glow. 9:48 p.m.

Whitney will be down in a minute.

She takes their mugs from the sideboard. Both have been chipped repeatedly over the years. Hers bears a faded sketch of the artist Monet as an old man. His cartoonish beard hides much of his face, but the eyes define his character, revealing insouciance, defiance. She will pretend that it is a souvenir of a trip to Giverny, or a gift from the artist himself. The other mug, Whitney's, is in better condition and bears blueprints for a range of Danish furniture in clear anatomical precision. He will say things like, 'I'll have my tea in the Danish mug tonight,' and make casual references to holidays that they might have taken together, years before, if they had been permitted. Often these episodes will culminate with tales of a famous design museum, which, he will claim, is where he bought the mug. He will say it had been raining outside, he remembers the puddles, and afterwards, instead of starting back for the hotel, they had gone to a concert at KoncertKirken Blågårds Plads.

'A trio of double-bassists in bowler hats,' she will add. 'Yes, I remember.'

She considers the mugs and her notebook, and it strikes her that, though much of their talk has grown perfunctory – discussions of dates, tests and the various forms that parole might take – music still finds ways of creeping in. A texture, timbre, a refrain. Her fingers walk the sideboard, and they have lost some nimbleness, but in her head she plays flaw-lessly.

Da-da-dum. Da-da-dum. Da-da-da-da-da-da-dum.

She used to practise while Max slept, with the piano lid lifted, and the hammers raised away from the strings; dead keys while the metronome clicked.

Clack–clack–back.

Clack–clack–back.

Upstairs the alarm goes, and she hears the roll of bed-springs. She pictures Whitney fumbling for the wristwatch on his bedside table. Something thuds on the floorboards. A book perhaps, and then the beeping stops.

She watches the door to the stairs. Like the door to the larder, it is composed of vertical slats, crossed by a wooden diagonal and fastened with black iron hinges. Up clicks the latch, and Whitney emerges, scratching his white stubble. He is ready for bed, wearing striped bottoms and a T-shirt beneath his dressing gown. He looks bleary-eyed, innocent, as though he has napped too little or too much. His dark eyebrows offset the white of his hair. They belong to a younger man.

Tea will enliven him.

The stovetop kettle whistles, and she adds a dash of scalding water to the pot, swirling it round, then emptying it over the sink. Stains mark the pot's insides; darkened patches that appear ferrous by candlelight. They will not lift no matter how hard she scrubs. With care, she prunes the plant that hangs in the window, transferring a small bunch of nettles to the pot, which she douses in water.

She lets it brew for a few minutes, then takes Whitney his mug. 'Did you sleep?' she asks.

He sips away the heat. 'A little. I wasn't intending to. I thought I'd be too keyed up.' He coughs, scrutinising the cylindrical white hulk in the corner of the room. 'I just can't stop thinking about parole. I can't believe it's almost here.'

She nods. 'You don't think the sheep could have anything to do with it, do you?'

He appears to mull this over. 'You think the Warden sent it?'

'Maybe,' she shrugs.

'To what end, love?'

'I don't know. A reward for enduring hardships.'

He laughs, distracted, and pats her on the shoulder as he heads for the short-wave radio on the wall. He lifts the receiver, clears his throat. 'Evening, Warden. This is Long Sky Croft.'

Nothing.

He waits a moment before speaking again. 'This is Whitney at Long Sky Croft. Come in. Over.'

Every night, he goes through this procedure, recounting little things from their days. Talking about the weather, the season. Things they have found on the beach. She finds it repetitive, monotonous, but soothing too. It offers hope, and a way to see the days through someone else's eyes.

As ever, he finishes with the chess move. 'Knight to B7,' he says. 'Check.'

They were each allowed one personal possession to bring with them to Long Sky Croft, and whereas she brought her pen, the music book and boxes full of cartridges, he chose this chess set. The pieces sit on the side, fresh from her dusting. It is commendable that he keeps it up. Three years since the Warden took his bishop, and there has not been a peep on the radio ever since. At first, they assumed the radio was malfunctioning, some technical issue, but as parole neared, Whitney started speculating that the silence on the line was part of a broader test. A ploy to see how they will act with nobody checking on them. And perhaps he is right. Perhaps this is all part of parole.

It is a tempting thought.

She looks at the board. She knows the arrangement better than he, and every so often she will change something, moving a piece, or re-introducing a pawn, just for fun. He has not noticed yet, or at least he has not said anything. As it stands, it is black to play, and Whitney could have mate in three, if only someone would pick up.

'Well, Warden,' he says, holding the receiver closer to his mouth. 'We'll expect you Saturday. Be well.'

He pulls up a chair beside her. 'What do you think it'll be like?' he asks, 'When we go back? You think the neighbourhood's still standing? The Arts Club still drawing a crowd? Or, maybe Baumbacher got himself elected. Wouldn't that be something?'

She smiles warmly. Just the thought of it. To be back in the city, among people. To be able to do what she likes, where she likes, when she likes ... The freedom to sit of an evening on the sea wall, uninterrupted, looking back at the lights of the North Sea Road. Or to play at her piano the whole day long, without ever moving from her stool. To be able to sleep past 6 a.m. ...

Her smile turns rigid, feels forced, and all these speculative futures seem suddenly built on something cold and solitary. Unease stirs. She wonders if he feels it too, that the closer they have got to parole, the more they have drifted apart.

9:57 p.m. The dial on the pill clock turns green. Whitney rises from the table. He places his thumb on the sensor. There is a whirr and a click and the mechanism dispenses a single pill in the collection drawer. She follows, and the clock dispenses a second capsule. Half red, half white, identical to Whitney's in every way. At 10 p.m., she places hers on her tongue, promptly bites the casing, and a gloopy, tasteless liquid is released. She washes it down with the last swig of tea.

'Come on,' says Whitney, setting his mug in the sink. 'We should sleep. It's a busy week ahead.'

A week, she thinks. Twenty-one pills. One hundred and sixty-eight hours. Then, this will all be over.

With a loud tick, the dial turns red once more.

3

Berm

I T RAINED EVERY NIGHT of their first week there. The roof
leaked and the wind toomed, and the only fuel was a small
stack of peat that had been left up by the shed. Poorly cut
and impossible to light, the briquettes smoked more than
they burned. She huddled with Whitney under the kitchen
table, in case the roof collapsed, and it was the quietest of
the rooms, away from the wind. 'You think our predecessor
made it to parole?' asked Whitney.

'Lionel, you mean?'

He nodded, carefully setting another briquette on the
stove.

'Honestly, I don't know.'

'I'm not optimistic,' he said, coughing. 'Not if this peat's anything to go by. It's absolute dreck.'

Besides some basic provisions, the Warden left them solar panels, a power inverter that needed wiring and the promise of a supply drop in the spring of each year. 'I'll come by boat in the middle of the night,' he explained. 'I'll leave a crate for you there, up on the berm.'

They had enough to get them started, and besides the peat and the roof, the drainage and the drystone wall also needed work. An endless list of things, which gave structure to their days, lent them purpose. And Whitney seemed to enjoy the physicality of the work. After a few days she did too, as a means to lose herself. Sowing seeds, building a cold frame, tasking herself with simple objectives. And once they sorted the basics, their scope expanded. The garden required clearer thinking, strategies for land management and pickling, and the work forced them to set their differences aside. It was a way to forget.

The morning of parole, the sea is calm. Grey. Almost entirely still. Boat weather.

She watches him, tall and skinny as a fence post, as he takes a final look around. It is amazing that they have survived. The two of them, together, alone for twelve long years. There is some pride to be had in that.

Hope too.

But the hours pass, and nothing comes off the sea but a breeze, and they take lunch early, in want of something to do. She picks lint from her jumper, rolling it between her fingers.

'There's no use fretting, love,' he says. 'High tide's at 3 p.m. There's hope yet.'

Hope ...

She has spent so much time, these past years, clinging to one form of hope or another. Hope for little things to lift the spirits: a blue-sky day; for clothes to dry; for the sound of birdsong. Hope too for broader forms of sustenance: that fish might run in the stream again; for a crate to appear; that beyond the perimeter, people will have endured. And above all else, hope for Max; that he will remember them; that a boat would one day come ...

Yes, she is intimate with hope. Knows the fickleness of its tides. Whitney should know better than to name it.

She stares at the radio. The coil hangs slackly against the wall.

'You know,' she cautions, 'this mightn't go as we expect.'

'You're thinking, what if no one comes?'

'I'm just saying, it must have crossed your mind.'

'They'll come, have faith. Look,' he points giddily out the window, and he is right, the sea is a pond. Perfect for a crossing. 'A few hours,' he adds. 'That's all. Then we'll be gone.'

He starts on the lunch things, and she takes the tea towel and helps him to dry, returning the bowls and mugs to the shelves. And as the minutes tick on, hope renews. She presses down on the oat-lid, squeezing the air out. Plumps the worn cushions in the nook, bolts the front door, and then, when there is nothing left to be done, they go out the back. She untethers the sheep from its stake so it can roam the garden, and it has food for a few weeks, after which, the thistles will be in bloom.

'Truce?' she asks. And she goes to pat its head, gently, as a sort of farewell, only the sheep shivers, and something stays her hand.

'What is it?' She follows its yellow eyes back up the valley. 'Were you running from something?'

The animal does not shift. Its hooves sink deeper in the mud.

Whitney's waiting for her up by the gate. 'Reckon you've an enemy for life there,' he says.

She takes a last look at the sheep and the croft. The white brick could use some paint, but it will be someone else's concern now. They set off down the track and it is like being carried downhill. Before them, the wide expanse of sea gently shapes the bay.

Whitney talks through his checklist. A pre-departure itinerary of all the last-minute tasks and chores. He has tidied the barn, sharpened the tools, returned everything to its rightful cupboard, hook or shelf. And he has mended all that needed mending. Fixed hinges. Cleaned gutters. 'You closed the gate?' he asks.

Aina nods. She takes his hand, and he squeezes hers in return.

They pass the dark ribbons of seaweed that she has laid out in the sun. It was the considerate thing to do. A kindness of sorts to ensure whoever follows has some of the essentials to help them settle.

The tide is coming in so they stick to the berm, passing the wheelhouse of a half-submerged tugboat. At the far end of the bay, the wreck of a freighter crowns the rocks. Twelve vessels in total; one for every year. All of them picked over and bare, testaments to their canniness.

Ahead, the ribs of the old trawler, Whitney's favourite, protrude from a bare patch of sand.

'Afternoon, *Rorvik*,' he says. 'Rest well, old friend.'

They had struggled so much that first winter without any practical knowledge of growing things or tending crops, and they would have fared worse were it not for *Rorvik*. The trawler ran aground in June the first year. Beached with no sign of the crew, no explanation, but with enough tins aboard to keep them fed, until the oats were ready to harvest.

A glint offshore. She looks to the horizon. A boat? No, it is just a momentary parting of clouds and the angle of the sun on the sea.

They walk on, and she wants for conversation but any comments or remarks that she might offer seem trivial or loaded, and better left unsaid. Whitney, too, has grown quiet. He carries a rough hessian sack on his shoulder, containing odds and ends, and two figurines, each a foot tall. A meagre collection of things really. Aina would rather leave it all behind: the pen, the music book, all the little treasures of shell and driftwood. She does not need reminders of this place.

He sets the bag on the berm, disturbing the pebbles. And she sits, a few feet away. A wave breaks, hisses up the sand. It was a mistake, his packing, she thinks. Presumptuous. A way of tempting fate.

'You ever wonder how far you can see on a flat sea?' she asks. The horizon is a grey clarity. A dark line under gathering clouds. 'What do you think, five miles?'

'Three,' he says, with absolute certainty. And he talks about an old nautical logbook that he found aboard the freighter, several winters ago. 'There was a formula: 1.17 multiplied by the square root of the height of the eye.'

'Right,' she says, nodding. She looks to the needles, pinnacles of rock that rise from the bay like church spires in a drowned valley. She used to swim to them when she first arrived. A half-mile out at high tide, she cannot remember why she ever stopped.

Two-thirty.

Three p.m.

The boat will come, she thinks.

And Whitney stalks the berm, impatient now. Back and forth, eleven steps. Crunch, crunch, crunch. A line of indentations in the pebbles. Shapeless divots, becoming craters. He pauses, looks to the sea, mutters to himself, walks on.

Three-thirty.

Four p.m.

And no vessel appears.

They stand out there, on the berm, all afternoon, waiting, as high tide passes and the undertow grows stronger around her ankles. The breeze picks up, and when the day starts to darken, she knows this is it. She does not want to leave him there, and she does not really want to be alone herself, but she has neither the patience, nor the hope, to remain.

———————

It was an awful thing, returning to the croft. She gathered the seaweed on her way back from the beach. Dried, she has sealed it now in clean glass jars. On a shelf in the kitchen, it awaits soups. Other meals too. She stands in the attic as colour drains from the sky. She cannot face the sea, so she looks out the back. The fuzz of the sheep, greyer than everything else. The worst thing was the stare it gave her when she came through the gate. Expectant. It hadn't seemed in the least bit surprised.

Long after dark, not long until their pill, and she is about to go looking for him when she hears the back door signal his return. She comes downstairs and there he is, dumping the contents of his sack on the table. A dreadful sight. Night gusts in the open door, flickering the candles that she has lit. He takes a breath, looks at the walls, the ceiling.

'You all right?' he asks.

She shrugs.

He nods, exhales slowly. 'Hungry?'

She had not thought to eat. She looks at the clock. It has gone nine-thirty.

'Come on. Let's just …' He runs the tap and sets a large pan of water on the stove.

The thought of dinner sounds obscene. A pretence. But she plays along. 'What are you in the mood for?' she asks cautiously.

'I don't know. What is there? Risotto perhaps?'

He sets a second pan on the stove and without removing his coat, he starts chopping an onion; one of last year's. He is careful with the knife. And it takes a while for the pan to heat – he grumbles about the peat, its inefficiency – but once the barley is added, everything starts sizzling, and he pours in two ladles of water, stirring the pale mulch aggressively to stop it sticking.

'Are you okay?' she asks.

He does not answer. He covers the pan, goes to the short-wave radio and takes a moment to compose himself. 'Evening, Warden,' he says. 'This is Long Sky Croft.'

Static crackles from the round copper grill.

'This is Whitney. Come in. Over.' He checks the frequency. 'This is Whitney … at Long Sky Croft …' His voice tapers. He swallows. Turns to the wall. 'Bastard, pick up.'

'Come away,' she says. 'Leave it. Sit.'

'I don't understand …' He goes on breathing in, his chest slowly rising, and he holds his breath as he hangs the receiver on its clip. He is silent for a moment, eyes searching the room until they alight on her notebook. He exhales. 'Are you sure it's today?'

'I'm sure.'

'You haven't miscounted?'

He does not mean this as an insult, but still an insinuation burns.

'Twelve years …' He goes back to the stove. Grips the wooden spoon.

'Look, why don't you leave that. Let's have a tea. Come on, love.'

'Tea?' He looks exhausted.

'Come on, sit,' she says. 'There's your Danish mug. Come on. Keep your spirits.' She rubs his back. Tells him that parole might be tomorrow … or, who knows, the day after … And her words sound empty, devoid of conviction, and as much as she wills them to be true, there is no denying the mounting evidence to the contrary. The empty boats, the sudden halt in food drops, three years without word from the Warden … Each of those things in isolation could be rationalised, but now this: parole has come and passed … and … nothing. A starker realisation presents itself: what if The Limits have been abandoned? They would be stuck here, trapped, indefinitely … She cannot admit her fears to Whitney. He is vested in the idea, sold on the premise that parole is their one route home. It has sustained him over the years, an axiom that has grown roots and taken possession. Felling it now might break him.

'Twelve years …'

She feels his muscles tense.

'Twelve fucking years.' He slams the spoon on the counter. Turns, cheeks flushed, eyes ridden with anger; they dart to the pill clock. 9:54 p.m.

'Whitney—'

'This isn't right,' he says. His eyes narrow. He snatches up one of his sculptures, wields it, and for the briefest moment, she thinks that he is about to inflict violence upon her, but he turns and hurls the figurine at the pill clock. The sculpture ricochets into pieces, and he takes the second one, feels its weight, and goes closer, winding back his arm, hammering at the casing until the figurine's plinth flies off and the legs twist free. Shoulders heaving, he inspects the dispensary, sees there is not even a scratch and drops the mangled sculpture to the floor. She watches him go to the larder, reappearing a moment later with the speargun. And he goes again, smashing the hilt of it over and over and over on the dial. The same spot. And the sound of it is almost musical – a harmonic sort of chime. She recognises the vacant look of determination on his face. He is pacing himself. And then there is a discordant sound. A deadening crack, like the impact of a body falling from height. The pink glow fades and the timer goes dark.

He does not see the zeroes blink.

Panic wells in her. It has never gone dark before … 'Whitney!' She grabs his arm. Electricity hums, something kicks over, and the dial resets. 9:55 p.m.

He is spent. The speargun clatters to the floor as he sinks to his knees. And she helps him up, helps him into a chair. Finds a cold flannel for his brow. She checks the dial, and everything appears in order. It does not appear damaged, thank goodness. 9:57 p.m. The pill clock turns green. She collects her pill, and she helps him with his, and he is like a child, having to be coerced. 'Give me your thumb. Here. Press. That's it.'

He swallows. The episode is over; another that won't be spoken of again.

'You really think parole is coming?' he asks.

'I don't know,' she says. 'The Warden said we'd be tested. Maybe this is it. Maybe they're watching to see how we react.'

He looks up. A glimmer of hope in his eye.

4

Needles

Aina cannot sleep. She is about to drift off when she sees the sheep, its pupils wide like letterboxes. *Clack-clack-back.* The animal blinks and its bright amber eyes turn pill-clock red. Flashing no-entry signs.

She slips out from under her blanket, toes numb to the air, and she moves with ease in the dark, closing the bedroom door with care behind her. She can still hear Whitney's snoring, the low thrum, as she avoids stepping on the creaking stair. In the kitchen, the pill clock's pink glow illuminates the dispensary. 4:51 a.m. Later than she thought. But she has time for a swim before her 6 a.m. pill.

She finds the wetsuit hanging in the cupboard, behind the ponchos and cagoules and the pair of bright yellow waders.

They have been waiting a week and no one has come, and everything about their routine remains. They do their chores. They take their pills. But they are both increasingly distracted. Several times, she has gone to the back door to ask if he wants tea, and found the only thing standing in the dirt is the hoe. It will take her a moment to spot him, down on the berm, gazing out to sea as the tide comes in, waiting for God knows what. And something nags at Aina too. It is not just what happened with the pill clock. It runs deeper, an elemental wrongness. They are stuck here now, the same as the sheep.

The morning is bitterly cold, and the garden is still. She has not been out this early in years. She carries the wetsuit underarm, and handles the gate with swift precision. Feeling eyes on her, she turns. The sheep nestles against the dry-stone wall. It does not look capable of swimming.

'All that wool …' she whispers. 'Must be heavy in the water. Weigh you down.'

The animal bleats, a loud reproachful sound, until she closes the gate behind her. Barefoot, she walks on, down to the beach, treading lightly across the berm. She is careful, watching for the glint of glass among the pebbles: jagged slivers of bottles and broken bulbs that are sharper than the splintered shells of the razor clams. She passes *Rorvik*, and comes to the spot where they had sat, a week before. Fissures of light crack the eastern horizon, but to the south the sky remains a Cimmerian black. The sea is blacker still, and bracketed by headland. And blackest of all are the needles, rising imperiously, out in the bay.

Wet sand – indigo in the dark – sifts between her toes, soothing after the discomfort of the pebbles. Waves break a few feet away; it is rare to see the tide this high.

She changes out of her jeans and the baggy grey-knit jumper, and sets them beneath a hunk of basalt. Her bare skin is tighter in the breeze, sticky with sea salt, and her shoulders are stiff from sleep. She clambers into the wetsuit. One leg, then the other. She needs several goes to get the thing zipped.

Pinpricks of spray carry, which she feels on her face and her forearms. Wind ruffles her short hair, and she rolls her neck in an exaggerated motion. Tendons splay across her collarbone. At fifty-two years old, there are aches, dull aches, and the suit is raw against her neck. She will feel better once she is in the water, and she folds one arm across her body and twists, gazing back up the beach. The sand, punctuated by her footprints – for Whitney, should he wish to follow.

She attempts a few squats; not much of a warm-up, but she only intends to have a quick dip. The wetsuit rumples about her hips as she walks, making her feel like a teenager again. She has made adjustments to the suit over the years: shortening the sleeves, stapling larger tears using rewound paperclips and painting worn patches with boat tar. She enters the breakers. Knees high, body tense, turning sideways to lessen the impact. The waves are sudden, icy about her legs, and she dives headfirst. She knows it is safe. She knows where the rocks are, and though she did not swim all winter, she is confident that nothing fundamental has changed.

When she surfaces, there is more water above her than she expects. She stands, bobbing, almost too short to touch the bottom. Her teeth chatter and she can hardly draw breath. The morning seems colder somehow, and her hair is pasted to her scalp. It is as though there is less of her.

But it feels good to be awake.

She bounces on her tiptoes – once, twice – and then she is off, and as soon as she is moving, she feels warmer. She has missed these ablutions; she does not recall why she ever stopped.

Leading with her elbows, she trails her fingers along her torso, up past her hips and her armpits. She sets her forearms as anchors. It takes effort, more than she remembers, and she feels leaden in the water. She tries to focus, imagining a pole running from her head to her toes about which she rotates. Another three strokes. She raises her chin to the little trough of air, but draws only a mouthful of the sea. She spits, coughs and closes her eyes. She is determined not to break rhythm, but all she can see is the sheep and the pill clock ticking, and in her throat, the tang of brine lingers.

How much time has she wasted, complacent, deaf to risk? In all these years, she has not learned a thing.

She first got a sense that something was wrong during their third winter. A small pleasure craft had run aground, the same as the others, and given its size, she let him tackle it alone. He came running in from the garden in a bluster. 'Come quick,' he said. 'You're going to want to see this.'

She had expected that he had found something on the boat of import. A map, or fuel, or music or something. But when she followed him outside, he pointed up at the sky, and she saw great streams of birds passing high over the croft, for-mations of interlocking letters flat to the horizon. Geese, starlings and meadowlarks. Other birds too.

'Isn't that something …'

She checked her bearings. 'They're heading north,' she said.

'So?'

'They're going the wrong way.'

Corncrakes. Gulls. Buntings. They all departed, and she cursed their leaving, but what else could she do? Autumn turned to winter which turned to spring and the tugboat ran aground. The Warden's annual seed drops became increasingly irregular, and then, without warning, they stopped altogether. And of the birds, only the magpies ever came back. She felt affinity for them, these few stubborn stragglers. They were tenacious, resilient, bold. She thought they might survive them all.

———

At high tide, the needles are a twenty-minute swim, even in the worst of weathers, and today the sea is calm, a flat serenity of darkness. She raises her head and blinks salt: the needles stand a few degrees to the west. She is a little off course, but it is probably just a shift in the tide. She adjusts her bearing. Twenty minutes there, twenty minutes back – thirty, if she's being cautious. She will be back by 6 a.m.

Onward. One-two-three. One-two-three. After a few minutes, she rediscovers her sleekness. She stops counting her stroke and just breathes, sometimes alternate strokes, sometimes as many as five. In through her mouth and out through her nose. Bubbles foam past her chest.

She comes up again. Waves lap gently against the pinnacles which tower ahead. Beyond, the horizon is brighter, giving a sense of distance.

You ever wonder how far you can see on a flat sea?

Three miles, roughly five kilometres. She runs over the calculation in her head, Whitney's formula: 1.17 multiplied by the square root of the height of the eye.

Whitney is close enough to six foot three not to make any difference. And the berm is elevated, adding another six feet. Or 12.25 once converted to a decimal. Square rooted, that is 3.5 on the mark. Multiplied by 1.17, equals ... what is that, 4.1 nautical miles, give or take a carry.

These little calculations help her stay calm, the way she used to do crosswords or play sudoku. She continues: 4.1 nautical miles, 7.6 kilometres ... Call it 4.7 miles. In her prime, she had averaged twenty-minute miles. But in the shape she is in now, she would have to swim the best part of two hours to ever reach the horizon.

She turns and looks back towards the beach. The croft looks so tiny. A white oblong of single-storey brick with two dormer windows. Up the valley, the moorland is obscured by low tracts of silver mist. Later, she will make a start on the peat, supposing it clears.

She should spot herself regularly, keep a check on her surroundings, but it feels good to be swimming. And she is in her rhythm now. She is thinking about the sheep, about how they have never seen a sheep, not in all their time on the island. An island – but that cannot be. Who ever heard of a sheep that swims?

Looking up, she expects to see the needles, but there is only open water ahead. It must be a trick. She thrashes around, trying to see how far she is from the shore. The needles are there, behind her, except they are more like drowned fingers than drowned spires now. She must be a quarter of a mile beyond, and the light is coming in the east: fast and bright. How could she have been so careless?

Her breathing is shallow. She cannot draw breath. Short, choppy waves pass like time-lapse dunes moving through centuries. She treads water. A thin trail of smoke rises from the croft's chimney.

Whitney. He must be awake. He will have seen her empty bed and presumed she has taken a walk. Or else he went out to check on the sheep. It is unlikely he will have checked the cupboard for the wetsuit, but with each passing minute, he will grow increasingly anxious, talking to himself with one eye on the pill clock, soothing, righting his fears. He probably lit the fire to give himself something to do.

'Jesus, Aina,' he had said, once, years before, when she had returned off the moor with barely a minute to spare. 'What were you thinking?'

The needles are matchsticks held at arm's length. She is drifting, but it is not the tide – this is a rip – and the strip of beach is thinning, and the croft, small as it is, grows smaller too. She tries swimming: kicking hard, keeping her body aligned like a spear, and it feels as though she is motoring through the water, but the water flows against her, vast quantities of it, making any progress seem more substantial than it actually is. She is rushing, failing to set her forearms properly, and her stroke is loose, sloppy, inefficient.

She tries to concentrate. Only two variables matter now: time until the pill is delivered, and the time it will take her to reach the dispensary. And if the latter exceeds the former, parole will be the least of her worries.

God knows how long she has got.

She tires quickly. Her legs feel spent and her arms are heavy things; she can barely raise them out of the water. One-two-three, breathe. One-two-three, breathe. So stupid of her. She is spluttering. Lungs bursting. Her neck and shoulders burn from exertion. More. Further. Faster. Draining reserves she did not know she had. One-two-three-four. One-two. One-two-three.

She is making headway. The needles are larger now. Almost within reach. She knows she should rest for a minute. Grab hold of the wet rock, take a breather, and then make a sprint for it. But she swims on, and it is easier now. She ignores all the aches and soreness. She just swims.

She imagines Whitney pacing the croft, with one eye on the dispensary. The pill clock, ticking onward to 6 a.m. He will be lining up a series of rebukes. *You should have told me you were going out …*

The water is warmer; she can touch the bottom now. The beach rises suddenly, and she scrapes her knees on the bottom. A wave breaks over her, and she is rolled in a churn; the water making a last attempt to drag her out, until she staggers free, on to the beach. Legs numbed. Not caring for her knees, nor her feet, she explodes into a run. Pain gathers in her chest. There is something in her throat – the burn of salt – and something worse clogging her lungs. She cannot breathe.

She trips on the pebbles, setting off a small landslide as she heads up the berm. The glass does not matter now. It must be almost 6 a.m. The sun is coming over the headland; it blinds her. Her lips swell, tingling, as though she has been stung. This is it, she thinks. The melting permafrost, the toxic spores. This is how the symptoms start.

She goes on. Running. Up the track, past the wall. All the world a blur.

Whitney must have seen her coming up from the marsh. He is halfway down the footpath, holding binoculars. 'Oh, Aina, no!' He looks aghast. 'Quick. Hurry. For God's sake.'

She does not stop. She crashes through the gate. The door to the croft is a rectangle of darkness. Inside, her eyes cannot adjust but she knows the layout by heart. To the corner of the room. The pill clock reads 6:03 a.m. She should be dead, but the dispatch is still green. Breathless, she places her thumb on the scanner. There is a whirr and a click and the mechanism dispenses her pill. The pain becomes excruciating, as though her body is trapped in a vice. She fumbles the capsule into her mouth, shaking now. Her mouth is dry. She can no longer stand. The pill is huge against her tongue. She shifts it between her molars and bites until the casing breaks and the serum is released, a detonation, like something nuclear pulsing through her, eradicating all pain.

6:03 a.m. Impossible.

Something clangs; air in the pipes. And then Whitney is there, stroking her hair. 'You're all right, love,' he says. 'You're in shock. You're all right.'

She is confused.

She wipes her mouth. Spit and seawater. Slowly, her breath comes back.

'What the hell were you thinking?' he says.

'I … I lost track.'

He must have taken his pill and gone out to the garden, scanning for her with the binoculars. But did he not see the clock? 6:03 a.m. She should be dead.

'You gave me a terrible fright,' says Whitney.

'I didn't mean—'

His face. What is it? Anger? Fear? He has seen something. Is her skin starting to blister? Whatever fate the pills keep at bay must have been unleashed. This is it, she thinks, wincing with pain. Not pain brought on by panic. But real, acute, nerve-singeing pain.

'Oh God,' he says. 'Your foot.'

She looks down. Her foot. The skin, usually plump and seawater soft, is blackened, crusted and sticky. Blood gushes from her instep where three shards of glass protrude. The glass is rammed tight; emerald green. Electrifying the bone when it is touched.

5

Maps

THE SUMMER THEY MET, she had been playing in a minimal-ist instrumental ensemble: cello, drums, her on piano. Delaney, the band's self-styled leader, had booked a series of concerts in old churches, abandoned railway stations. He had mentioned it to Lucia at the Arts Club, asking if she knew anyone who could mock up a flier. Delaney was explicit – he wanted young, talented, cheap – and she steered them to Whitney, who was supposed to be all of that and more.

After rehearsal, Aina would let the conversation get away from her. Delaney would go on ranting about something, berating Smith for switching up the tempo during the coda, pushing Aina for her support. Assenting, she would spot

him, Whitney, stooping through the club's basement door-
ways, or stationed on a stool with a book, with one eye fixed
on the quartet up on stage. He was not handsome by any
conventional measure, and his hair was longer then. Sometimes he wore it tied back, but when it was loose, it would
come to his shoulders. Always wearing the same dark jeans,
same dark boots, same black shirt with a pocket on each
breast. One time he looked up, and Aina smiled involuntar-
ily, a moment too long, surprising herself, and he raised his
hand in what she thought was a wave, until Lucia skipped
down the bar with her smile and her easy manner to pour
him a beer.

Occasionally she would see him on the platform, waiting
for a train, or he would walk by the coffee shop as she waited
to pay.

Oh, hi, I'm just, how are you, I'm just—

Rehearsals going okay?

Going great, thanks. We're almost there.

She did not know what else to say. She could have asked if
he would be there, but having pasted his flier all over the
Quarter, he surely knew the time, date and place.

Friday 22 September

7 p.m.

—THIS ROUGH BEAST—

St Luke's Church, Fisk

You should have shown it to us first.

Like a commission? Come on, Aina, I usually get paid for those.

But you changed our name. No one will know this is us.

Artist's prerogative, no?
Delaney thinks you approached this like a branding exercise.
And what do you think?
It has that feel.

St Luke's, the night of, they waited in a stuffy little room off the chancel. She had not been to Fisk in years, a run-down coastal neighbourhood north of the Quarter, the only place Delaney could get a permit. He was convinced that no one would show. He fretted, wanting to make last-minute changes, but Smith shut him down. He was a perfectionist, Smith, cold, logical and constantly snacking, like most drummers she knew. She remembers unlatching the chancel door and seeing the faces. So many of them, fanning the air with magazines, old hymnals, whatever they could lay their hands on. Smith gently pulled the door closed. 'Think of it as Schrödinger's church,' he said, offering her a slice of square yellowed cheese. 'When the lights go down, they don't exist.'

Walking in: Smith ahead of her, his drum sticks stuffed down the back of his jeans. She remembers the warmth of the spotlights, polite applause and the flicker of candles in the nave. Darkness beyond as she sat to play. She looked at Delaney, looked at Smith and counted backwards from ten. The rich hum of a bow-rung cello. Whisk of drums in a tick-tock manner. Her fingers set off traversing the keys, unravelling notes in a wider arpeggio. One-two-three. One-two-three. One-two-three-four-five. The disparate pieces are bound together then pushed apart in a sparse overlapping soundscape. Tempos converge. She loses all sense of time.

When it is over, the last echo of Smith's wordless vocal hangs in the air. There is a split second of quiet, the sound of her breathing. She glances over at Delaney, feet planted astride his cello, as applause breaks through the church. And when the lights come up, she spots him, tucked in an alcove, ten rows back. Dark shirt. A pocket on each breast. Whitney. Stood tall, clapping loudly.

She would be glimpsing the flier for months, its blue-black font, half peeled, half scrubbed on the lampposts and tram shelters. The image, a woodcut: the head of a ram on a lion's body, the thing floating above a church roof like a gargoyle in flight. Piano-key grin, curved horns spiralling into clefs.

———

In the afternoon, Aina takes to her armchair in the nook. She keeps her bandaged foot elevated, and the view up the valley is obscured, partly by low cloud, but also by the condensation that has formed on the inside of the window. Beside her, the peat fire glowers; helixes of smoke twirl upwards, infusing the croft with the aroma of clover and petrified bog wood. The briquettes smoulder in the hearth. Black little cuboids, burning orange within.

She will have to make a start on the peat soon.

From the bookcase, she takes her notebook. She finds her page, uncaps the pen and marks the previous day. A draught licks her toes. The wind seeks her continually, even indoors, as though her presence creates some sort of barometric anomaly. Always it finds a way in, between the walls or under the boards, whistling through the croft at all hours. If only she had a sock to cover her foot; there is one in her dresser that would fit nicely over her bandage, but she does not feel up for tackling the stairs.

She limps to the kitchen and finds Whitney there. She had assumed he would be down at the beach all afternoon, harvesting more of the seaweed, but here he is. Her wetsuit hangs on the back door, dripping occasionally as it twists in the breeze.

'Can you close that?' she asks.

He turns, oblivious.

'The door,' she says.

Before he can reach it, the wind rises, the door slams, and the whole croft shakes. 'Sorry.'

He removes a large pan of steaming water from the stove, and sets it on the floor of the hearth. 'Could do you a bath tonight, if you'd like.'

'Maybe after dinner,' she says. 'What are you making?'

'Turnip and beetroot.'

He takes a small frying pan from the cupboard.

'Sautéed?'

'I think we deserve a treat. Don't you?'

There is only an inch of oil left, but she does not argue the point. She is grateful for a little indulgence. 'I'll get some sage,' she says.

Whitney disapproves. 'Take the weight off,' he says. 'Relax. I can do this.'

She fires him a look, and he knows better than to push her. She gathers a couple of sprigs from the garden. Velvety, almost purple. And when she returns, he has gone to the short-wave radio on the wall. He has the receiver in hand. 'Evening, Warden. This is Long Sky Croft.' He continues along the usual lines, without waiting for a response. 'Weather's improving here. Still a bit of wind, keeping us invigorated. We could do with some bandages. Some antiseptic too, besides the lightbulbs and fuses. Aina had an accident, nothing serious but … we'd rather not take any chances. Sky above. Earth below. Heaven within.' He pauses. Their eyes meet. 'Knight to B7,' he says. 'Check.'

He motions at her bandage. 'How's the foot?'

'It's okay,' she replies. 'It'll heal.'

He nods, glances around sullenly.

She hates having to coax him. If something is on his mind, he should just come out with it, but instead he takes a board and a small worn vegetable knife, and he starts chopping the turnip without bothering to peel it first. She lays the table, hobbling back and forth between it and the dresser, and it is only when she sits again that he says, 'You were lucky. You shouldn't have gone out so far.'

She smiles. She cannot help herself. 'That's what this is about, you want me to stay out of the water?'

'It was a reckless thing, you going off like that.'

'It was an accident, Whitney. A riptide. It wasn't intentional.'

He moves on to the beetroot, patiently slicing it into cubes. 'Still, I've been thinking about what you said, about parole. How this might be something bigger. Some kind of test.' He speaks calmly, diluting any accusation. 'Maybe we've just got to keep our heads down. Play the game. Have faith.'

'Have faith? That's not what I said at all.'

He shrugs. His fingers are stained pink from the beetroot, and he has sold himself on this, she thinks. Lost the ability to see things as they are. He lays the knife parallel to the board, taking her hand before she can withdraw. 'Even so,' he says, continuing. 'Let's not risk everything on a whim. It's not like you should stay out of the water altogether. Just keep to the shallows. We have to stick together, prove loyal, like the Warden said.' He strokes the back of her thumb with his own.

She does not speak. She clasps her thumb away, keeping it hidden, inside her fist.

———

After dinner, she retrieves the old hand-drawn map from the sideboard and sets it out on the kitchen table. They drew it together on the reverse of an old sea chart found in the trawler; the first of the boats to wash ashore. The paper is worn – a palimpsest of creases and folds, marked with crescents of tea and held together with tape – but it shows the island in remarkable detail. Twenty-four miles long, five miles across at the widest point. A maze of coves and inlets, battered by the sea and the wind.

When they first arrived, Whitney would run every day. So much training, fuelled by vast quantities of homegrown oats; she had even shared her portions with him, believing he could use the extra. And on Sundays, he would attempt to extend the map. A longer run, looking for a settlement, a village, another croft. Anything. He was hopeful then. She was too.

The map's largest portion – year one – is shaded green and includes the valley, the croft and the cliffs along the southern shore. The Northshore is shaded yellow; windswept and less accessible, it was not mapped properly until their second year. And there are smaller territories in other colours besides. Red for the peaks of the island's spiny ridge, which Whitney summited in their third year; blue for the moor with its treacherous bogs, which Aina finally mapped the year after that. And beyond the ridge, the eastern seaboard tapers into a long straight spit. A violet point. The most inaccessible part of the island, and the only territory that she has never seen for herself.

Outside the sheep bleats.

She looks at the pill clock. Their leash. Restricting them to these eight-hour excursions. But she missed the pill by three minutes. No disputing. Maybe she could last even longer. Maybe she could—

Something comes to her. The tip of something not fully formed.

Back when they first arrived, desperation got the better of them and they tested the pill together, to check its effectiveness. A tug on the chain, so to speak, just to see what would happen, but the pain was immediate, unbearable. Inflammation in the face, the hands. Constriction in the throat. They had not lasted a second from the moment the pill clock turned red, and she had always taken her pill promptly after that, precisely as the Warden instructed. They both had. But what if the science is flawed? She looks over to the dispensary. There is a faint crack on the dial from Whitney's efforts with the speargun. Maybe he damaged it somehow. Changed something. She remembers the dial fading. The sound of the machine rebooting. Could that be it? Or could it be something else? Something simpler, biological. In twelve years, might her body have adapted to the toxic air, building up some kind of immunity that allows her to go eight hours and three minutes between pills? In any case, if she can delay taking her pill, she can steal minutes incrementally. She considers the logistics. It would be quite complex. She would need to receive her pills at their regular times – 10 p.m., 6 a.m. and 2 p.m. – but she could take them on delay, like a piano played slower than everything else.

10:03 p.m.

6:06 a.m.

2:09 p.m.

Her mind is alive with arithmetic: three minutes, three times a day. Within a week, the lag would constitute an hour. After two months, she would be able to take her lunchtime pill at night and save her night-time pill for the morning, and she would effectively gain a spare. An eight-hour cushion, meaning she could take a sixteen-hour trip away from the croft. Over a year she might build a stash, or she could give her spare to Whitney; he could travel further. He could fix up a boat and he could use her pill to map the coast. Maybe he would see something they had missed. A place where there are sheep. She could give it to Whitney. Or—

She could keep it for herself. She could just pretend to take the pills on time, and do it all in secret. Why not? It would be simpler. She would not have to get his hopes up. Would not need his permission. And if he is right and this is all part of parole, he would at least have deniability.

'Will you go paddling tomorrow?' he asks, looking up from his book. 'Saltwater will be good for that foot. You don't want it getting infected.'

'Maybe,' she replies. 'Or maybe I'll start running instead.' That has his attention. She waits for him to mark his page and close his book, then she turns the map to him and says, 'I'm going to ask you something, just once. And I need you to be absolutely honest with me, okay?'

He looks sceptical, verging on perplexed.

She points at the violet-coloured sandbar. 'Is there any-thing there?' she asks. 'Out east, beyond the hills.'

He picks up his book. Smiles placidly. 'Only ocean, as well you know.'

'So you're sticking to it, this claim, we're on an island?'

'Aina, I'm sticking to the truth.'

She persists, 'There's no causeway? Maybe at low tide … No possibility of a peninsula. No other islands?'

He shakes his head. 'The map's a true rendering. It's accur-ate, I swear.'

'So the sheep must have swum.'

'Yes,' he says, a hint of irritation in his voice. 'It must have.'

He turns a page, and to the casual observer it would appear that her concerns have been quickly superseded by the intricacies of his novel. But she watches him closely. His eyes skip and dart. They skim a paragraph. He is only pre-tending to read.

She looks at the dispensary. The little red numbers. Tick, tick, ticking.

Her mind is made up. She will wait for the 10 p.m. pill and try again. She will wait as long as she can. As long as she can bear it. And she will find out how long she can last. She will time herself. Whitney has the watch, but there are other ways. Older ways.

6

Enamel

S HE STRIKES A MATCH in the dark, igniting sparks of blue, green, butterscotch candescence.

The flame cowers and blows horizontally. It rests, retreats, and for a moment it is rounded, weak, and looks set to go out until she shields it from the draught, and the flame putters higher. She bows the match to a waiting candle, allowing the wood and the wick to touch. The light yields a bright doppelgänger, which burns brighter, competitive in its luminosity, while the match kindles down leaving a brittle withered splint; shaped like a figurine, or the silhouette of a distant man seen against a backdrop of white sky.

She lays the dead match on a saucer and carries the candle to the kitchen. The shadow of the dangling light socket sweeps across the ceiling. In the corner, the pill clock stands, resolute. It appears larger, somehow, a trick of dimensions.

9:48 p.m. Whitney comes in from the barn. He has clean goggle marks around his eyes and the rest of his face is smudged with grease. As he washes his hands, he tells her about a new project that will be bigger than anything he has attempted to date.

She hums, offers nods. The patches on his overalls need re-stitching. 'Denmark tonight?' she asks, filling the kettle.

'Oh, yes, yes please,' says Whitney, drying his hands.

She collects their mugs from the sideboard. Her fingers trace Giverny's chipped porcelain. And a few minutes later, he is in full flow. 'You remember your birthday, in Copenhagen that time. The night we met those Spaniards in the bar in Vesterbro – all that singing – and the herring at that little all-nighter. Wasn't that terrific? The taste! On rye bread, with a pickled onion. My goodness, what a treat. I think it was your thirtieth.'

'My thirtieth?' She stops abruptly.

The kettle whistles. Whitney's eyes linger on her mug. 'I'm sorry … I didn't think.'

She recalls distinctly retrieving the two mugs from the small sailboat that ran aground in their second year. She returns Giverny to the shelf and chooses a plain enamel one instead. It is white, glossy, smooth, with a simple blue trim.

'Everything … okay?' he asks.

'Yes,' she says. 'Everything's fine.'

She finishes making the tea in silence and when the clock turns green, Whitney approaches the sensor and collects his pill. She follows, collects her own, and with a tick, the dial turns red once more. 10 p.m. They place the pills on their tongues. Whitney swallows his with the dregs of his tea and takes the candle through into the bathroom.

As the light recedes, she traps the capsule under her tongue and counts, the way her grandmother taught her: *Yan ... Tan ... Tethera ... Methera ... Pip ...*

At first she feels nothing. She focuses on her breathing and stands, innocently enough, pretending to drink her tea as she watches him through the frosted glass. He is humming to himself as he brushes his teeth. The clock moves to 10:01 p.m. Whitney is scraping the back of his tongue with his brush. He spits down the sink and starts flossing. She feels nothing. Nothing at all. She feels fine.

10:02 p.m. She stops counting and just watches the clock.

The thought that they might have been a placebo seems absurd, but what other explanation is there?

At 10:03 p.m., something changes. At first, it is simply that her limbs become cumbersome. But within seconds it feels as though her organs are taking up too much space in her body. Her heart feels engorged and she can no longer stand. She is gasping for breath. The light of the candle, even muted by the glass, sears her retinas. It is too bright. She sees Whitney hovering over her, mouthing words that she cannot hear. He is a dark shadow. She sees Maxime's features in his face. She cannot take any more. She moves the capsule between her molars and bites.

'Can you stand?'

Whitney is helping her into a chair.

'It's your foot, isn't it. It's infected.'

'Just a spot of dizziness,' she croaks. 'Please don't fuss.'

49

He wants to get the thermometer. He insists. The glass tube feels foreign in her mouth and her jaw aches. She wants to vomit. When he takes the thermometer from her tongue, he simply looks at it, puzzled.

'What does it say?' she asks.

'Thirty-seven.'

'See? I'm fine.'

'You don't look fine.'

'There's nothing wrong.'

He seems unconvinced, and she tries to sit straighter.

'Here's your tea,' he says.

Senses are coming back to her. The ladderback chair. The ting of enamel at her fingertips. She takes a swig, but it tastes foul and has lost its heat. She has to spit it out.

'By the way,' she says, wiping her mouth, 'I'll need the watch tomorrow. I'm going up to the moor. To start on the peat.'

'Tomorrow?' He scratches his chin. 'Is that wise?'

'What's the alternative? I'll go crazy sat round here all day, I need something to do. You've got your project. It makes sense that I take the watch.'

'You think?'

'I wouldn't want to lose track of time.'

'Ah, yes.' He nods. 'You're right, not with parole. Now, if only our Warden was as punctual …' He rolls his eyes at the pill clock, fingers the watchstrap. Pauses. 'Maybe I should come with you though. What with your foot—'

'There's really no need.'

His eyes narrow. 'But if something were to happen … If you were to slip in a bog, or fall and break your leg, what then?'

'Whitney, I'm not going to drown in the bog, don't worry.'

'I have your word on that?'

She smiles.

'Because I'd have a hard time explaining that to the Warden.' He laughs, genuinely relieved that she is okay, and he is off, talking about parole, trying so hard to be positive, but he has pitched this all wrong, and all she can see is the seeping blackness of the water. And she tries to picture Maxime, tries to imagine where he may be, but she cannot conjure him. And that is all she wants right now, to see his face.

Night rattles the door.

'Aina?' he says, holding out the watch. 'We're going to get out of here, you know. Today, tomorrow, this week or the next. Someone will come.'

Her smile feels thin on her face, and she takes the watch. Kinetic, water-resistant, it is warm in her grip.

'You don't believe me?' he asks.

'I'm tired, Whitney. If you want to believe this is all some sick game, fine, so be it.'

'Aina—'

She brushes past him on the way to the bathroom.

'Aina, stop.' He follows her to the doorway. 'There'll be an explanation for all this. They might be held up. A problem with the boat, or the fuel. Or—'

'Or what, Whitney?' She fastens the watch about her wrist. 'He's not coming.'

'We're going to be okay.'

'Maybe you're right … you and me, we'll be fine …' She speaks evenly, watching the candle flame bob like a child starved of attention. 'But what about Max? Where does this leave him?'

He has nothing to say. He turns, slowly, vacating the space in the doorway, and she stares at the mirror as the flame settles on the wick.

She runs the tap. The water is cold upon her face.

7

Day Sixteen

As the days pass, the moon grows bigger, and the tides rise higher on the berm. The Warden is nearly a month overdue, and there is still no sign. No boat. No word on the radio. Practically speaking, nothing has changed but the weather.

By the stream, the first catkins dapple the willows. Whitney bounds down to the berm each day, undeterred, in short-sleeves, while the oats are harvested, and the back field is tilled and replanted. He suggests they leave the front field fallow, at least until autumn. Autumn, she thinks? Autumn feels such a long way off, a theoretical construct, and time stretches out, unscripted. An infinite coda that be must improvised, without any sense of what lies ahead.

She bounces between this future and the past.

The twelve years spent clinging to the prospect of parole and the chance, however slim, that by playing the Warden's long-game, she might be permitted to see Max again. Twelve years … all those nights dreaming of him, where he is frightened, calling out *Mama!* without having aged a day … All those years wasted, for what?

In many ways, the pills are the only things keeping her sane.

For two weeks, she has delayed taking each one by three minutes. The effect is cumulative and the lag builds, and though she is cautious, it helps having something tangible to work towards. A reward. A pill. Something to counter the weight of uncertainty.

She needs that now, more than ever.

Her method for preserving the pill is straightforward. At dispensation, she lodges the capsule beneath her tongue, removing it from her mouth when the opportunity presents. She might excuse herself and go to the bathroom, or if Whitney is in the kitchen, she might go to the nook, and if he is in the attic, she might go to the larder or the cellar; the important thing is that she is someplace he is not. Then, for safekeeping, she stows the capsule within the body of her pen, which she has threaded with twine, so she can wear it about her neck at all times. Next, she unfastens the wristwatch. She has kept possession of it for the last two weeks, and Whitney is yet to object. She programmes three silent alarms with an interval of eight hours and three minutes between them. But keeping track of these times is proving difficult; the accumulation of minutes makes her brain ache. It is simple arithmetic, but so much rides on it, and doing it day after day, she is fearful of making an error. It would be catastrophic to get this wrong. But she has an idea. A way to document the process.

It is not yet morning and she has barely slept. Whitney loiters in the kitchen as she prepares for her run. 'You're up early,' she says, the pen feeling obvious about her neck. 'Busy day?'

'Hoping to get the kiln lit.' He drains his tea in one gulp. 'There's more tea in the pot, if you want any.'

She stretches, tense and stiff, and when he goes to the bathroom to shave, she takes her notebook from the sideboard and opens it at a new page. She changes the watch to a twenty-four hour setting, making it easier to track. Today, she will take her morning pill at 08:12, two hours and twelve minutes after it was dispensed. Then, eight hours and three minutes after that, she will take her lunchtime pill at exactly 16:15. And finally, she will take her evening pill at 00:18. She pops the lid off her pen and writes:

08:12—16:15—00:18

In the same way, she plots out the rest of the week:

08:21—16:24—00:27
08:30—16:33—00:36
08:39—16:42—00:45
08:48—16:51—00:54

And on she goes, programming the watch and noting the times. It is easier having it all written down, and, if all goes to plan, in six weeks, on the evening of Day Fifty-Four, she will take her lunchtime pill at 21:57, and then the evening pill she will not have to take at all. On the morning of Day Fifty-Five, she will wake and take the 06:00 pill as normal, and at that point she will have her spare.

It is a risk, to leave a record like this – it could serve as evidence against her – but what else can she do? It is the only way to keep track.

———

She spends the morning in the garden. The thistles are starting to flower, spiked urchins with their lavender-coloured hats. The colour has come early this year, too soon, and they will need cutting back. At the vegetable patch, she checks the squash and the kale for blemishes, slugs or signs of blight, but there are none. The netting is secure. The courgettes are in, the potatoes will soon be dug, and the manure is working a treat. At the top of the garden, the sheep watches her, chewing side to side. It is such a strange-looking creature, with its elongated nose and mechanical eyes, its face a prominence of bone.

The animal bleats, a hot blasphemous sound, a warning or a curse. It rubs against the gatepost, leaving thin strands of wool like cirrus clouds.

Whitney approaches up the track. He has overloaded the barrow with wood and he struggles over the uneven ground. At the dog-leg, the track veers away from the beach and there is a big slab of rock as wide as the path. The pitch is too steep and too sudden and the little wheel on Whitney's barrow cannot make it up. He lets the barrow roll back and takes more of a run-up this time, but still his momentum is lacking. She waggles her fingers into her tatty old gloves, watching as he becomes increasingly irate, and he is all head, neck and hands, shoulders sloping as he strains, still holding the barrow, as though to set it down would be to admit defeat. He snags himself on a bramble, and in the end, he gives up. Beyond him, the sun shines down on a half-mile of beach. The tide is further out than normal, revealing the sandbanks and the needles in full, and for a moment he is perfectly positioned, looking up at her, or the croft, or the length of the path, and as he catches his breath, the waves break in the distance, twisting in white spears that skewer his midriff and then his chest.

Earlier that morning, as she looped back to the croft from her run, she had spotted him along the beach. A figure in the mist, crouched alongside the old trawler. She drew near, observed him placing a hand on *Rorvik*'s hull; he whispered to the boat, a huntsman offering veneration to a downed deer. 'Bless us, O Lord, for these Thy gifts, for the doors You have opened and the doors You have closed ...'

She coughed, and he looked up, startled. She saw the crowbar. He let it slide through his fingers until he held it by the hook.

'What're you doing there, Whitney?' she asked. 'That boat might be our way off here.'

He turned back to *Rorvik*'s hull, started working the tapered end between planks. The wood popped and splintered as he yanked the bar free. 'Not without fuel it isn't.' He worked the crowbar vigorously, pumping his arms back and forth, using his own weight as a cantilever. 'It's barely even a boat.'

'Yes, but …' She nodded, attempting to align some kind of argument. 'What if no one comes?'

'Let's just focus on the things we can control.' He straightened and smiled and patted his brow with a folded handkerchief. 'The Warden will come.'

She could not grasp the logic in his actions. 'But what do you need it for, all this wood? We've peat for fuel,' she said. 'A whole moorland of the stuff.'

'It's not for the croft. It's for something new I'm working on. A piece in bronze alloy. I've been experimenting.'

'In metallurgy?'

'Charcoal will burn hotter. You'll see.'

He steers the barrow past the boulder, taking the path with stiff little steps. She can hear him grunting now, and he is aware of her, making a show of his efforts. She goes hacking at the soil with a trowel, breaking the earth into smaller clods. Why does he fill his days with these tiresome endeavours, she wonders. These selfish little projects that distract him for a month or maybe two, until the limits of his abilities become increasingly apparent, and his interest dies. Then what? He will mope like a man betrayed, sulking for a month before starting something new.

Usually, she would enjoy watching this play out. Waiting for his enthusiasm to wane, for his critical self to start laying bare the ways his project has departed from his vision. Those cracks will emerge, becoming chasms, and she might speed things along with a word or a look. Ah, the doubt that can be sown with a look. Even an elevated eyebrow or a simple nod of agreement. And off he will go, back to his studio, ranting about the lack of materials. How he must make do with the same tired techniques, rehashing the same imagery, and everything culminating in the old familiar lament, how everything is derivative of something ...

She watches through the fence as he unloads the barrow. He has dug a shallow pit in the fallow field a little way beyond the barn, and he begins layering the wood according to some principle known only to him. She goes back to her trowelling. The soil crumbles. Dry, parched, they are due rain. The sun is higher and she removes her pullover and hangs it on the spade. The sun feels good upon her arms as she returns to the task at hand. She feels something bordering on affection for the thistles, the plant's stubbornness, the way it repopulates the land. Lifting back a leaf, she sees the tiny tentacles upon the stem. Seedlings, waiting to be blown or brushed by some passing animal. Hitching a ride however possible.

A weed. No different to an idea, once it takes hold. An idea, like parole. It is always there, channelling things, like a sunken rock at high tide. If only she had kept her mouth shut ...

She hears the barrow, bouncing, empty now; Whitney steers it with ease along the path. He is whistling. And then the whistling stops and she looks up, and he is leaning on the fence post, tilting it forward. The wind does enough without him making it worse.

'A couple more loads ought to do it,' he says, wiping his brow with the back of his arm. 'Then it'll be ready to light.'

She looks up the track to the fallow field. She does not speak. She waits for him to fill the silence with words.

'You'll want to get those thistles,' he says, squinting. 'The sheep … It won't do well with thistles. They'll make it sick.' He starts on about the weeds, about how they might affect the quality of the manure. And she stoops, trowels, goes to stand but something stiffens in her back, a sudden compression, and all she can do is draw breath. And she thinks of Maxime; everything leads back to him. The apartment. Night-time. The blackout blinds are drawn. She feels the plush carpet underfoot, newly laid to dull any noise. The kitchen sleek with appliances. Everything white, set in recesses. The fridge door is open. A bowl of half-eaten leftovers on the marble counter. A dropped spoon. Rice, like maggots on the carpet. Maxime, grey-faced and vomiting. It is her fault. And Whitney wants to take him to hospital, but she cannot. She must refuse.

Get Nangelis then!

No!

No?

I'll deal with it here. She convinces him. Anything but the hospital. They would ask questions there. Difficult questions, like who is this boy and who are his parents and why is he not registered on any system. In the end, the swiftness of his recovery only flattered her stance. He was a pound lighter and that was a lot for a toddler to lose.

'Well, make sure you get the roots,' says Whitney as he surveys the garden.

'Yep.'

He stands awkwardly. 'Lunch in a hour?'

'Uh-huh.'

She watches Whitney go, knowing it is not enough to get the roots. The ground is loose and full of tiny stones, and the thistles will grow back, they always do. She is as vital to their propagation as water or soil or the sun, with her thick gloves, ribbed cotton on the back side of her hands. The little thistles barb to the material, and all she can do is smile, knowing in a week she will be out there again, doing the same thing all over. Picking at the thistles and making matters worse. She looks at the sheep, and on its coat and around its face, there, too, a mass of tiny bristles.

'Jesus, look at the state of you.'

The rest of her day takes shape. She will attend to the seaweed once she has finished in the garden. It will need to be rinsed and dried and boxed away. And there is the question of the wool; she would be wise to gather it, else it will blow all the way to the Northshore. It will be summer soon and the sheep would be glad for a trim. She will use the scissors as shears. And she will find a couple of sticks among Whitney's kindling that she can sand and smooth for knitting. She will spindle the fleece into yarn. The days might be growing warmer, but she will want for layers if she is to cross the spine.

A thought strikes. She removes her glove, approaches the sheep, slowly, and it does not fear her hand. It goes on chewing, half tame. It knows people, she thinks. And she strokes its flank, its hind quarters. The wool is knotted with dirt, seeds and sharp bits of wood. Thorns perhaps. She unpicks one, lets it rest in her palm for closer inspection. A needle of pine.

The sheep regards her briefly then shunts off towards the patch of lawn on the front side of the croft. She looks from the marsh to the stream and up to the moor. All the land unbroken but for rocks and gorse and the few stunted willows.

'Travel far, did you, sheep?' she asks.

———

With a hard day's work in her haunches and arms, she should be quick to sleep, but her mind is alive and firing. She pictures majestic trees, tall hillsides of pine, and she thinks of their map. Whitney's portions. The places she has never been. He never mentioned any trees. He will claim the needles have come from abroad. But the more she dwells, the more it does not make sense. How could they have stayed snagged to the sheep, all the way across open sea?

The low-level pulse jolts her wrist.

00:18.

She takes her pill discreetly, watching the room. On the far side, under the eaves, Whitney lays motionless. Asleep, or else pretending.

8

Trimester

D AY EIGHTEEN. SHE WILL take her pills two and a half hours
after they are dispensed. Her back aches. There is a
basket of washing folded at her feet, and she sits at the table
with the pieces of jigsaw spread before her. It is a jumbled
rendering of an old Escher lithograph; 750 pieces, so claimed
the box, and she had no reason to doubt the figure, until
she counted the pieces from boredom and came out ahead.
Seven hundred and sixty-eight, total. She stores the pieces in
a ziplock bag now, the box long since used for firelighters.

She glances at her notebook. Day Eighteen of fifty-five; a
third of the way there.

The secrecy around timings and dates, the careful planning and the harbouring of anticipation are all painfully familiar. The toil … the wordlessness. The expectation … the hope. Of course, if this were a pregnancy, she would be sharing the news about now, telling friends, family, whoever would listen. And then there would be the application for Permission to Conceive. The prime minister had ushered the policy through at the start of his second term, once Councillor Baumbacher was unseated and any meaningful opposition had melted away. The laws had passed like submarines coming into harbour. Barely a ripple.

Permission—

Repulsion twists through her at the wrongness of it.

She stares at the pieces of jigsaw.

She remembers vividly the dinners with friends and old acquaintances, taking over the big long tables in the Arts Club. There would be a few faces missing, late cancellations because someone's childcare fell through, and everyone else sat in huddles, catching up on gossip, Smith loudest of all, pipping everyone for bitchiness. And they all just assumed that her and Whitney's childlessness was either through choice, or else the result of some misalignment of luck or biology, something they could fix with recommendations for pills, injections, things to eat, things to avoid. *You'll get there*, they would say. *It'll happen. Have faith* … She found the condescension forgivable, even when, between main course and dessert, they would begin discussing the so-called merits of certain positions. But, try as she might to put a brave face on, over time the good news of friends and colleagues became something harder to endure. She soon knew all the intimate looks that couples shared, wordless preludes that signalled an announcement would be imminent: lingering eye contact, a smug little half-smile. The couple would clasp hands, savouring that last moment of quiet happy coupledom before the room is made incongruent by a knife on glass. *Ding-ding-ding.* Here is one now, Delaney this time. She is not surprised. *Excuse me! Everyone … if we may … we've a little news …* He lets that sit for a moment, showing teeth, while Lucia bathes in the hopeful looks, immaculate. And while Aina pours herself a larger glass of wine, there is some mild shushing as Smith finishes a joke. But there is no denying the couple their moment, the news is shared with grating faux modesty, and it all sounded so simple. Lucia looks suddenly stupid and bovine, fluttering at the adoration, and yet for Delaney, as father-to-be, there is a special kind of congratulations reserved. And all she can think of is him holding the cello with his knees, so firmly, and she wants to be sick. And to appease the back slapping, he comments almost regretfully, *Actually, we'd only just started trying … pity really …* Some laughter. She catches Whitney's eye and he smiles wincingly, embarrassed. Inevitably, the champagne arrives, and her spite dilates, and the couple take questions, talking nonchalantly about their trip to District Hall, recounting the steps required to get the pregnancy approved. *How nervous we were. It seems silly now … Just a few formalities really.* Of course, Delaney and Lucia had no cause for concern. They were upstanding individuals, of good stock; Permission to Conceive was always granted to folks like them.

People are saying:

Heaven help us, they'll hand them out to anyone now.

Course, it was harder in our day. It used to mean something.

Standards must be slipping.

The jibes continued, and though she smiled politely, tittered and fawned, the more it went on, the more she wished that someone else would be denied permission, just so she might feel less alone.

———————

Assembling the jigsaw from memory makes it trickier, but she feels equal to the task, and what used to take her three days can now be completed in a single sitting. She sets the watch to timer mode. Maybe tonight, she will post a new record.

She has forgotten the name of the picture, but, if she remembers correctly, there are seven staircases, and sixteen figures spread across three different gravitational planes. And when complete, some figures will stand horizontally, and others will walk on the underside of the stairs. She begins, and the perimeter emerges as a series of dots and dashes, like sandbanks at low tide. It helps to have focus; keeps her mind from wandering. With all the edges in place, she starts scanning the remaining pieces for sixteen featureless heads. The pieces are long familiar. A diagonal bit of banister. A foot. Disembodied legs. They look like quavers and crotchets. Deftly she sifts, sorting like with like, arranging each in turn.

She remembers the piano, the stool, the apartment filling with morning light. Maxime feels nearer today. And her fingers move lightly, a sort of tarantella, up and down the table, as she hums. *Da-da-dum. Da-da-dum. Da-da-da-da-da-da-dum.*

The window of sky above the sink is darker. She looks up, startled. There is a hand. A face, smudged with charcoal. Whitney leans in the doorway. She has no idea how long he has been standing there.

'You're flat,' he says, grinning.

She hides her hands beneath the table on instinct, and there is an awkward moment as neither of them speaks. 'How's the kiln?' she asks finally.

He steps inside. 'The charcoal's working a treat,' he says, seeming genuinely pleased. 'Nine hundred degrees. A new record.' He smiles shyly, wiping his grubby hands on a tea towel.

She nods at the basket. 'If you've washing, can you do it now while there's room on the clotheshorse?'

He considers this but thinks better of it. 'Reckon I'll wear these for a few days yet,' he says.

She turns her attention back to the jigsaw. She has located fifteen of the heads. One remains. Outside in the black, rain patters the window.

When their evening pills have been dispensed, he gets to his feet, makes a show of stretching and says, 'Okay. Well … think I'll turn in.' He is mumbling on about the charcoal and the kiln and she is not really listening. He crosses behind her on his way to the stairs.

She clutches her pen, feels a vague smug sensation rise. She wants to tell him. He ought to know, and she wants to get it over with. She launches into words before she knows what to say. 'Whitney … there's something you should know …' She clasps her hands together. 'About the last few weeks …'

She becomes aware of him, physically, the way he stops abruptly at her shoulder. And she cannot see his face but she can sense his eyes being drawn to the pieces. And he cannot help himself. He reaches around her and picks one up, connecting it to the ghostly torso that presides over the landing.

The last head.

'Sorry, what was that, love?' he asks wearily.

She stares at the piece, feels tension in her stomach hardening to anger. 'Just … I meant to say, well done again on the kiln. That's really terrific. I'm really proud.'

She catches a faint smell of lavender on the air as he kisses the top of her head. 'You'll be up soon?' he asks, and his casual off-hand manner is deliberate, concealing something.

She grips her pen. Stares at the table. 'Actually, I'm pretty into this,' she says. 'I won't be long.'

The door closes behind him, the latch clicks shut, and the room suddenly feels larger; the air carries a pleasant chill. No doubt he would appreciate knowing, but it is nice having something of her own, and he would only jinx it. She does not need permission. And besides, there is still something about the sheep, something off about it, which stokes a lingering mistrust.

She refreshes her tea, resets the watch and breaks apart the completed section of jigsaw so she might start over. Seven hundred and sixty-eight pieces, spread and shuffled upon the table. She begins again. The same approach, grouping like with like. Edges. Corners. The first piece slots in. Tap-tap-tap. It is a satisfying sound.

9

Thumb

Her bed is uninviting, and candlelight does little to warm the attic or her blankets, but it casts enough light that she might consign the day to paper. She opens her notebook, takes the pen from about her neck. Five weeks to go; at the first sign of summer she will be ready.

She sits, watching the shadows on the far wall. It is past midnight. The jigsaw took her three hours to complete. It is getting too easy. She imagines sitting, emptying the pieces from the ziplock bag, laying them face down and constructing it wrong-side up, making a solid blue rectangle. Given time, she would learn the pieces by the shape of the divots and wedges, but to begin, simply finding two that slot together would occupy her for hours.

It would certainly help pass the time.

Five weeks …

She remembers five weeks ago. The week that the sheep appeared, one week before parole. The mad rush of cleaning, the preparations. She checks her journal entries for any note that she may have made, but the days were indiscriminate with little to mark them apart. Five years ago … that was the year the freighter washed ashore. The freighter, whose plumbing they welded to make the two single beds, which creak now as she sits and she splays her feet, channelling pressure through her toes. The floorboards feel cold and dense underfoot. Impossibly solid. She pushes harder. The nail on her little toe grows sharp and triangular and bites the soft flesh of the toe beside it. She finds the scissors in her tin, starts clipping methodically, and the brittle nails take flight on unexpected trajectories. Short on calcium, short on vitamin D, but the undersoles of her feet are hardening fast.

At the far end of the room, Whitney is awake. His eyes shine like scimitars in the dark.

She switches feet and goes down the line, working from big toes to small. Her fingernails are next, how fast do they grow? A millimetre per month. Faster than the peat … She returns the scissors to the tin, and her fingertips tingle as she presses the lid tight.

The candle dies, and her bed is no less cold in the dark. She will sleep fully clothed, and she pulls the blanket tight about her as best she can. There is a creak from the far side of the room. The yawn of bedsprings. Movement, and she sees his triangular form, he is sitting up. His eyes blink silver, and he stands, crosses silently towards her, and she feels the rush of air as he draws back her blanket. The bed is small for one and it dips with his weight and she rolls slightly into him. They are side by side. He does not speak. He is waiting, perhaps in hope that she might initiate something.

Her face is raw from the pumice stone and the air is crystal.

He smells different. Smoky, but not of peat, of wood. Beechwood, perhaps. Or whatever the boat was made from. Poor *Rorvik*, she thinks. She tries not to inhale any more of him.

He reaches out and touches her arm. This is how he begins. He does not rush. He is saying, Look: I am considerate. Look: I am tender. His hand moves up her thigh and he slips it, fingers first, down the front of her jeans. He builds himself room with his knuckles and here they come, those bony fingers, sternly applying pressure. He has manoeuvred his other arm out from under him and is attempting to unbutton her shirt, one-handed. His angles are wrong, and he cannot prop himself on his elbow and work the shirt buttons at the same time, and in the end he rolls on top of her, and removes his shirt instead, and in the moonlight he is skinnier, and there is something almost pitiful in his leanness.

A creak on the stair. She looks to the door and the door is open and she has the sense of being watched, but it is just the croft. The darkness has seen all this before. He is kissing her neck. His lips are dry, parched and abrasive, and she thinks of the land. The garden. The fields. She catches the smell of lavender; her soap, which he probably used in an attempt to conceal the woodsmoke. And now there is a change of pace. Sitting astride her, he begins unbuttoning her shirt. The pen

71

is about her neck, getting in the way as his fingers fumble hurriedly. He kisses her breasts, pulls her jeans lower.

The pen—

It will be almost time for her pill.

She tries to check her watch but he takes her wrist and pins it above her head. He clambers forward, clumsily on his knees, and he whispers a joke about keeping three points of contact with the wall at all times. She draws her head away from the curve of his neck, and he must take this as a form of acquiescence. He enters, bunting into her, and she angles her neck against the bedstead, and the metal frame shunts into the wall. The mattress sags under their weight. She can feel the jut of wire mesh – coat hangers, twisted using pliers.

She taps, almost politely. 'Whitney—'

He pushes down on her breastbone, steadies himself. There is weight behind his hands. The pen is pressed into her chest. She tries to move. His fingers curl. Her pill, what time …? She searches for some glimpse of intent. And he interprets this eye contact as the granting of something, a licence or permission, and his jaw clenches mechanically. The blanket is off him now. His eyes are shut and his shoulder judders into her face.

She struggles, pushes him. The watch's electromagnetic pulse zings her wrist.

'Whitney!' She gasps, tries to wriggle free but he has his hand across her mouth, and his fingers are bitter, acidic. Charred. His thumb probes the inside of her cheek. She bites, tastes blood, and he yelps, tries to disentangle himself and falls off the bed. On to the floor. He staggers back, speechless, clutching his hand.

She feels her throat starting to tighten. Harder to breathe.

He crouches over her, a hand on her shoulder.

'Get off!' She kicks him. 'Get away.'

Under her blanket, she unscrews her pen, slips the pill into her mouth.

'Aina?' he asks, feeling for her with his hands. 'What was that? Aina love, are you okay?'

She bites. The capsule breaks and the dose hits.

'Just go to bed.' She pulls the blanket tight, rolls close to the wall, tense until his footsteps recede.

10

Stitch

SHE PINS THE SHEEP between her knees, straddling it, and she snips methodically with the scissors, working towards the hindquarters. Occasionally the sheep attempts to wriggle away, but soon it settles, perhaps understanding the process intuitively, or maybe it has been through this before. There is a notch in the soft felt of the sheep's ear. A wedge made by a knife to signify ownership or the year of its birth. She looks towards the spine. A clear sky. Blue. Hardly a cloud.

It takes a day to clean the fleece, untangling it from a variety of dried mud, shit and thistles. She shakes out the dirt and stuffs the fleece into hessian sacks. Filling one, then another. The sheep is a different animal without its coat. It looks vaguely annoyed.

Whitney sits at the table. She can feel him trying to catch her eye.

'I made you tea,' he says.

'Thanks.' She looks up, sees the Giverny on the side, steaming. 'I'll just see to this,' she says. She has had a long day, and there is nothing for dinner, and once she has collected her pill and slipped it into her pen, there is still more to be done. She collects the hessian sacks from the back door and carries them through to the bathroom.

'I was just remembering,' says Whitney, loudly over the sound of the bath. 'That hotel on the main square. The funny little porter, the night of the storm, you remember?'

Cold water splashes from the tub. She speaks, loud enough that he might hear. 'The night of the storm, we stayed at the d'Angleterre. We had a suite. Maxime was with us then.'

He looks confused. She has corrupted his game. Turned his fiction back on itself.

She continues, 'The day before, the Saturday, we visited the National Aquarium. And we visited the amusement park. Tivoli Gardens, you remember? Max was so tired. The rain was lashing down.'

'Aina, please—'

'Tivoli Gardens.'

He eyes the radio, nervously, and asks, whispering, if this is something to do with last night, something he did, and she is so far misunderstood, the question does not even warrant a response. Instead she takes a sack and dunks it in the tub, sloshing it until all buoyancy is lost, and when she lifts it from the bath, heavy and cumbersome, water trickles darkly from it.

'Aina … listen …'

She dunks it again, empties the wool. Swirls it with a stick. Pine needles spin like tiny canoes.

'Aina, is it him?'

She wants to throw the stick at him. She wants to beat him in the chest and hold his head underwater. But it is too much effort, too much effort being angry. And he hasn't done anything wrong. He's just … Whitney. Looking at her with those sad mopey eyes. She feels herself swaying. Fingertips on the doorframe. 'You remember how happy we were?' she asks.

He nods. 'Yeah.'

'Then stop trying to crase him.'

She closes the door softly, and she stands with her back to the wall, hidden from view, waiting for him to retreat to the nook. She undresses, folds her clothes neatly on the chair and lifts the pen from about her neck. Candlelight from the kitchen enters weakly through the frosted glass in the bathroom door. It does not reach the tub, whose filthy water smells vaguely of lowlands – pine, loamy – and as she clambers in, her skin constricts. Her body is a rock and the rock is porous and the cold reaches all parts of her, takes her breath away.

Max—

She picks out the pine needles, laying them on the rim of the bath to dry.

Max—

She used to go days without thinking about him, memories just another thing she learned to ration. When they first arrived, she would focus on tiny details, specifics, as a way to cauterise the wound. The wrinkle of his nose that would pre-empt laughter. The tiny lines crossing the palm of his hand. She would allow herself a minute per day, reliving childish moments in the saferoom, where they would play their little games. He would flip the dimmer switch and the room would go dark and he would switch the light back on and she would pull a new face, and he would giggle harder. She would arrange his futon and say, 'Okay now, that's enough, time for bed.'

She knew it worried Whitney, keeping this great ticking timebomb cooped up in the apartment. The metronome on his nightstand, punctuating the seconds, clack-clack-back, to help him sleep. *Where'd you learn that?* he asked. And she thinks of the piano, lacquered lid, shining black. He was right, they should have gotten rid of it, but it was an heir-loom, bequeathed to her by her grandmother, and it did not matter that it took up half a wall. And as Maxime grew, tod-dling, curious of things, he would reach for the keys, stretching nearer with every passing day. Whitney warned her so many times that she fashioned a lock for the lid, and each time she left Maxime alone in the flat, she would turn the key and hang it about her neck. And when Maxime was old enough to grasp the notion of risk, and he knew not to leave his cubby during the day, she began giving lessons again, and she resumed playing in the tin-tiled lounge of the Arts Club. Once a month. A short set. Jazz standards. Some blues. Over the years, the crowd had thinned, but she recog-nised a few faces. They never offered compliments or applause, but she would catch them sometimes, smiling inward, whispering a lyric or two. Notes. A half-forgotten melody.

Clack–clack–back.

She thinks of his toes, his hands, and the more he grew, the more she felt that she was denying him something. She misses him more at night, always has. A tiny sentinel, he was drawn to the window, and she would tell him to come away, warning him over and over lest his father catch him. But he stood defiant, face tilted, gazing at the lights, pointing as he repeated the words she had taught. *Up, down, in, out, mama, dada. Dada!* She did everything she could to keep him occupied. She bought books. Dictionaries. Grammatical guides. An atlas. At night, she tried to distract him with old street maps of Riga, Milan, Copenhagen. She would turn the pages and ask, 'Where do you want to go tonight?'

He turned to the window, pointed. 'Out.'

As the weeks turned to months, it sounded more and more like a threat, and reluctantly she began exploring itineraries. Day trips. If they could just make it through the summer … Whitney would be off visiting his sister, and there was the possibility of a whole week together, her and Maxime. If she could just …

Alone in the apartment, she began teaching him to swim. 'Imagine this is water,' she said. 'This whole room. Can you do that?'

His face … nodding. Turning from side to side, wriggling on his stomach, he swung his arms up past his ears. He listened. And she had to impose so many conditions and stipulations, at times she wondered if it could ever be worth it. But there was a pool across the city; she felt sure they would not see anyone they knew. And she just needed to handle the risks consistently, logically. She would devise playbooks in case they became separated, or he tripped and fell and hurt himself, or someone else. She would draw maps, and they would rehearse all manner of scenarios until every possible contingency was accounted for. She made a game of it.

'You're not to breathe a word of this to your father,' she said. 'You understand? And if anyone asks ...'

He looked up at her. 'I will tell them I am your nephew and you are my aunt.'

'And from where are you visiting?'

'From south of the river.'

'And what are you to do?'

'I am to nod politely.'

'Show me.'

He turned his eyelids inside out and waggled his tongue. 'Like this.'

'Okay,' she said.

'Really?' His smile—

'Tomorrow.' She patted his knee. 'Tomorrow. We go.'

———

She steps from the bath, and her body tingles warmer as she stands on the mat. She feels her abdomen. The two waxy scars. One a smile; the other a frown. There is no way she could ever get pregnant again, not even if she wanted to. Time and knives have seen to that.

She adds the needles to those she has already collected, wrapping them in a torn strip of paper that she slips into her cardigan pocket. In the kitchen, she arranges the wool on the rack, restocks the fire and sets fresh water atop the stove.

The tea in her mug is long since cold.

11

Peat

DAY THIRTY-ONE, THE SECOND week of May. She will take her pills four and a half hours after they are dispensed. And every pill feels like a small triumph, as though she is gaining time. She carries the spade over her shoulder as rain patters her cagoule, and she follows the track up the valley, hiking through low cloud, past the line of stunted willows bending leeward; each one slightly taller than the last. It is a month since she started digging the peat. The pain in her foot is barely a twinge now.

She halts, shields her eyes. There is something or someone up ahead. Where the path splits, a figure stands veiled in mist.

The scratch of her cagoule and the sound of her breath fill her ears. She drops from sight and crawls, flat to the wet grass, in behind a lump of granite. She lowers her hood. Looks around. There is nowhere she can run without being seen, so she waits in the hollow, listening intently for the squelch of mud up the track, anything, but the mist dampens the reach of sound and minutes pass. A muted stillness descends. Cold too. She places her face to the rock. The mists part and she risks a look, and whoever is there has not seen her. He has not moved at all. It takes her a moment, and then her breath comes steady, and she clambers up around the rock, feeling foolish to be covered in mud. The figure is one of Whitney's sculptures. Cast in bronze, an inhuman senti-nel. A wire blindfold covering the eyes. It is the third that she has seen.

The first presides over the bay, looking out to sea. She had spotted it on the morning of Day Twenty-One while coming back from her run by way of the beach. Low tide, blue sky reflecting in the wet sand. She had assumed it was Whitney from the posture and the build and the way it graced the berm. But as she approached, it did not move. And then she saw him, Whitney, up in the fallow field behind the croft, and she stopped short, unable to process the scene, and she snuck back the way she had come to warn him. She felt her cheeks redden as he explained her mistake. That he found it so amusing only unnerved her further.

The next morning, while feeding the sheep, she had found another, seemingly identical, watching the croft from among the reeds at the back of the marsh. She dumped the scraps, went looking for Whitney and found him rinsing courgettes in the sink. She asked bluntly, 'How many more are there?'

Whitney smiled. 'A few. They shouldn't be too hard to find.' He placed the last courgette in the colander, looked up at her. 'I'm sensing a reservation ...'

'They're kind of hideous, Whitney.' She pointed down the beach. 'Everywhere I turn it's like I'm being watched.'

'You've misread the intention. You're projecting.'

'But they're all *intended* to look like you, aren't they? Your height, your build? The shape of your face—'

'There'll be similarities, differences too, though maybe they can't be seen from afar.'

She felt anger rising, as though his intention was simply to provoke a reaction. 'Are you just bored?'

He chuckled. 'No, Aina. No, no.'

'What then? Explain it to me.'

'It's like ...' He took a moment. 'The body's the only real prison there is.'

She looked out across the marsh and something clicked. 'This is your way of escaping?'

His face relaxed. 'To make amends, we must first face up to what we did.'

'*We?*'

'The both of us.'

'For parole?'

'Exactly.' He nodded. 'We have to confront the past, Aina. Leave something of us behind.'

Beneath the wire, the sculpture's face is featureless like the back of a spoon. An oversized chess piece. She repositions the spade on her shoulder and continues swiftly along the left-hand fork. She has started taking her notebook with her whenever she leaves the croft, carrying it in a waterproof ziplock bag and filling it with sketches. The sketches are landscapes, amateurish impressions of the beach, the valley and the view over the moor; they will offer justification for her recent attachment to the pen, should Whitney ever question it.

At the top of the valley, she stops, takes her pen and starts drawing. From above, the croft looks so serene. An idyll. The two solar panels on the cottage's roof are the same colour as the overcast sea. In the garden, the sheep is a speck beside the washing line, and she can see Whitney in the field beyond. She thinks he might be another of his sculptures, but it is him; his chequered shirt moves against the colourless land.

She draws the curve of the bay, and the boats, dotted at ease along the berm. It does not take her long.

A stream chatters nearby. It joins with other tributaries down the valley, becoming visible as pure white over rocks. She used to know all kinds of words for specific types of streams. Ones that run only in summer; they had a name. And ones that could be heard but not seen; they had a name too, but she has forgotten now. Now everything is simply a stream or a brook and she does not know the difference. They babble down the valley, and from here the croft looks cut off, an island surrounded by the sea, the stream and the back-reaches of the marsh.

To a fresh page, a new sketch. She draws: a boyish mop of hair, a mischievous smile, a kink in one ear. Maxime. It is basic, and the eyes fail to capture his liveliness, but it will do. A gust of wind blows down the valley and she looks back down the path. Wait. The angle of the head. The broad-backed posture. The sculpture is not Whitney. It is Maxime. A projection of him. Grown, as he would be now: a young man.

The realisation creates a disturbance within her. Memories percolate and merge, unfolding across time. Clack-clack-back. Forwards and back. Forwards and back. A sink, a room, a pool. The voices of children from the local swim team echo through the changing rooms. Whitney has taken his annual week of leave as usual, and Maxime is delighted to get back in the water. His face, all goggles and smiles as he grips the float and kicks. He is nine. She remembers walking the deck with her stopwatch in hand. The smell of chlorine in Maxime's hair; the green tint it would leave. She will need to be careful about that ... And that last time, after he sets off on a length of crawl, she waits for him to surface before starting the timer.

'Eighty-seven seconds!' she says, when he touches the wall. 'A new record!'

Clack-clack-back. The metronome. His bedside. The second hand of a clock, mounted high on wall.

In the next lane, a steady procession of youngsters flip-turn off the wall. One after another – barely a second between them – their elongated bodies ripple off underwater. Maxime watches them too, and she knows there will be questions tonight. He wants to go with them, and each time he asks, she forbids it, telling him it is not safe, that he is especially vulnerable. In the last year, her lies have become increasingly elaborate, becoming intertwined with reports of melting permafrost and toxic spores in the northern canton, and she uses these stories to her advantage, as grounds to procure vitamins, which she gives him at mealtimes, as a means to keep him healthy. His dependency grows, but what else can she do? There are rumours, coming with increasing frequency, of families of illegitimates being rounded up and forced to choose. Husbands, wives, mothers, fathers, children being separated and taken off to a place of internment. It does not bear thinking about, if he were to be found.

At the sound of a whistle, Aina looks up and there is something familiar about the team's coach. She looks different in tracksuit bottoms and a white polo shirt, and her face has aged badly, but it is her. Aina knows from the voice, the manner in which she consults the swimmers and offers instructions. The stern insistence. The woman reaches the end of the pool, turns and begins walking back towards her. Lucia, swinging a whistle around her finger. 'Okay, everyone,' she shouts. 'That'll do for today.'

Aina wants to slip away but she cannot leave Maxime. And now Lucia halts beside her. They stand side by side, the two women. Lucia's focus is solely on the boy. 'He shows promise,' she says. 'Has he been swimming long?'

'About a week,' Aina replies.

'How's his backstroke?'

Maxime bobs at the far end of the pool. Together they watch him swim over to the steps. Water drips from him as he clambers out.

Lucia turns and finally looks at her. There is a flicker of recognition. A silent gasp. 'Oh, my God! Aina, so good to see you!'

And she talks too much and too fast, everything in some way an explanation, and Lucia's smile hardens on her face.

'This is your son?' she asks. 'Isn't he lovely.'

She hears the patter and slap of wet feet over her shoulder. Here he comes. Lithe-limbed with pre-emptive biceps and the faint trace of yoghurt-pot abdominals. She wraps the towel around him. Rubs his back. She has planned for this. The denial rolls off her tongue. 'No, no. This is my nephew,' she says. 'He's staying with us a few weeks. Max, this is my friend, Lucia. Say hello.'

She nudges Maxime but he does not speak. He shuffles in behind her. Clamps to her leg.

'He's a little shy,' she says, noticing how Lucia holds her clipboard tighter across her chest. Behind her, the girls of the swim team whisper and exchange glances as they head towards the changing room.

It is suddenly awkward. Lucia's countenance has changed, and she is stiff. She goes to speak and then stops.

A tickle in Aina's throat. And to break the silence, she asks after Delaney, and Lucia tells her he is fine, well, in fact. And the pool is suddenly empty. Water glugs in the overspill. A lone man sits in the spectator seats, high above.

'I'd better be going,' says Lucia. 'We've got two now. They're such a handful.'

'Yes. Of course. Well …'

'Well?'

'It was so nice to see you again.'

'Yes.' Lucia begins hurrying away. And it seems so obvious, as she looks back, this heightening sense of her own misjudgement. She was becoming numb to the risks. Brazen even. Of course something had to give.

On the moor, the heather is greening up and the sphagnum moss is in flower. The bank that she has cut from the peat is three feet deep and a hundred wide. Despite the recent rain, the topsoil is dry, brittle almost, and it takes the better part of an hour to strip the layer of turf. She rests, drinks tea from her Thermos and then continues. The spade's handle is smooth and she is quick with it, lifting neat rectangular blocks with an economy of movement. She is an old hand at this now.

She thinks of the peat as a repository of time. A dictionary of years, storing all sorts of measurements, the way some glaciers used to trap pollen and log atmospherics. She found a boat in the peat once, several years before. A wooden thing, possibly Viking, that Whitney hung from the rafters in his studio. Keel, beams, oarlocks, all preserved in remarkable detail. Wood smooth as cooked bones.

She half expects to find a body out there. Lionel's, perhaps, curled around a rock, his face a death-mask frozen with fear. And the deeper she digs, the heavier the peat becomes, and soon the blocks resemble oversized slabs of fudge. She moves methodically down the line, heaving them atop the bank, calculating as she goes. Once dried, a slab will yield four briquettes that will burn for an hour each. For an average winter, they will need anywhere between fifteen and twenty per day. Four thousand briquettes total.

All morning, she lays the turf on top of the bank. A mist rolls in. By her calculations, the peat banks grow at a rate of one millimetre per year, and she stands there, hour after hour, cutting through centuries.

In a way, she thinks, she will miss this once she leaves.

12

Broadcast

DAY FORTY-SEVEN. SEVEN HOURS gained. Rain hammers the skylight, and she cannot sleep. She tries breathing exercises, memory games; she tries reciting old poems. She counts in French, in German, in Latin. She counts in Japanese, Korean, Russian. She pictures the sheep: *brebis, oveja, kondoo.* What is the Flemish for sheep?

No answer comes to mind. Only the sounds of the croft and the night and the clog–clog–clog of her consciousness. Gears. Wheels. She imagines a tugboat sailing towards open water. Seawater dripping from the main line that rises from the water. The line is taut, and is connected to a vast harbour wall. A tether. Like the lead of a large, powerful dog, which drags her down pathways, into brambles. Into places where there is no path. The dog meanders and is off again and her arm yanks in its socket, unexpectedly, and the line is like reins, like toddler reins, and then the line goes slack. She pulls, keeps pulling, but the line has been cut. She is alone in a blackthorn thicket, watched by amber eyes. An animal: dark zeroes of nostril sniff the air. And suddenly she is awake. Jolted. Not even aware that sleep was coming up on her. 04:56. She dimples the watch, takes the pen from about her neck and tips the pill into her hand. The pill feels large, oversized. She places it between her teeth. Checks the watch. Counts the way she would when leading into a solo. *Yan tan tethera*. She feels that first constriction in her throat, then she bites. Not rushing. Not even a hair ahead of the beat. 04:57.

The pill. Her pen. A key.

She can do this with her eyes closed.

The screen on her watch goes dark, and she lies still, blinking. Retinal echoes of the watch face appear: rectangles of indigo, becoming rhomboids, kites and nameless quadrilaterals whose angles fold and bend and refract like the angles on a sundial, until what is left of the shapes disseminates into a shower of violet sparks. There is the faintest smell of matches in the room. She inhales, slowly, and there is Maxime, sat hunched at the piano. Was he drawn to risk through inquisitiveness, curiosity, a defiance stoked by the simple imposition of boundaries? Or was it something inherited? Did he learn it from her?

The croft is a place of quiet distillation. The sound of the wind is gentle, soothing, and the waves come as murmurs. Must be the tide is on the turn; she pictures the beach exposed under a gleaming moon. She hears a rustle of air. It might be snoring except, at the other end of the attic, she sees the ripple of white bedsheets. Whitney is not in bed. His covers are drawn back. He is up, and she thinks that he might be standing at the bottom of her bed. She stares hard into shadow until her eyes adjust to the dim.

Bidden, curious. She crosses to the staircase. At the bottom, the door is ajar, and a sliver of light jags upon the stairs. She steps down. Traces her hand along the uneven wall. Leaning closer, she hears Whitney's voice, low-timbred, mumbling, 'Warden. Come in … Warden, this is Long Sky Croft.'

A soft crackle like the sound of a small fire in an empty room. Static. Then … she strains … hears the sound of breathing on the line. Something connects, and it should feel like relief, but a coldness washes over her. An icy vulnerability. This is a threat to her plan.

She approaches the bottom of the stairs. The door is cracked. And she thinks of Maxime in the saferoom. Alone in the dark, peering out at the world.

Whitney stands with his back to her. He is so close. He moves a piece on the chessboard. 'Knight to B7,' he whispers. 'Check.'

The sound of the wind, or a chuckle, comes through the receiver.

She takes a step forward. A slight compression beneath her foot. The board squeaks.

Her breath hangs in the air.

Whitney turns and she ducks back against the wall. Panic swells in her. She holds her breath, hears the click of the receiver – the slack of the coil against the wall – and she starts retreating swiftly upstairs. Across the attic, to her bed.

It is still warm. She pulls the covers up to her neck. Wind passes through the chimney breast above her. She hears the sound of the latch closing. The scuff of footsteps on the stairs. A form appears in the doorway. He stands, pauses. A silvery outline of a man until the door closes and his image melts away. Darkness. She cannot tell if he is inside the room. She clasps the pen about her neck.

She hears footsteps – or the throb of blood in her ears.

The bedsprings creak on the far side of the room.

'Goodnight, Aina,' he says.

13

Tor

I T IS NOT YET 7 A.M. One week to go.

She has finished sanding each piece of the jigsaw, front and back, leaving 768 wooden segments, all of them double-sided, all of them blank. This complicates matters, and the jigsaw can now be completed upside down or right-side up. It is like being simultaneously in the Antarctic and the Arctic. Never quite sure which is which.

'Ingenious,' says Whitney, patting dry his clean-shaven face. 'I'll give you that.'

He makes little humming sounds and tuts, as if he wants to help, but she offers no encouragement and he has no idea where to start. The pieces are all broadly identical, and after hovering a moment, he pours himself a mug of tea, and she watches from the corner of her eye, wary of his good mood. He goes to the larder, returns with the seed crate. 'What shall I plant?' he asks cheerfully. 'Any requests?' He sets the crate on the sideboard, fanning the packets like playing cards. Fifty seeds per pack. Enough for another year, or two at a stretch. They are marked with faded stencils; a picture of a vegetable and the words: Keep Dry. 'I'm thinking onions, broad beans. Maybe a few tomatoes.'

'Sure. If you like,' she says. 'Go with the beans.'

He looks over. 'I know it's not much,' he says, 'but there's enough to see us through.' Beyond him, the window is pale and bright with morning. 'Who knows, perhaps in October, the salmon will run.'

But October is such a long way off, she thinks. She looks up: Whitney has stopped what he was doing and is gazing straight at her with piercing eyes.

'You're still worried about the Warden?' He steps towards her. 'Look, he'll probably come when we least expect it. A watched pot and all that. And this,' he gestures at the seeds. 'This is just a precaution. More for whoever follows. We've got to keep the ground ticking over, you know that.'

'Have you considered, though … What if you're wrong?'

'About parole?' He smiles coyly, shakes his head.

She continues on with the jigsaw, turning pieces around in her fingers. Sometimes they fit and sometimes they do not, and when they do not, they go back into the pile. Whitney goes back to his planting schedule, and something like a minute passes and the wind whistles through the croft, rattling the windows and doors. She watches as he fills his Thermos with tea. It is the complacency, the way he is so sure of himself, nonchalant. Was he always this way? She stares at the table, works her thumbnail into the wood, and the next time she looks up, he has gone, either to his studio or the garden. She consults her journal, makes a note of her pill times, and prepares to head out. Hat, scarf, layers, pen.

The notebook's pages flap in the breeze.

She spends the morning barrowing peat down off the moor. Safely, she can carry upwards of fifty briquettes per trip, and she has made four trips so far. Back and forth. Every stone, rut and furrow on the path is known to her; the barrow's wheel churns stripes in the mud, deeper heading down than on the way back up. It will take the best part of a week to clear the haul. And then another four months for the peat to dry. Maybe Whitney's right. Perhaps she will be long gone by then. Maybe they both will.

When she has finished with the peat, she goes along the cliff to a large formation of boulders, the tor, made of broad granite discs that balance precariously, like a stack of plates left by some giant's hand. On the highest slab is a small cairn. Eleven flat pieces of rock. She finds a twelfth in the marram grass, and adds it to the heap of stones, one for every year.

———

She sits on the floor wearing a mud-stained fleece and shorts. The earthenware tiles are cold against her legs as she lowers her forehead to her knee, and holds the stretch. She is becoming increasingly limber. The pill clock blinks – 13:56. A minute passes. Watching the barn, there is no sign of movement. She has a sudden awareness of quiet.

What if something has happened?

'Whitney?' she calls. 'It's nearly two ...'

The pill clock turns green. She has not seen him since breakfast. She is quickly to her feet, calling again, 'Whitney?'

Where is he?

She is through the door and into sunlight, momentarily blinded.

His head appears between the rows of early-season chard. He seems stiff, frail. His knees are muddy. 'Did you call?' he asks.

She taps her finger to the watch. 'Two p.m.,' she says. 'Come on.'

The pill clock is still green, and she stands to one side, letting him go first. He saunters in, brushing off the mud, and scans his thumb. She follows. The pill clock whirrs and clicks. He heads to the larder, and she slips her pill into her pen.

'The magpie's back,' he says, returning with a tub of oats. 'She's been following me all morning.'

'Uh-huh.' She scoops two servings of oats into bowls, pausing as he collects their mugs from the drying rack. The Danish mug and her enamel one. Then she gives her bowl an extra scoop, hoping that he won't see.

'You know,' he says, motioning at her bowl, 'maybe you shouldn't take so much.'

She pours hot water over her oats and stirs the mixture into a vague amalgamation of liquid and solid.

'And it's bad for your digestion to run on a full stomach.'

'I don't recall it ever bothered you.'

His shoulders tense, but he lets it lie. 'Point taken,' he says.

She sprinkles dried seaweed liberally and eats from her bowl, standing up. The food has an uninviting texture but it is nourishing; the seaweed gives it a pleasing bite.

Whitney blows on his spoon. 'Are you composing again?' he asks.

For a moment she is confused and then she sees that her notebook is open on the kitchen table. He runs his finger down a page. Her breath quickens. She has too much food in her mouth – can hardly swallow – and her instinct is to bat him away and snatch the notebook, except doing so would only make him more suspicious. She must have left it there all morning. Rows of numbers on display: her pill times. What was she thinking?

'Actually, I've been drawing.' She takes the chair beside him, flicks backwards to a page showing a sketch of the moor, turning the notebook so he can see.

He looks askance. 'Drawing? You …?'

'I needed a way to … process things. Engage with the land. There's no music for me here.'

His face softens and he smiles, knowingly. 'Did I ever tell you how sounds continue to reverberate long after we're able to hear them? They say if you had a powerful enough microphone you could hear conversations that took place years ago. Did I ever tell you that?'

'You did.'

'And?'

'I don't believe that's true, Whitney.' But she is keen to keep him onside. 'Anyway,' she shuffles towards him, 'what do you think?'

He studies the drawing intently. 'You rely too much on shading to give a sense of distance,' he says, licking his finger and smudging the line of the brook. 'And you'd be better off using a pencil instead of a pen. But a change of medium can do wonders. You're right about that. Perhaps if you tried charcoal …?'

His teeth scrape the spoon as he talks and eats at the same time. She nods occasionally, and upon finishing his critique, he turns the page. Flicks ahead. The sketch of Maxime gazes up at them. The next page will be her pill times. Her schedule. The steam coming off his porridge moves slower than the steam coming off the tea.

Whitney is still. Fingertips on the edge of the page.

She places a hand firmly on the journal, stopping him from turning the page. 'I see him everywhere,' she says. 'In mirrors. In you. The statues.' Her words bubble up. 'I'm dreaming of him too. I can't control it. I dreamed he was sat where you are now. Lighting matches.' She meets his eyes, staring intently. Appealing to his vanity is the only way. 'What you said before, about confronting the past … I think it inspired me.'

Whitney halts. Oats harden like concrete on the rim of his bowl. 'That's good, Aina.' He exhales slowly, leans back in his chair. 'I'm glad to hear it. Focus on the things we can control.'

She has drawn his attention from the page, and she leans forward, folds the notebook closed and holds it stiffly to her chest. She looks up from the table. 'Right, like parole.'

Her sarcasm misses its mark. 'Precisely,' he says. 'The radio, the broadcast. Last night, there was someone on the line. You heard him too, I believe. The Warden.'

His focus has shifted away from her notebook, and she feels a little more confident. 'You're sure it wasn't the wind?' she asks.

'We'll see now, won't we.' He sizes up her attire and adds, 'But if you want my advice, you should spend less time running and more time sketching. You might find it helps.'

She shrugs, unwilling to yield.

'How far will you go?' he asks eventually.

'Twelve miles.'

'East?' He raises an eyebrow. This is his little joke. A way to bridge the distance between them. She has no choice but to head east, since west, there is only the sea, and the little plinths of islands visible at low tide.

'I'll go up to the tor,' she says. 'Then probably loop back inland via the moor and round to Whit's End.'

He thinks on this. 'That's more than twelve miles. Whichever path you take.'

She nods. Sometimes it is easier to just nod. And they talk on, and it is not unfriendly. She runs her hand along the edge of the table, circling the black knots, and they talk about paths, tracks, trails, ones that hold well in the wet, and there is something shared here. He asks her how many miles that will be for the week, and she tells him, 'About thirty.'

'Your legs feel all right?'

'A little tight in the hamstrings. Pretty good on the whole.'

'And your foot? It's healed okay?'

'It's fine.'

He sits back. 'You must be averaging close to ten-minute miles,' he says.

'Eight and a half, with the wind.'

The faintest trace of a frown crosses his brow. 'Ah, but you won't be able to sustain that across open country. And if the wind's with you on the way out, you'll need to be extra careful coming back.'

For his longest run of forty-eight miles, he had needed to maintain ten-minute miles for a full eight hours. She is closing in on this, but he is right. Until now, she has kept to paths and the beach; she would be wise to vary the terrain. Still, she is making progress, faster than he imagined.

Something changes in his face. The way he scratches his cheek. For whatever reason, he is more threatened by her running than her drawing. And she knows she should not push him, but she cannot resist. 'I'm thinking, next week I might cross the spine,' she adds.

Whitney's eyes tighten, and his mouth narrows. 'I see,' he says, nodding, carrying his bowl to the sink. 'The spine? In this weather?' He chuckles, dismissively. 'It's not just time and wind you need to account for; there are traps, snares.'

'I'm careful,' she says, scraping the last of her bowl.

'But why risk it?'

She chews. 'Maybe I'd like to see for myself.'

'Waste of time,' he says.

'Really?' She meets his eye. Holds his stare. And she should just let it go, maintain the peace and stick to her plan. But instead she takes the wrapper from her pocket, and empties the small collection of needles on the table.

He prods the heap with his finger. 'Is that pine?'

'Uh-huh.' She nods. 'They were snagged on the sheep.'

He leans back against the sideboard, arms folded. 'So?'

'So it walked pretty recently through a forest.' She gestures at the door, at the window. 'You see an abundance of pine round here, Whitney?'

'It must have come from some other isle, like I said—'

'Right! You expect me to believe the sheep swam here, all the way from God knows where?'

'How should I know? Maybe it's been here all along,' he scoffs. 'Maybe there's a cove that we missed on the Northshore where pine needles wash in, and there's a small rabble of sheep that frolic thereabouts on the sand.'

His gall is incredible. 'Can you hear yourself? Twelve years and we've never once seen a sheep. This isn't an island, is it? This is a peninsula, and we're connected somehow to the mainland. Just admit it, for pity's sake!'

'Aina ...' He glances towards the maps on the sideboard, hunches down beside her. 'I don't know how else to say this, there's nothing but sea. I promise.' He reaches for her. 'Aina—'

He is either lying or he is blind to it. She pulls away.

'You really think everything'll go back to how it was, don't you?' she says. 'That we'll do our time here and everything will revert. You'll go back to the DER. I'll go back to the piano ... as if he never existed.'

She thinks of the piano, the soft yield of the keys.

'Aina. We're almost there. They'll be coming, any day now.'

'Parole? Please. No one's there. Something's happened—'

'A test, that's all. Our debt is nearly paid.'

'Our debt? Whitney, they took him from us. Our son ... They took him from us and they sent him out here alone. He was a boy, Whitney. You talk about debt. About confronting our past. *They* owe *us.*'

He gestures at her notebook. 'I understand the guilt you feel, but we must atone; we have to show remorse. And our remorse must be for what we did. Not for getting caught. That's how we get to go home.'

'You're fucking nuts, Whitney. You're playing around with your stupid kiln and your stupid sculptures, while he's out there, alone, trapped, waiting. Not knowing if we'll come.'

'He's not a boy any more, Aina.'

She feels her face harden, a rock, impervious to his glare. She meets his eye. 'It's like you want to abandon him all over again.'

'For God's sake,' he turns sharply, sweeping everything from the table. The needles, their cutlery. Her bowl smashes across the room. 'I'm not abandoning anyone!'

She stands, feels an impulse towards violence. And she is shouting. They both are. Their voices are indistinct. A babble, like the streams running down off the moor, and she can no longer hear herself. He is like the stupid sheep, tied up in the yard, tamely waiting out its days, and she cannot bear this: parole, him, the croft. She has to get away. She barges past him and out the door, running. Through the gate and along the track. The wind against her, and she is glad for it. She sprints to the beach, and the sand is wet and heavy, and it saps the energy from her legs. But she pushes on, picturing Maxime. His face, as he would be today. Eyes unblinking. And time is running backwards. He is younger now. And his face grows youthful, increasingly familiar, increasingly distressed.

She runs, and someone catches her, and holds her back. The wind. The terror of it. The apartment is overrun. The carpet sodden. People in uniform, they have her boy, and they are dragging him from the cubby. Someone is holding her back, and there is nothing she can do but watch as they carry him out, legs kicking. He screams, *Mama!*

In the corner of the room, the lid to the piano is up. The white keys. And the metronome ticks. She runs. Yan tan tethera. Yan tan tethera. Yan tan tethera methera pip.

Clack. Clack. Back.

Clack. Clack. Back.

Clack. Clack—

Running. Past what is left of *Rorvik*. The trawler's wooden hull reconstituted as charcoal in the barn. She runs into the dunes. Slower. The incline saps. Come on, come on! She wills herself up to the moor, barely quicker than walking pace, but she makes it. She is famished. Dizzy. She will never get by on oats alone; she needs something else. The land stretches out and in the distance, a thin band of rock waits. The spine.

Something makes her hesitate.

She looks back the way she has come. The valley, the marsh. The first drops of rain fall, and she squints at the gathering clouds, the sky, the sea. She spots something bobbing, two miles out, past the headland. A lone mast on the turbulent sea. Foresail curved, bulging in the wind. The next second it has gone. The sail has been reeled in, or blown away, or perhaps she imagined it, and the horizon is closer now that the boat has vanished. There is just a jumble of whitecaps, emptiness in her stomach and a keeling in her heart, telling her something is wrong.

14

Mutton

SHE IS WET THROUGH by the time she makes it back to the croft. In the kitchen, she finds the binoculars in a drawer, goes back outside. The gutters are overflowing and mud squelches thick in the yard.

'Did you see it?' she asks.

It takes Whitney a moment to understand. 'A boat?' he says. 'You're sure?'

'Hundred per cent. Some kind of cutter. It must have rounded the headland.'

'And the sails were up? In this weather?' He gestures for the binoculars, scans the ocean. 'Maybe a Fata Morgana. A trick of the waves and the light.'

'I know what I saw. Someone's out there—'

'In a sailboat?' The squall whips his hair about his face. 'No, it must have been a patrol.' He nods, pensively, handing back the binoculars. 'The Warden. The test … of course.'

She calls after him, 'What would the Warden need with a sailboat?', but he does not answer. He simply goes to the kitchen, leaving her out there alone.

All week it rains, and nothing comes off the sea. Not a thing. She is famished. Her mouth aches. A tooth is coming loose and she is awake when the silent alarm goes. 05:42. She retrieves her pen, takes her pill, and downstairs, the pill clock blinks. She has half completed the jigsaw, and it should be getting easier now, but in all likelihood she will never get it finished. Not that it matters. In two days, she will have her pill. Forty-eight hours, that is all.

The pill clock blinks green and they collect their morning pills. She does not tell Whitney what she is planning. After breakfast he heads to his studio, across the yard, and she has no stomach for another circuitous debate. She clears away the jigsaw, wipes down the counter and sets up a makeshift brining station by the sink. With all the mud and water, the threat of bacteria is high, so she sterilises the empty airtight jars, using boiling water from the stove, and dries them thoroughly with the cleanest cloth to hand. In each jar, she pours measures of sugar and salt. Hanging space in the hearth is limited, so she will only smoke a little of the meat, wet-curing the bulk of it. She sharpens the scissors and a long shanking knife that she will use for filleting.

She decides on the spade instead of the speargun, and runs the whetstone along the shovel's edge until it shines. She is better with the spade, she tells herself. After all those hours spent up on the moor, the skin on her palms is as thick as leather soles. The spade feels like an extension of herself.

Outside, her hair blows in tufts. The rain soaks her jeans while the animal nibbles at what little grass remains. Most of the garden is mud now. The only sound is the clanging coming from Whitney's shed.

She looks up at the sky, and then she straddles the sheep, pinning it behind the shoulders with her knees. The animal writhes as she rests the spade on the back of its neck. With one hand on the handle and the other on the hilt, she measures the blow, and she digs as if cutting through centuries.

The clanging stops.

Whitney emerges from his studio, and when he sees the sheep, he stops short. 'What have you done?' he whispers.

The fringes of sky darken with a gathering storm, and she knows what she must look like, matted in blood with her arm up to the elbow in the animal's innards. She brandishes the spade at him. 'Don't,' she says calmly. 'Turn around. Back to your shed.'

'Aina—'

'I said: Fuck off back to your shed.'

15

Proxy

D AY FIFTY-FOUR. this is it, she knows the rest of the schedule by heart. She collects her lunchtime pill, slips it into her pen. She will take it at 21:57. Then at 22:00, when her evening pill is dispensed, she will not need to take it at all. It will be her spare. Fifty-four days, delaying each and every pill by three minutes, and she is almost there. One last dispensation. That is all. And at that point, with time to hand, the choice over whether to stay or whether to go will become hers. It will be her first real decision in years.

She spent half the night hacking at the sheep's carcass, sealing the joints in brine, and now a shoulder roasts slowly over the hearth. Fat sizzles, dripping on hot stone, as she slides a dull blade into the joint and the meat comes away with ease. It burns crisply on the outsides, staying silky within.

Whitney approaches slowly. She knew he would not be able to stay away once the smell of the mutton reached him.

'Go on then,' he says, propping himself on her armrest. 'Cut me a slice.'

It feels like a victory of sorts – hollow, shame filled, sweet – and she tries to focus, to prepare herself mentally for her journey across the spine. A last night, and then in the morning, she will be gone.

She was twenty-six, the first time she became pregnant. They had been married a year. He was doing well at the Department for Energy and Resource, and she had been offered a semi-regular spot with the Philharmonic. There was no reason for them to be worried.

She had told him immediately when she found out. It had come as such a surprise. 'Are you happy?' she asked, uncertain. 'Is this what you want?'

Whitney looked at her in disbelief, but he smiled and she found herself laughing with him. 'Of course!' he said. 'It's going to be a boy. I can feel it.' And he made her lie on her back as he dangled a threaded needle above her belly, waiting for it to move. 'It's swinging,' he said. 'No. Wait. No, it's circling.'

'Circling?'

'Yes.'

'Is that a boy?'

'I don't know,' he said. 'I thought you knew.'

Under the terms of PTC, they had to apply retroactively, once the pregnancy was confirmed. Everyone complained that it made the whole process so much worse, so much more inefficient, but the minister who sponsored the bill said that the important thing was that the initial choice still lay with the couple. And that would never change. Autonomy – or the appearance of autonomy – was vital, and the government should (and would) only intervene as a last resort. And the policy achieved its aims. Uncertainty made for an excellent deterrent; cheap and efficient, it stoked people's fears. The birth rate tapered, then dropped, then plummeted with the introduction of a three-strikes rule. A mandatory hysterectomy and ex-habitation for anyone unlucky and stupid enough to fail the PTC three times. It was the vulnerable that suffered most. Those on the periphery. Residents of the city's poorest quarters. People like Delaney and Lucia, they were fine, skating along. And Aina assumed she and Whitney would be too. They lived in a bracket of ignorance – not rich, not wealthy, but nowhere near poor – and she had no trouble obtaining the relevant assertations, checks and testimonials. She filed promptly, ahead of the preliminary deadline at eight weeks, and it felt like things were aligned. They looked good on paper. People would be rooting for them. A simple formality ...

But the letter back was weightless, prompt as it was curt: *Permission to Conceive denied.* Somehow they had come up short.

There was no explanation. The mandatory termination was booked for the same week.

'There must have been a mix-up,' she said. 'There must be something we can do.' She suggested they might obtain the necessary paperwork through backchannels. She had an old school friend – Amal – at District Hall, who might help. Or they could forge one. 'Maybe you could speak to your boss,' she said. 'Do you think he'd appeal on our behalf?'

Whitney shook his head: they would be mad to risk it, mad to tell anyone, especially his boss, and he was right. There were no concessions. No lottery. No bribes. It was law; every child needed a permit, and theirs had been denied. It seemed so unfair. So ridiculous to have to apply, after the act, *ex post*. It was vindictive, cruel, exploitative. But there was no way of fighting it now. There was no appeals process, no form of recourse. What choice did she have? On the date shown, she took a taxi up the North Sea Road, to the address in Ullamoor, printed on the slip. The clinic was rundown, above a noodle shop, not far from where she grew up. A backdrop of refineries and the broken dome of the old LNG terminal. A nurse buzzed her in. A flight of stairs. 'You the ten a.m.?' asked the nurse. 'Come in, please. Don't tell me your name. You should have a slip, a piece of paper … Thank you. Dr Nangelis won't be a minute.'

Dr Nangelis. Tall, thin, with age spots on his hands. He spoke calmly about what would happen. There would be a blood test. An ultrasound. One pill that she had to take in the presence of the nurse, and another to be taken at home two days later. The first would shut off the pregnancy. The second would flush it out.

———

The sun is starting to dip. Soon she will light the candle. Twelve hours now. It feels tangible; the culmination of so much hard work. Only her restlessness affects the tempo of the day; the minutes span out in widening plateaus.

Daylight gradually wanes and early-evening raindrops settle on the window; each a prism for the grey sweep beyond. She watches them, fed by tiny tributaries until adhesion is lost and one jags away down the pane. It closes in on another, fatter drop. Buffeted by the wind, it edges closer until the two collide, and a single drop runs on.

She has been doodling. Her music book is open on her lap. On a fresh page, she lines up the five horizontal staff lines so that the shadows of the raindrops fall upon them. She circles some, adds stems and fixes them as notes. A tune rises. A familiar melody. She hums: one-two-three, one-two-three, one-two-three-four-five.

Her second pregnancy was unintended. An error. It followed quickly after the first. She had been drunk. And neither she nor Whitney had contraception to hand. She told Whitney it did not matter. She said she was at the wrong point in her cycle, and that it would all be fine. And he did not take much convincing. She just wanted to forget the process, its mechanics, to enjoy a few minutes of carefree abandon for a change. But she woke, the next morning, and she knew right away what was coming. Dreading everything, it was almost a relief when it was confirmed. Whitney called her stupid and reckless, and he did not speak to her for days. It would have been easier to just skip the PTC altogether, manage it off-book, but the tiniest sliver of hope convinced her otherwise. She should have known better. The result was another letter. Another trip up the North Sea Road to see Dr Nangelis. Blood test. Ultrasound. Two pills. Kept in overnight this time.

In the months that followed she barely spoke to anyone. What could she say? She certainly could not speak to Whitney. Instead, she began to imagine a dark cubby under the stairs in their apartment. A place for hiding. One strike remained, and the months wound on, and her rage crystallised, turned dark, beyond despair into something resolute. Grit, or stubbornness. She could not tell.

Whitney coped in the most unimaginative way possible. He threw himself into his work. Scared, feeble, but he was busy. She saw it as a weakness. She did not want to be rid of the pain, or to smother it somehow. She wanted to endure it. Outlast it. To fortify. And soon they were moving into a nice new apartment in a smart high-rise where they kept to themselves. And the apartment became her chrysalis. Almost without trying, their credits started to tally. Whitney won a promotion to the press office, handling strategy and communications, and occasionally she started going out. She felt aged. Her smile a fabrication, drawn. She cut ties with the Arts Club, and took up swimming. And she started playing at luncheons and dinners. Private recitals at rich people's houses, taking their money, watching the kids eating long-tailed tempura with quiet disdain. Meanwhile, Whitney was made a director. And he had an inside track on things now. Status. More things to lose.

Night. Cufflinks in the saucer. A dossier in hand. 'You want the good news or the bad?' he said.

She sat curled on the sofa with an ice-cold vodka, watching the lights of the city beyond. 'Let's go with the bad,' she said.

'They're bringing in a new law. An amendment. If you're not pregnant by thirty, that's it.'

'What do you mean *that's it?*'

'I mean' – he patted his midriff – 'No more chances.'

'Who told you that?'

'Doesn't matter. It's coming. Trust me.'

Her birthday was months away, not that it would make any difference. 'What's the good news?'

He slid her the dossier. 'Early birthday present.'

She did not understand at first. The dossier was slim. Their whole lives, tallied up and weighed. He explained what it meant, explained how he had paid a high-end consultancy firm to carry out a special type of credit check, something off-book. He insisted they were reputable. 'Just think about it, please,' he begged. 'This puts us in the clear. Fully vetted. We can try again. It's safe. This is our green light.'

And yet, to move ahead on this, it felt like a concession of sorts. She did not want to go there again, to tread in those dark rooms. But she could not shake the thought. The possibility … it gnawed at her. She had to appraise the situation logically: in a few months she would be thirty, and after that, all hope would be extinguished. What was there to lose? She looked at their file. Their score was off the charts.

'Okay,' she said.

'Okay?'

'Let's do it.'

She would turn thirty in eight months. Then seven. Then six. And it happened with five months to spare. The euphoria … And Whitney's smiling eyes. Her veneer softened. She filed for PTC a third time, and she did not feel anxious, nervous or threatened. She let herself believe that things were under her control once more. And she felt a warm serenity take hold. Pleasure in simple everyday scenes, on the tram, at the park, watching kids on swings, which made it all the worse when the same letter came back. Wafer thin. A slip. The address of the clinic in Ullamoor. Permission denied.

He took it worse than she did. He wanted to go down to District Hall, flash his status and query the decision in person, but she talked him out of it. And instead, without his knowing, she went alone. All morning, in the lobby, waiting. A clerk in a plum blouse passed in the corridor, the girl from the year above her at school. 'Amal?' she asked. 'Is that you?' She did not have to play up her distress, but she made out that their meeting was happenstance, and Amal took pity on her. She was on her way back from her break, had a meeting to get to, but she told Aina a time and a place, and they met in a coffee shop nearby.

'It's the not knowing,' Aina said. 'I just want to know … My husband had a record …'

Amal had kindly dug out her file. She was not supposed to, but she was discreet and there was no harm in it. 'You're right. There's a history of malfeasance,' said Amal. 'But it's not on his side. It's yours.'

The coffee in her mouth tasted suddenly dank. 'What? How?'

'Your grandmother's listed here as Kithi Nieminen.'

'Yes?' Aina still did not see.

Amal continued, 'According to this, she wrote some kind of protest song in her youth. She was embargoed.' She looked up. 'I'm so sorry.'

Knowing was worse in a way. She told Whitney, she had to. And he was furious. 'You didn't think I had a right to know?'

'I had no idea—'

'Your grandmother wrote "The Bridge of Tralloon".'

'She was a farmer, Whitney. That's all I knew.' She pauses. The date on the slip was two days away. 'Oh, Jesus, what do we do?'

'What can we do?' He touched her belly. 'Nothing will overturn that.'

Another taxi. And this time it is all the worse. She remembers the engine's low thrum, her shoulders wet against the seat. Wipers eradicating the queue of tail lights ahead as the driver taps the gear-stick. Flooding on the North Sea Road up to Ullamoor. Everywhere backed up. The wipers going faster, flapping down, bouncing back. One-two-three-whump. One-two-three. The driver changes the station. Jazz. Country. Static. Serious tones. He switches it off.

'There's a diversion round Tillerson,' he says. 'Miscreants, probably.'

She is going to be late. One-two-three-whump. One-two-three. They edge forward. Halt. Everything underwater. She tells the driver to pull over, she will walk from here, and by the time she reaches the clinic, she is drenched. The noodle shop is boarded up. She rings the buzzer in the doorway. Up the stairs. And this time Dr Nangelis greets her himself. There is no nurse. Just Nangelis, skinnier than ever. Pallid, like he has been coughing up blood.

'Ms Ollasson? Come in. I'm on my own today. Won't be a minute.'

———

Ten p.m. The pill clock turns green. She places her thumb and her pill is dispensed, and she stashes it in her pen, quickly. The euphoria is brief, and she is mistrustful of it, and with every passing minute, the pen grows heavier and she grows less assured. Can she really leave Whitney after all they have been through … And this choice, to go, risking everything without knowing what she might find … the plan seems suddenly absurd. And even if Maxime is alive, and he is out there somewhere, how will she ever find him? It is a gamble, and how can she do that to Whitney? On what grounds? On the presence of a sheep. On Whitney's minor imperfections. Whims, them all, feeding an impulse, derived from time and rage, emotions that would otherwise be directed at herself. For Whitney is not a bad man. He never was. It is just … all this time … together … distorting things.

Maybe she should leave a note. He will assume the worst otherwise. But there is something exquisite in the idea that she might simply vanish. No body. No sign. No knowing at all what happened. Maybe then he will understand what she has suffered, all these years.

Night has fallen. Raindrops cluster the window like spiders' eyes.

Da-da-dum. Da-da-dum. Da-da-da-da-da-da-dum.

Whitney looks up from across the nook. 'That tune …' he says, listening intently. 'Is that …?' His eyes light up. 'Friday 22 September,' he says. 'I'm right, aren't I? Seven p.m. St Luke's.' He crosses the room, peers cheerfully over her shoulder at her musical notation. Her body is alert to his proximity. Shift of his head. Breath on her neck. His warm staccato, *Da-da-dum. Da-da-dum. Da-da-da-da-da-da-dum.* She stares at the wall, grips her pen, and he hovers, kisses the top of her head.

He is right, but she will not admit it. 'It's "The Bridge of Tralloon",' she says, lying. And though the night is loaded with insinuation, he doubts himself just enough not to push her on it. He stands, colour draining from his face. It was a mean thing to say, but it was not meant in spite. This is her choice, and she needs to get on.

'You'll be up soon?' he asks, instead of pressing her.

She tells him to go on ahead. 'I'll be a while yet.'

If she is to leave at 6 a.m., she should pack her bag now. It will help occupy her mind, having something practical to do. Mutton, oats, binoculars, a few extra layers for crossing the spine. Nothing much. He just needs to think it is another of her morning runs.

'Well, goodnight,' he says.

She watches him go, waits for the door to the stairs to latch, then quietly sets to work.

16

Departure

THE GROUND IS SOFT beneath her feet. Softer than she would like, but she feels nimble, running barefoot, scrambling, repeating her mantra: *Long sky. Charged earth. Warm fire.* She heads up the valley, following the brook and the line of dead willows whose branches have been stripped bare by the storm, and she is fast, quicker than ten-minute miles, even with the incline. She knows the route, knows the path is clear of traps, and for the first time in years, she feels full. Her legs, strong. The mutton has seen to that.

At the sculpture, she takes the right-hand fork, crossing the stream and doubling back up the headland. She has been going a mile, and the crosswinds blow stronger as she comes out of the valley. She concentrates on her gait, keeping an efficient stride as she runs on, leaving the croft behind. Ahead is the tor, then the next two miles are across open fields, and there is no trail. The ground is uneven. There is rain on the wind, fat cold drops, but running is like the opposite of wind chill, it makes her feel warmer.

The sound of thunder rolls, a rumbling cannonade that she mistakes for the sound of waves until the grey sky flashes green overhead. Lightning tears slogans across the sky. It strikes somewhere behind her, and her shadow steeples across the headland. She stumbles, trips and falls headfirst into undergrowth. Brambles. Blackthorns. A thicket. Up ahead, another detonation strikes the clifftop and rocks tumble down to the ocean below. The weather is deteriorating, the rain torrential, but she cannot turn back. She breathes, pushes on. She has never seen it like this.

She skirts close to the cliff. The tide should be on the way out, but diesel-black waves angle in towards shore, shooting spray up the cliff. Once the mist clears, she sees it. A speck out in the bay. The boat – the cutter – it is back. She slows to a walk. Drops her bag in the dirt. Why does it have to be today? She watches as the boat is tossed violently; every passing wave pushing it closer to the needles.

She curses the wind as she is buffeted again, and sinks to her knees. The cliff is impassable. And the pain at turning back is a physical thing, as real as the burning in her lungs and the aching in her legs. But there is no alternative. To carry on would be a decision born from bloody-minded reck-lessness, and it is too great a risk. She must turn back. There will be something aboard that boat she can use. And she needs every edge. Every advantage.

She will delay a day or two, that is all. Sometimes it can be worthwhile to wait.

17

Håvsra

THE WEATHER BECOMES PROGRESSIVELY worse, and by the time she makes it back to the croft, she has lost sight of the vessel. The sea is angry, vengeful, and it takes her a moment to locate the boat again. It is wedged, dead centre in the middle of the bay, high between the tallest two needles.

'Whitney, come quick!' she yells. 'Look!'

He squints for a long time as the rain pastes his face, and when he sees it, he goes running back inside. He re-emerges with the speargun and three harpoons. Clack-clack-back. He loads the barrel. 'Better we have it to hand and not need it, than want for it and not have it.'

She makes no objection. The gun is oiled and gleaming, and he checks the mechanism before slinging it on to his shoulder.

'Have you seen the binoculars?'

Her cheeks flush, burning hot, even in the rain.

'The binoculars …' he repeats. 'They're not in the drawer.'

She takes them from her bag, passes them to him, and he looks slightly confused, but he does not wait for an explanation. He trains them on the boat, scans a little to the left, the right. Then he hands them back, returns inside, and she hears him in the kitchen, saying, 'Warden, we have an unidentified sailboat trapped on the needles. A yacht. Thirty feet long. No sign of any crew.'

She takes a look herself. The boat perches above the sea. Someone has made repairs to the hull, but even with the binoculars, it is impossible to tell the extent of the damage from the way the boat is fixed, like a grain of rice between the prongs of a fork.

Whitney's voice comes, muffled from inside. 'Requesting permission to make a preliminary investigation,' he says. 'The time is zero-eight-forty-three.'

He hangs up the receiver as she enters the kitchen.

'There's no going out in that,' he says. 'We'll have to wait until low tide.' He smiles, suddenly, buoyed by some idea. 'You think this is it?' he asks. 'Do you think they've finally come?'

'Who?'

'The Warden.'

She thinks about it for a moment. 'If it were the Warden, there'd be an official vessel. A landing party. He wouldn't wash ashore in an unmarked yacht.'

'Maybe that's part of the test. Parole, remember. It fits.' He disappears into the cupboard and returns with rope, the waders and a wetsuit. He coils the rope and hands it to her. 'Do you mind taking this one?' he asks. 'Only my back's killing me. And, if I remember right, I did the last one.'

She does not argue. For one, she is the better climber, but there is also the lure of having first dibs on the hoard. There might be food, or a compass, or a new pair of boots. This way, she can have her pick of the wares.

———

At mid-morning when the tide is as far out as it is going to go, there is a break in the storm and they set off. He goes with her, as an escort, carrying the speargun in case. She has the rope, hanging from her shoulder.

The sand is a wet sponge and the tide is so low that they can walk all the way out to the needles. Whitney follows behind in the waders, carrying a bundle of netting. The vessel is twenty feet or so above the water. The sails might have ripped off in the storm, or else they have been stowed away for safekeeping.

'You see that,' says Whitney, pointing at the barnacles. 'Been a while since this one's been inside a dry dock.'

He is right. But the keel and the rudder appear in reasonable condition. The sun comes out and she has to squint. There is every hope that the engine might still work. There might even be fuel.

As they near, she sees that the boat's original name has been painted over, and below it, in whirling calligraphy, there is a new name. *Håvsra*. Pebbles rush against her feet with the current. She knows that word. She read about it in the atlas … The seabed is uneven and the outgoing tide sloshes up past Aina's knees and soaks the neoprene. The breeze makes her colder still. Seawater drips from the hull in dots and dashes. Beneath the stern, the propeller creaks as it turns in the wind, and from the hawsepipe, a rusted, anchorless chain scrapes uselessly on the rocks.

Whitney slips the speargun from his shoulder. One hand on the barrel, he offers it to her. 'Here. In case anyone's home.'

She ignores him and sets to work.

The wood groans, and she can see just how precariously the boat is wedged. The rock is too sheer and slippery to climb, so she hurls half the length of rope, still coiled, over the bowsprit. Whitney retrieves the end, and without comment or instruction, he passes the rope behind his back, favouring a rudimentary belaying technique.

'You should wait for the tide to come in,' he calls. 'It'll be easier then.'

'No,' she says. 'If I wait for the tide, maybe the boat breaks up on the rocks, or maybe it will wash away altogether. Better to go now.' While there is time, she thinks.

The rope is wet and she feels some spring as it takes her weight. One arm over the other, she climbs, feet together so she twists and swings as little as possible. Beneath her, Whitney struggles against the combination of the current and her weight. Halfway to the bow the rope slips and catches on something – a turnbuckle or the windlass – and she flails in mid-air. The coarseness of the rope and the salt burns her hands, but the peat-digging has primed them for this. Discomfort will only be temporary.

Hand over hand, she continues.

This is the hard part. The bow is an arm's length above her head. She stretches for it – too far – she has misjudged her reach. She spins into the hull, taking the impact on her shoulder. She kicks out, trying to get a toehold, but she is tiring and the barnacles are sharp. She steadies herself, and she reaches again. Her fingertips brush the wood. A little more. Fingers splayed, and she has one hand on the pulpit. She lets go of the rope, swings one-handed, dangling from the prow.

Her body is deadweight.

Legs useless.

Fingertips numb.

To fall now would mean broken legs at best.

'You okay?' comes the call from below.

She reaches with her free hand and grabs the rail. Her biceps feel like old elastic. Straining, she pulls her chin up and hooks her knee over the side. With a final effort she tumbles to the deck, and lays there on her back, listening to the waves below; now she can breathe. It is not pretty, but she is aboard.

Whitney calls, 'What do you see?'

A line of flags flutter from the mast. A blue triangle with a red cross. A white triangle with a black circle. Their message is meaningless to her.

She pulls herself to her feet. With one hand on the guard rail, she inches cautiously past the forward hatch, towards the stern. In the cockpit, the wheel rocks, turning a few degrees, then snapping back. The key is in the ignition. She turns it, and presses a few random buttons, but the engine does not sputter. It might just be the battery. She flips the

cushions from the benches and checks the storage compart-
ments. Things are in order: tarp; emergency drybags; a torch
with extra batteries. Life jackets: there are supposed to be
six, but two are missing. As is one of the life rafts, and there
is no flare gun, no hammer, no axe. But that is not unusual.

All in all, it promises to be a good haul, the best in years,
and she allows herself a momentary gloat. Surrounded by
dark, backlit clouds, the bay is suddenly illuminated, and she
basks in the sense of vindication and relief. It was the right
decision, turning back at the cliffs. This was worth sticking
around for.

She secures the boat as best she can, looping ropes and
cables over the top of the needles and winching them tight.
Her fingertips glide on the banister as she heads below deck.
In the galley, everything is wooden and glossy, and smells of
fresh polish. Above a small breakfast bar, plantlets dangle
from a hanging basket. Some kind of spider plant, its name
escapes her. No doubt old Lionel would have known. There
is a spray bottle on the bench, half filled, and she squirts a
fine mist into the air. The plant appears healthy enough, as
though it has been recently watered.

The marine oven pivots gently. Blood pumps at her tem-
ples, and the walls groan around her.

'Hello?' Her voice is steady, assured. Hearing it quells her
unease. She tries the light switch, but either the fuse is out or
the bulb has blown, so she takes the torch, slaps it against
her hand. A beam pierces the dark passageway. It is a different kind of light to what she is used to. Cold. White. Constant.
Like the light of the saferoom. Ahead, a door swings gently
on its hinges. She walks forward. Inside: a cramped cabin.
Headroom is limited, even for her. Twin beds curve with the

hull; their mattresses are thick with old sweat and sea salt. But there is order here. A sense of procedure.

A sound in the darkness. A splintering of wood, and the boat shifts slightly.

A bottle comes rolling towards her. She stops it with her foot. Glass, a cork jammed into the neck. She shines the torch. A greeny-golden-hued liquid sloshes about. Urine, she thinks. Or it might just be stagnant water drawn from a dirty pipe.

Back in the galley there are cables for what appears to be a radio and a laptop, but any hardware is missing. She finds the cupboards stocked with spices. Paprika, turmeric – such colours – and a range of dried herbs: tarragon, parsley and a smart type of salt, which seems like a ridiculous thing to take to sea. In the back of the cupboard, there is cumin and a bottle of hot sauce. She places the jars on the sideboard. The last contains cardamom. She unscrews the lid and shakes a pod from the jar. It is the size of a pill. She breaks the husk with her thumbnail. Inside a string of grey seeds nestle together, surrounded by wisps of cottony threads. She brushes them lightly with her finger, and inhales deeply, bringing on a cascade of memories: dosas, fish curry, the apartment hallway. Quickly, without thinking, she places the seeds on her tongue, and at once her mouth is awash with saliva. A tide lifts the seeds. And now the taste. Not pepper. Not spice. She is expecting something aromatic and sweet as vanilla, but it turns bitter on her tongue – liquorice – and she spits out the seeds on the floor.

The toilet in the stern hardly seems used. Above the small sink, chalky white residue patterns the mirror. There is an empty tube of toothpaste in the bin, but no sign of any toothbrush. No shower either, though there must be one on deck. Wouldn't that be glorious, she thinks, to shower in the rain on the open sea, or in the dark, under moonlight, as the world slips past.

In the panelling above the banquette seats, there is a recess that doubles as a small ornate shelf. Backgammon. Travel chess. A book of crosswords filled out by a child's hand. A guide for tying knots. There is nothing new here.

Around her, the whole cabin shakes, the sound of wood grinding on rock. She drops the book. Starts hurrying, filling the drybag with plasters and antiseptic creams from beneath the sink. She is careful, precise, and wastes little time. A last sweep; she might not get the chance to ever return.

———

Whitney is waiting for her when she climbs down the rope. 'You're certain it's empty?' he asks.

'Same as the rest,' she nods. Only something does not feel right … Normally, she would leave a wreck with a vivid impression of a smuggler, or a stowaway, or some fisherman trawling the deep. Going aboard would be like walking into the middle of some catastrophe. Things would be strewn about, cereal boxes all over the floor, things upended. Only with *Håvsra*, everything is so neat, tidy, and any face stays hidden. It is like someone planned to leave, and they took all their personal effects with them. Everything except the plant.

She stares back up the rope. 'Maybe he fell overboard,' she says. 'Or he was trying to fix the anchor, and the boat drifted away.'

Hope sags in Whitney's face. 'I really thought it was them.'

'Them?'

'The Warden.'

She has no time to think. The tide is coming in, and she fashions a makeshift raft from one of the cabin doors which she loads with the heavier items and those that are awkward to carry: a toolkit, two new wetsuits, a snorkel and fins. She secures the raft with the old fishing net.

'Here, help me with this, will you,' she says.

Whitney takes a last look up at the boat and begins dragging the raft through the waves.

She loads up with drybags. The sea comes up over her ribs and a wave drenches her, sending water trickling down the back of her neck. She quickens through the breakers. Emerging from the waves on to the beach, the sun is past the yardarm. She checks the watch; half an hour until their lunchtime pill, but even so they should hurry. She walks on, carrying the two drybags, one slung over each shoulder, and she is halfway up the beach when she realises that Whitney is no longer beside her. She looks back. He is standing in the shallows as the raft shunts forward on a wave. The underside scrapes the sand, threatening to spill its wares. He just stands there.

She goes back and drags his raft clear of the waves. 'We should hurry,' she says. 'We haven't long.'

He does not move. He looks at her feet, and then at her face. He might be looking beyond her. She cannot tell. His brow tightens.

'What's wrong?' she asks.

He points up the beach, beyond the accumulation of broken bulbs, bottles and plastic, towards the drystone wall and the waterlogged fields. 'I thought I saw someone,' he says. 'Up there.'

She follows his arm. Beyond, the hill rises up to the moor. A hazy purple line on the horizon. All of a sudden the beach does not feel right. There is no cover. No tree. No shade. The sun shines down, and sweat stings her eyes. She feels horribly exposed.

'A man?' she asks, raising her binoculars.

'A child. I think.'

The cold draughts between the neoprene and her skin. She scans the beach, the dunes and the marsh for anything incongruent, anything that might not have been there before. Something reflective glints, high on the hillside, above the marsh. A figure, standing indistinct and featureless. A man, it must be—

She adjusts the central wheel, brings the face into focus.

'It's just your sculpture,' she says, handing him the binoculars.

The head is a black dome against the paper-white sky.

18

Phantom

INSIDE THE CROFT NOTHING seems amiss. The water in the sink is murky grey, cold to look at. Their breakfast things rim the surface like volcanic atolls. Breakfast – so long ago. She will leave tomorrow, a day late. Nothing in the scheme of things. She deposits the drybag on the table. The snorkel, fins, wetsuit. A rich enough bounty. Worth the wait.

The house creaks, resettling upon sodden foundations. They take their lunchtime pill, and having completed the cycle, she takes hers at the top of the hour. No point in pushing things now. Whitney paces the kitchen nervously. His doubts percolate the room.

'Tell me what you saw,' he says. 'Every detail from the moment you boarded. Don't skip a thing.'

'The boat's still there, Whitney, you can go see for yourself.'

'Please. Had someone been aboard?'

'For a time … at some point … but …' She considers the various wrecks: the tugboat, the pleasure craft and the freighter down the beach. 'It's like the others, there's no telling when.'

'Someone's out there,' he whispers. 'I can feel them.'

The cold rises up into her lungs; she needs to keep moving. And for a moment she considers what it might mean if he is right. What if someone has come ashore … *Håvsra* had not been fitted with a dispensary, not like the Warden's official vessel, but there are ways to survive out here, and if she discovered the pill clock's deficiencies, maybe someone else has too.

She clutches the pen about her neck.

Water drips unseen.

'Aina, come on. You said: *Maybe he fell overboard.* You're sure it was a he?'

'The toilet seat was up.' She tries to speak plainly, reasoning with him. 'But man, woman, child, what does it matter? If someone came ashore, there'd be footprints in the sand, in the field, crossing the berm. There'd be some sign.'

He shakes his head. 'Not if they took precautions, say they came ashore at high tide.' He looks up at the hillside. Tendons taut on his neck. 'That's what I'd have done.'

The sound of metal tinkles from the barn. Pulleys and chains just shifting in the breeze. His eyes shine. She can practically hear the inner workings of his brain.

'You think maybe they crawled down the hillside, hidden in the creek? Or maybe they're slinking across the marsh, right now, approaching as we speak. Is that what you would do? Or maybe they're already here. Did you check for porridge? Did you check for oats?' She whispers, 'Did you check the nook?'

If he senses her mocking, he does not let on. He motions for quiet, and goes to the door, mouthing numbers, *one … two … three …* then pulls, hard and swift on the handle, and disappears down the hallway with an exaggerated sense of stealth. He is enjoying this, she thinks, having a new purpose, but his composure is paper thin, like a warm front in winter. She hears him going room to room. Drawing back the curtains by the front door. All he will see is fifty feet of beach and nothing else besides. Into the nook, more clatter, the fire iron scrapes against brick. In a moment he is back, hunkering a little less. He unlatches the door to the stairs with the speargun's tip. The stairs creak as he shucks mud all up inside. His footsteps reverberate from one end of the attic to the other. Eleven paces.

Aina glances up at the hillside. She sees nothing and goes to the sink. The weather changes by degrees and a coolness envelopes her. There is a void in her stomach and her hunger is sudden, stoked by the morning's exertions. She swallows. The wind rips along the side of the house.

Footsteps clobber the stairs and Whitney reappears: master of the watch, at ease now his rounds are done.

Minutes pass. He asks if she would like tea, and though she does not answer, he goes about making her one anyway, clipping leaves from the nettle on the sill, loading the stove with peat from the stack on the leeward side of the house, filling the kettle. The water from the tap runs dark and he lets it run longer than is necessary. At the stove, she warms her hands briefly. Her skin is raw, rubbed with sea salt. The wetsuit itches. Brambles are snagged in the black neoprene. She picks them out, one by one, and heads upstairs, changes into her fleece and running shorts. She is not planning anything extensive, just a few miles to stay loose. She will need to conserve her energy for tomorrow. A few lunges, some stretches. Downstairs. She feels his eyes on her as she crosses to the back door.

'You're not thinking of going out, are you?' he asks. 'I'm not sure that's wise.'

'I'm sorry, what?'

He stands, moves slightly so he is half blocking her exit, maybe on purpose, maybe not, and he looks at the floor and shrugs. 'I know what I saw up there.'

'You saw a statue, Whitney.'

He inhales deeply. Immovable.

'There's no one here but us, you know. You're being ridiculous.'

'No more runs, okay?'

'I'm not asking permission.'

'And you won't ever need it, but come on.' He props the speargun against the table. 'We stay put,' he says. 'We stick together. That's what we do. What we've always done. Come on. At least until we know what's going on.'

Outside, the land darkens. Rain drums on the roof, and she looks to the ocean. Sheer battlements of cloud are building once more. It is not the right time, she thinks. And she makes a show of compliance, letting him guide her to a chair, where she sits, a picture of quiet assent, sipping her tea, as she explores his logic for gaps. She is alive to his stubbornness too, the lines he has drawn. If she pushes harder, he will only dig in, becoming further and further entrenched. But he is right about one thing, there will be no more running today, not with that brute of a storm.

She can only wait, bide her time and be ready. The moment will come, always does.

19

Tides

Darkness. She imagines blue tints, shapes, and she hears someone scratching. A ticking. Whitney? No, someone else. Here he comes: a man. His movements are languid, youthful. His arms are slack, as though he has been carrying something heavy like a crate of oats, or a box full of sheet music. She sees him, or she thinks she sees him. Shapes, shadows, pixelated forms. Maxime.

A tumbling sense of falling—

She kicks herself awake and momentarily she cannot tell if she has woken, or what she has woken into. She half expects a splash or an impact, but there is only air – wind – vast quantities of it, rushing past her ears.

She blinks. Checks the watch. 9:48 p.m. She has only been asleep for a few minutes. Above, the wind rages on.

The cellar is steeped in candlelight. Saws pinned to the walls in order of size; their blades caked in various degrees of rust. The pair of waders now hangs from a joist. Her eyes adjust and she sees hoes and trowels and warped shelves that are stacked with cans of oil, solvents and two tins of ships' tar. At the foot of the stairs, a dusty metal desk is piled high with refilled bottles of water. Her sacks of wool wait in the corner; it was thoughtful of Whitney to have brought them down.

He had suggested relocating to the cellar as a precaution-ary measure, and faced with the storm and the prospect of a night under a leaking roof, she had seen the logic in it. She needed rest, a full night's sleep, and from the noise of the wind above, it was the right thing to do. They spent the afternoon squeezing their mattresses through the small trapdoor in the larder, and now, the earthen floor is cold through the makeshift futon. Heavy breaths, the smell of damp earth and wool. She pulls her blankets closer, exposing her feet, and she shuffles around, trying to regain some sense of comfort, only the floor slopes down towards the shelves, and it is horribly uneven from years spent attempting to excavate the pill clock. Not that the slope bothers Whitney. He has set his mattress on the far side of the cellar beneath the stairs, and sleeps, content and unfazed, despite the wind.

The gale sounds angrier. It courses through the kitchen and the nook above, searching for her as it always does. She can understand why the Norse devoted so many gods to the wind – the Greeks too. It is probably the same reason

Whitney still persists in making reports to an absentee warden: a way to keep things onside.

The wind is a hard thing to visualise though; never a seen thing, but a rendered effect. Like dimples moving across the marsh with the choreography of birds seen from afar. Something is blown over upstairs, sending dust motes falling around her. She begins whispering, 'Aeolus, Zephyrus, Notus ...'

9:50 p.m. The watch's alarm sounds, progressively loud. But even at its loudest, it does not wake Whitney. Not above the wind. She switches the alarm off and carries the candle over to the stairs. She could leave him sleeping there, adrift in his dreams. She could just clamber on out and lock the trapdoor behind her. It would be easy enough.

But when she sees him, actually sees him – helpless, trusting, peaceful – she remembers that none of this is his fault. He honestly believes that someone is out there, caught in the storm. He is just doing what he thinks is right. She almost pities him. She kneels beside him and touches him on the shoulder.

He takes a moment to stir. He knuckles his eye and looks startled.

'It's time,' she says, pointing at the watch.

The wind extinguishes the candle as they exit the trapdoor and the kitchen is pitch black, darker than it should be. The floor tiles are damp and littered with all kinds of shrapnel. Plates. Glass. Curtains whip past her face. She bumps into things. The table. Chairs. Everything that was domestic is now a hazard of sorts. Where's the pill clock? Why is it so dark?

'Whitney!' she shouts, but she can hardly hear herself over the roar.

She feels her way to the wall. Past cupboards, whose doors hang on hinges, to the hearth. The stone, cold. Wet. She knows where she is now. The sideboard has toppled, obscuring the pink glow of the pill clock.

Whitney helps her clear the path. 'Resistant to hammers, crowbars, blizzards,' he shouts. 'A bit of rain is nothing by comparison!'

They are just in time. The dial is already green. 9:59 p.m. In turn, they press their thumbs to the sensor, and the mechanism promptly dispenses two pills in the collection drawer. Whitney hands her one. 'Careful!' he shouts, as she slips it into her mouth.

In the cellar, she lights a fresh candle from the box, squashing it down in the holder. The smell of matches fills the subterranean space.

Whitney stops picking at the mutton between his teeth and inhales deeply, as though the smell intrigues and repulses him in equal measures. 'You know why smells are so good at triggering memory?' he asks, keeping his eyes lowered on the flame.

She knows this one. 'Because the olfactory bulb connects directly to the amygdala and hippocampus,' she says.

He nods, and then he sits back, slightly disappointed. 'I still can't smell a match without wanting a cigarette. Ridiculous, isn't it. After all these years.'

She smiles wanly. The smell triggers other things too, she thinks. Campfires. Lighting the pudding at Christmas. A little boy, playing with … She inhales, but the smell is less distinct, as though the receptors in her nose have grown accustomed and stopped transmitting.

Whitney looks up at her and smiles. 'I'm sorry about all the stuff with the sheep,' he says.

She can see he is trying to be civil, trying to keep her onside. He has always exploited adversity to that effect. But if he is making an effort, maybe she should too. Being civil has advantages. It takes less energy for a start.

'Well,' she says. 'The manure was a good idea. It would have worked if not for this weather.'

'And now this. It's been one thing after another. And the boat … We just have to take stock. Just until we know what's going on. I know it's not ideal, what I'm asking. I know your running's important.'

'Yes, it is. But …' She is too tired for another fight. 'Like you say, there's no chance of running in this.'

She holds the candle close. The wax is soft and a drop spills, hardening into a white tear on the shaft. She shields the flame so that it might settle, and the light grows bolder, perpetrating vision and shadow alike.

'You know,' he continues, gazing intently at the candle, 'in a desert, you can spot a naked flame at a distance of thirty miles. Conditions have to be right,' he continues. 'No moon, of course.'

She does know. 'Cold too, I expect.'

The walls of the cellar sink back into darkness. Perhaps they are on an island after all. Something lurks in the recesses of memory. Regret? Pity? If Whitney knew there was a way to escape, might he see things differently? It is a slow, halting concession. She could tell him about the pill, she thinks. Does he not have a right to know, a right to choose; a luxury she was not permitted? Part of her wants to quash these sentimental notions. These moments of doubt are temporary, she thinks. They will pass. They always do. And Whitney will do something, or he will say something obtuse and condescending. Her ire will be familiar and true. Comforting. It will yield anger. She just needs to wait.

But watching him, his eyes search the room, and finally they meet her own. She sees a different quality in his eyes. Pain or a certain vulnerability. Two little windows into his mind. The prospect of conversation glimmers as delight in his eyes, and his hair shines. He brushes it from his face, the way he would when he was young. 'You know,' he says, 'it's safer over here, statistically speaking, beneath the stairs.'

———

She wakes in blackness with an arm resting heavily across her. Whitney's breath warms her neck. Disorientated, she reaches for her pen. It is not there. Her logbook is not there either. She panics, and goes groping around until reason overcomes instinct. The candle has gone out. She is in the cellar. Behind her, the mattress sags.

'What is it?' Whitney's voice is heavy from sleep.

'Nothing. Go back to sleep.' She goes crawling back down the slope towards her own bed. She sees the crinkled gleam of the ziplock bag. Inside is her pen.

'You okay?' Whitney asks from the darkness.

'I'm fine.' Her voice is tense. She tries to relax. 'I just … couldn't find something. That's all.'

'Your notebook?'

She hesitates. 'Silly, isn't it.'

'Not at all,' he says. 'I mean, I get why it's so important.'

She feels a compression in her chest. Her heart races. She hears him shift about across the room. His voice sounds clearer, as though he is sitting up. 'It's your pictures,' he says. 'Isn't it? The ones of Maxime.'

A stillness. The wind has dropped. She is aware of everything. His breath. A dryness in her throat. She asks, 'Don't you ever wonder what happened to him?'

He waits, and she is not sure if he heard her. Then he says, 'I do, yes. All the time.'

'You never talk of him, though.'

The floor grows colder in the silence. 'Of course I miss him, Aina. I miss him so much.' His voice waivers, and he pauses to steady himself. 'It's just … I never know how you'll react if I do.'

She does not know what to say. She stays extremely still, looks down where her hands should be and sees only darkness.

'I miss him too,' she says, finally. 'I just can't bear to think of him out there somewhere, trapped like us. Not knowing if he's even alive, that's the worst part.'

'Hey, hey,' he says, moving clumsily to her. She feels his arms around her. One hand clasps her head, pressing her cheek to his bony chest. They hold each other, and when the silence becomes unsettling, he talks, trying to soothe her, and his words help. He is saying, 'Sometimes, I think of him, I picture him surrounded by trees.' And he

147

describes the sun angling through the branches. The sound of water. And she can see him momentarily, Max: he walks, trailing a hand behind him, gently strumming the shafts of light.

She knows this is just speculative, that Whitney is just trying to lift her spirits, but the scenario is so seductive, so idyllic, she longs it to be true. 'You really think he's okay?' she asks.

His voice is a whisper. 'I'm certain of it,' he says. 'He's out there somewhere. Waiting, like us.'

———

They finish the last of the cold-cut mutton, and for the next three days, they eat only oats. The storm rages, and there is no differentiating day from night. They keep to the cellar, ration the candles, and she moves her mattress closer to Whitney's. It is the only way she can hear him over the wind, side by side in the dark. She finds it comforting, talking to him without seeing his face.

The wind grows stronger; she thinks of her years at the croft. She sees the days superimposed over one another. Her ghosts walking in circles: in the front door, through the hall, out the kitchen, to the garden, round and round like the figures in the Escher picture, walking up the stairs and making orbits of the croft, ambling along the beach or up the valley, past the willows to the tor, and back inland, passing the peat bank. She sees herself clutching the spade, loading the barrow and running. So much running, along the cliffs and the marsh; watching the shore, watching the horizon, over and over and over again.

Speeded up. A flattened overview of time. She moves among echoes, trapped in an etching with so many versions of herself.

On the fifth day, she wakes. A pale watery light streams through the floorboards above, and she peels her face from the mattress. Her cheek is cool, wet. Not wet with sweat. She does not feel feverish. She brushes herself down, and her hands feel stained with something coarse. Her clothes are too heavy – everything chafes – and the ground is softer than before; it squelches underfoot.

The wind has died, and the only sound is that of water trickling over rock.

'Whitney,' she hisses. 'You awake?'

He stirs, groaning, 'What is it?'

She reaches for the matches. The first is soggy and will not light, but the second scrapes into a flame that she holds to the candle.

She sees Whitney, sitting on the mattress. They lock eyes for a moment. And then he looks through her. He is pointing. 'Oh shit. Shit. Shit. Shit.'

She turns. Arcs the candle around: the seed crate shunts alongside the oat-filled plastic tubs and tins, bobbing like flotsam. In the lowest corner of the cellar, a dark triangle has seeped up through the floor. Water.

'The seeds!' he yells. 'Quick, get them out!'

'Where?'

'Somewhere dry. Up there, on the stair. Help me.'

He wades down into the water, towards the crate. And then he stops. It is no use. The water rises quickly, bubbling up from underground. The whole of the floor is covered now. So much water. It is coming from above and below.

Cascading through the floorboards. Running down the trap-door. A vast sluice.

'Oh, Jesus,' she says. 'The tide must have broken the berm.'

20

Stairs

THEY HURRY, SHIFTING THINGS from the cellar to the kitchen and from the kitchen to the attic, and the boundary between order and disarray grows ill-defined. Everywhere the air feels different. Heavy. Dense, contained. And everything is cluttered. There are no exposed surfaces. Things are discarded. Others are simply forgotten. What matters is surviving. The two of them. Everything else can wait.

Bits of jigsaw float down the hallway, pliable and over-sized. So much has been ruined, or else lost.

In the attic, bowls sit within pans, and cups within mugs, and things that are carried in boxes and crates are stowed wherever there is space. She squashes the air from the hessian sacks and wedges them under her bed. The wool will have to wait for spindling.

It is hard to gauge whether the waters are still rising. She looks out at the sculptures dotting the headland. The one on the backside of the marsh is almost completely underwater. It stands, buried to the neck, a condemned seafarer awaiting the tide. She finds a new hook for the waders, stashes their maps in the chest of drawers and leaves a pile of clothes and coats in a heap on her bed. Everything is damp. Nothing will dry. She runs a length of rope from one end of the attic to the other. The line is slippery in the wet, and she needs help fixing it in place. 'Whitney,' she says. 'Grab the other end, will you, please.'

Together they pull, tautening the line, and Whitney fastens it at the second attempt. She tests it for weight and begins arranging their wet clothes, spacing them evenly.

'A fire might help,' suggests Whitney cautiously. 'We could use the bucket as a brazier. The ladderback chairs as fuel …'

He is trying to be proactive, and she does not wish to discourage him, or damage the sliver of trust between them. But his plan is flawed. She leads him downstairs. The water is at the second stair, over a foot deep, and it takes him a moment to understand her logic. 'The chairs must stay downstairs,' she says, watching his face, sunken and pursed. She tracks his gaze to the pill clock, the old stanchion, and the barricade of chairs and furniture that she has arranged as a brace on either side, supporting the weakened wall.

'For now, that's our priority,' she explains. 'We protect the dispensary.' She sloshes across the room and lifts one end of the kitchen table. 'Here, help me with this, will you?'

Dusk. A smuggler's moon rises over the moor. She stands at the window. The sky is the colour of lint. A clear night, the first in a week, but this is no ordinary tide. The breeze shifts, and still it rises. Water laps the wall below, reinforced as best they can.

They eat the last tin of tuna. A treat. She works the tin-opener. Savouring the moment when the lid is pierced and the brine gurgles out. She prises back the serrated metal disc. Inside, compressed flakes of boneless fish, compacted into whorls. She forks the fish between two plates, and it disintegrates readily. There is not much, and they eat it in one sitting, leaving only the jars of mutton and the oats. The seeds are ruined, the barley too. But, for Aina, there are more immediate concerns.

In a matter of days, the pill clock will be completely under-water, and it is hazardous enough, wading across the kitchen three trips a day, but having to swim will be even more treacherous. She is conscious about the pen around her neck. In the water, she could lose it so easily, erasing all that effort in an instant. She should stow it somewhere. Her notebook too. That would be prudent. But where? Higher ground, perhaps. On land.

Whitney joins her at the window. She is certain he has his own hiding places. She hears him at night, scratching on the floorboards, easing the wood apart. Finding voids that he fills with his sentimental trinkets. His figurines. Clay models. Woodcarvings.

He rests his hand upon hers; she leaves it there. 'You've been in the water too long,' he says.

He is right, her hands are pruned. White, soft. And wrinkled to the point where she can barely sense his touch. Dead man's hands, he calls them; the body's way of giving improved grip in the wet. By contrast Whitney's hand is smooth. She traces the scar on the webbed flesh between his thumb and forefinger. He had been making something for Maxime, a wooden ark; it was to be a Christmas present. He spent an entire weekend locked in the study, chiselling away with a brand-new set of tools. Saws, hammers, drills. She remembers his gasp and the patter of blood. The sight of the gash. Blood welling up. The cut was deep, damaging the nerves. He still suffers numbness.

'Do you remember the ark?'

He nods.

'Whatever happened to it?'

'I've no idea.'

She remembers him, sanding and sawing, and each evening, before Maxime would wake, he would sweep up the dust, shavings and offcuts, and dispose of them down the rubbish chute. And as he worked, she would watch him. Noting his diligence. His precision. How he did not rush. He took pride in his work, applying final touches and paint, bright paint, each aspect a different colour, red, yellow, a turquoise blue – leftover from the poster – and she felt a warmth creep up her neck; an intensity of love that she could not really explain.

'You know, I've been thinking.' Whitney is propped on his bed, with his book open on his lap. 'When all this is over, I might start running again. It'll be something we can do together …'

'Really?' she says, sensing an opportunity. 'Because you might have a job keeping up.'

His smile is strained.

'But you're right,' she says. 'I miss having land underfoot, something solid.' And she explains that there are things that they could do together, besides running. Practical things … Peat to cut. 'You know, there's no reason to wait,' she adds. 'We could go up to the moor, just for a few hours each day. Think about it. Be nice to escape the wet, if nothing else.'

And as he mulls it over, she thinks about where she might stash her pill. The shieling, the dunes, the tor. There would be any number of places …

But Whitney shakes his head. 'I don't think so, Aina, not with these tides. They're too unpredictable.'

'We can swim it.'

'Too risky.' He is resolute. 'And besides, we've still no idea who's out there.'

That anyone made it ashore seems like a stretch. 'You really think someone could have survived out there? A five-day storm, Whitney? Gusts topping 150 miles per hour. Think of the exposure.'

'That's exactly what I *am* thinking about,' he says quietly. 'We've got our pills. The croft's on sturdy ground. The safest place is here.'

'But for how long?' she asks. 'If the waters keep rising, we'll need a plan B.'

'We'll deal with it, Aina, don't worry. We'll find a way, always do.'

In the kitchen, the ceiling feels closer than ever.

She goes to her bed and, casually, trying not to draw attention to it, she takes the pen from about her neck. Glancing at Whitney – he is again absorbed in his book – she places her pen in the drawer of her bedside table. It will do for now. In the bottom of the drawer, light crinkles on plastic and she spots her spare ziplock bag. She has no need for it now the jigsaw is ruined, and she offers it to Whitney. 'For your book,' she says. 'To keep it dry.'

At the first hint of morning, she rolls out of bed, ducks beneath the washing and goes to the stairs. Darkness. Quiet. A third night trapped in the attic; the wall is damp as she descends. The stairs creak. Yan tan tethera, methera—

Even with the wetsuit, the water is cold. Ice traverses bone. Toe, arch, ankle. Her shins are conduits. Rigidness seizes her Achilles. Down, and the water comes over her knees. Her thighs. Her lungs constrict, compressing her breath. She feels around for the handle and latches the door to the wall. Better to keep it open, she thinks, and the sweep of the door sets off a wave that rebounds across the kitchen. Things bump and knock, wooden things, but the barricade is intact and the wave comes back to her, dissipated, but making her colder still. She hears the bedsprings ease and footsteps above. Whitney appears in silhouette at the top of the stairs.

'Where's it now?' he asks.

'The eighth stair,' she says.

As they wade across the kitchen, she feels the drag and pull of the current. She leans. Grips. Watchful for changes in the tide. It would be dangerous to be caught in the kitchen when it turns. In the corner, the pill clock stands resilient. A gleaming white monolith, designed to withstand fire and flood. The sensor's light casts an eerie underwater glow. Pinkish, then green. She holds her breath, ducks beneath the surface and cups one hand to the dispensary, forming a seal. Her thumb is wrinkled, but the sensor reads it without delay. The mechanism clicks and whirrs and the pill deposits into her hand.

They take their pills and are ascending back up the darkened stairwell when they hear a muffled eruption from outside. The rumbling grows. Upstairs, they approach the frontside dormer. Whitney cranes, points. 'Look!'

It's coming from out in the bay. The needles. There is a loud crack. Wood ruptures, and the yacht, *Håvsra*, slides and halts and rests momentarily, precariously, before a final series of pops splinter the foredeck and the boat is drawn towards the water, disintegrating in fizzes and shards.

'Well,' says Whitney, drawing his head back inside. 'It's a good thing we got to her when we did.'

21

Bowline

ONLY THE TIPS OF the needles are visible in the bay and long stretches of the berm are submerged. The broad surrounding waters offer no means to measure distance. The beach, the marsh, Whitney's drowned statue. Even the headland appears further away. Closer to shore, the bay is jumbled with pieces of the wrecked yacht, and as the tide goes out, a section of mast becomes wedged in the window to the nook. An entanglement of rigging and cables becomes caught upon it, trailing down the side of the croft. Whitney is right to be fearful, she thinks, the currents are swift.

She spots something yellow carried on the tide. One of *Håvsra*'s inflatable rafts.

'See,' says Whitney. 'There's proof. Someone came off the boat and made it ashore.'

They hook the raft, reel it in, and the rubber is punctured, torn in places. Aina sets about mending it, but she does not see it as proof of anything. She accuses him of speculating. 'The one we salvaged was lost in the flood,' she says. 'It could be the same one for all we know.'

'It's been used,' says Whitney. 'The toggle's been pulled.'

She refuses to concede. 'It could have just snagged on the rocks,' she says. 'And in any case, it doesn't prove anyone made it to shore alive. If anyone was aboard *Håvsra* – and that's a big if – given the state of the sea that night, and the state of this raft, I'd say there's a good chance that they drowned.'

'Now who's speculating?' Whitney smiles, in an odd paternal fashion, as though her stubbornness is something to be charmed. But he has no counter, no rebuttal. Instead his eyes flick about the room, his hand goes to his neck, and his smile slowly dies on his face.

She is aware of something prescient. An awkwardness in him. His eyes have settled on the raft. 'What is it?' she asks. 'What's the matter?'

Eventually, he speaks slowly. 'Do you remember that storm, a few years back? We were holed up in here for a week.'

'The blizzard?' she says. 'It was four days, it wasn't a week.'

'Right. And you remember the sea ice?' he asks with nervousness, holding his breath.

Again, the hilt of something, but she is not clear how this relates to the raft. 'The ice, yes. It preceded the storm, I remember, it'd been so ... unexpected.' But there were signs, she thinks. Unusual things. Like how, in the days leading up to it, the temperatures had suddenly dropped. She remembers the cold; cold as she had ever known cold could be, the kind that made the air seem thinner, and she thought that she could see the distant peaks of snow-capped islands across the straits. The faint trace of land gave shape to the horizon, and shimmered like a mirage. She spent hours with the binoculars trained on them, looking for a wisp of smoke, a block of colour. Finding nothing. And that afternoon, the weather rolled in. Skies descended. White carriages of snow-laden clouds approached fast over the ice, bringing a blizzard that obscured the islands and smothered the sun, and with it the stars and the moon and any sense of a world beyond. Four days straight. It took them another day to dig themselves out, and they emerged into bright daylight to find their world had been reconfigured. White shackled everything, and an armoury of icicles spiked the croft. Icebergs jammed the straits, some the size of a house. Aina had been convinced that by walking out on them, she could make it to the islands.

Only Whitney talked her out of it. 'They aren't islands,' he had said. 'It's just the passing ice seen from a ways away.'

She feels the weight of his hand on her shoulder; something confessional about it. 'It was land,' she says. 'You knew, even then, and you lied.'

He is quiet for a long time, and when he does speak, it is barely a whisper. 'I did,' he says. 'I did. You're right.'

For the first time she has a sense of the shape of things out there beyond the spine. She turns sharply towards him. 'And the maps, they're lies too?'

'They're just … incomplete.' His voice is calm and rational. 'I'm sorry, I should have told you. I thought it would be easier this way. But now, with this boat, parole, this test, I realise that was a mistake.'

There is something in his tone. Something cajoling.

Easier for whom?

She pushes him away. 'You made me think we're out here alone.'

'But we are. That's what exile is.'

She shakes her head. 'Tell me, what's out there.'

He breathes deeply, trying to regain a sense of calm. 'It's just forest. Trees as far as you can see.'

'Pine?'

He nods. 'In the distance there were hills. And there was smoke—'

Her sense of vindication is wrong, curdled; it yields dismay. She stands. The attic is too cramped. She needs to move.

'Please, Aina, listen to me.' He moves closer, trying to grab her arm. 'It might have been a croft, or a camp, who knows, it might have just been wildfire,' he says. 'It was miles away. And there's a river, an estuary, dividing the territory.' He pauses. 'I never had enough time. Never found a way to cross it.'

'I knew you were lying,' she says. 'I knew it the instant the sheep showed up.'

His hand covers his mouth, goes to his neck.

'Tell me, truthfully: did you see anyone?' she asks.

'All I saw … there's a ruin of an old distillery on the far bank. Trees growing up out of the roof. And in the distance, to the east, there were mountains.'

'That's it? That's everything? You're certain?'

His eyes are drawn to a chipped bit of skirting beneath the dormer. Eventually he shrugs. 'Does it matter?'

Her rage is hard-edged, elemental. 'Course it fucking matters. You should have told me. Why didn't you say?'

'Why do you think?' He meets her gaze. 'I tried for months to find a way across. The channel's half a mile wide at low tide. This is as good as an island, I swear. I wasn't lying about that, and I was going to tell you, just as soon as I found a way across. I was just trying to protect you.'

'Protect me?' She spits the words at him.

'You don't know what that kind of hope does … To see something, so tangible. To see smoke … to have it there constantly in your mind, always just out of reach. It drains you of everything.'

She thinks of Maxime, how they kept him locked in the apartment, night after night. But this is different, Whitney has knowingly misled her. Kept her helpless, reliant, a gullible fool. She is shaking. Her chest is heaving. The truce is ruptured, in tatters now. 'You gave up, Whitney. Your choice, not mine.'

And he tells her he just wants to be honest with her. That it's important they leave with a clean slate. And he is quiet for a moment, contemplative, and she thinks he is about to offer an apology. But he shakes his head. 'What with parole—'

'Parole?' A snort escapes her. 'Whitney, no one's coming. They lied.'

'Don't be foolish, Aina. Don't take this stance. I won't let you—'

'Listen to me. Listen! You won't have to *let me* do anything.' Her hand goes to her throat. She stares at the drawer, where she has hidden her pen. Steadies herself. 'You can stay here rotting just as long as you like. But our son's out there, and I'm going, I'm gone. When the waters subside, I'll find him.'

'And how in God's name are you going to do that?' he asks.

'Patience, Whitney. You'll see.'

———

She watches from the window when it rains. The surface of the water vibrates, a million dimpled chops, like sand on a taut drum. And as the floodwaters rise, the croft becomes less and less distinct from the water and more a feature of it. The air is thick with moisture and everything now has a damp sheen. The water abrades, exerting a force from outside and within; counteracting the foundations, it permeates the brickwork and lends buoyancy to the timber. There are breaks in the rain when the clouds part and the flooded rooms assume a brightened quality. The ceilings dapple refracted light and everything is pliant. The floorboards, the walls, her memories.

Maybe she should have left when she had the chance.

Their clothes are cold and heavy and brown with mould. The washing line sags. She unties one end and it thuds to the floor.

Whitney looks up from his book. 'That for downstairs?'

'Uh-huh.'

'No point us doing the washing now, I suppose?'

'Nope.'

She scoots the washing to one side, coils the line around her elbow, and enters the flooded stairwell alone. She can tell that he wants to help, but it feels like a tactical move, a trap; a little prison built on indebtedness. And if she were to accept his offer, she would also have to cede the moral high ground, dial back her anger. Better to let him writhe a little.

Clambering down, the waters come up to her chin. She is on tiptoes and she pushes off, swimming out into the dark. The sideboard has shifted away from the wall and she climbs on top of it. She braces herself against the ceiling, and begins fixing the rope to the top of the pill clock.

She is downstairs an hour. It is difficult, working by the soft glow of the pill clock with all that water, but she is methodical, and when she is finished, she threads the rope through a series of cast-iron brackets that she has fixed to the ceiling. A safety line. She ties it off in the stairwell, using a mnemonic that she learned in one of the guides. She makes a loop near one end of the rope, the rabbit's hole. Pokes the other end up through the loop, the rabbit emerges. Then rabbit runs round the tree, hops back down the hole, and she pulls fast on the rope. The knot tightens and the rope goes taut, fan water cascading. It should be sufficient to hold them both.

Apart from the water that laps gently, the croft is suddenly quiet. There is no movement from above. Whitney must be asleep, or else he is still engrossed in his book. As she returns upstairs, she expects to find him, sprawled on the bed where she left him. She emerges into the attic, and halts. Without the washing line, it takes her a moment to appraise the room. Something is amiss. A gentle gust shifts the curtains.

The skylight is open. His sheets are tangled and his bed is empty and the drawer to her table is slightly ajar.

22

Cartridge

'WHITNEY?'
She stands on the chair and looks out of the skylight. The water is calm and flat. Dazzling. The sky is vast.

'Up here.'

She turns and cranes her head. He sits cross-legged on the roof. Hunkered over her music book, which rests, open in his lap. He has her pen, her pill, and he is sketching something. She must stay calm. She clambers up through the skylight and on to the roof, fingertips to the tile, so if she falls, she falls forward. Stupid to leave her pen unattended. Stupid to think he would not go riffling through her things. She must stay calm.

The rafters feel soft beneath her feet. Some of the tiles are loose. She squats a few feet away. 'What do you think you're doing?'

'Peace offering,' he says, without looking up.

'You think you can make amends with a picture?'

'Maybe.' His face seems to glow. He gestures at the scene and smiles. 'There's something about the light …' He holds the notebook slightly away from her, grips the pen in an unconventional manner, directing pressure through the soft nib.

'Give me that.' She claps one-handed at her pen and the book. 'Both of them. Hand them over.'

'One moment please. I'm almost done.'

She moves closer. She thinks it will be a landscape. The waterlogged fields, or the headland, but the brushstrokes aren't quite linear enough for that.

'I don't know what prompted it,' he says. 'Maybe it is the light. But I can feel him. I can see him so clearly.'

In the picture, Maxime is no longer a child. He has aged, a young man. She can see herself in the picture, and she can see Whitney too, or the trace of Whitney around the nose and the mouth, a resemblance to the man she met in the Arts Club all those years before. Shuffling over to their table. Patting his shirt pocket for his tobacco and matches.

The nib scratches on the paper. He pauses. The ink is running grey, thinning. And he holds the nib up to the light and flicks the shaft, but the trough is dry. She knows what is coming.

'Have you more ink?' he asks.

She stares at the waters, which have spread half a mile up the valley. She cannot move. 'Don't,' she says. 'The pen. It's delicate, the thread is worn. Let me,' she says. 'Please.'

He has the pen in two parts now. The barrel and the nib. And she is sure that he knows. When she reaches for the pen, he holds it away from her.

'It's okay, Aina,' he says, with a half-smile. 'I can manage.'

The empty cartridge is exposed. Sheened, with globules of ink clinging to the inside. He looks inside the barrel. 'Ah, there it is.' He tips the barrel and the replacement cartridge slides into his palm.

She nods, helpless and stupid.

'You always were so good at rationing.' He hands her the empty. 'Keep that,' he says. 'I'll show you how to make your own ink.'

She just stares. If he were to look inside the barrel, he would see the tiny wad of tissue. It would stoke his curiosity. *What's this*, he would say ... And he would pull it free. And the tissue would unfold like a flower in his palm, and there in the middle he would see her pill. The spare. Half red, half white. He would take it between his thumb and forefinger and hold it up to the sky.

She grips the chimney to steady herself.

He slots the new cartridge in slowly, prolonging the agony, and he screws the barrel back in place. He takes his time finishing the picture. The sun goes. Something channels the air. And she sits there on the roof, barely able to breathe, silently cursing her foolishness, until some minutes later, a summer rain begins to fall.

He closes the lid of the pen, hands it to her with the music book.

'It's for you,' he says. 'I know it isn't much.'

'Fuck off inside, Whitney. And stay out of my shit.'

He nods, goes. And she wants to tear the picture and ball it up but she cannot bring herself to do it. The brown water

169

slides by, full of silt, as she hangs the pen about her neck once more. She swallows. Relief tastes brackish, of salt and brine, and she is suddenly aware of the dirt. In the creases of skin about her neck. Under her nails. The irony of it, to be surrounded by all this water but never able to get clean.

23

Light

Dawn's first murk paints the walls blue, and when the morning alarm sounds, it is followed by a strange creaking in a different part of the croft. She reaches the stairs before him. Some mornings the water is mineral, others it is onyx. Today it is glass, noiseless, sleek, hiding movement. The furniture that was once piled on either side of the pill clock has shifted to the far side of the kitchen.

There is something different about the tide, but they cannot wait. She takes a breath, grips the safety line and enters the water. There are various hazards to contend with. Chairs and flotsam bump and shift and knock. She will have bruises on her ribs, on her elbows. The red glow from under-water switches green. 5:57 a.m.

Only the top of the pill clock rises from the water. There are no handholds, nothing to grip, and the current is stronger on this side of the room. She lets go of the line, cups her left hand around the dispensary and places her right thumb on the pill clock. Nothing. She presses harder. Tries again. Maybe the water has finally seeped through the seals and shorted the circuitry. 5:58 a.m. And then the click. A definitive sound, muffled by the water, but definitive. She cups her left hand tighter and feels something drop into her palm. She kicks back to the surface. She gasps air, lungs burning, as Whitney goes under without a word. There is no reason to wait; she puts the pill in her mouth and bites. The cold liquid trickles into her throat.

She can feel Whitney kicking around. The water is choppier. It must be the current. It will be difficult for him to stay steady. She grips the line tighter overhead. She can still make out the faint green light, pulsating through the water, but something is wrong. Whitney breaks the surface in a panic. Snot runs from his nose.

'I dropped it,' he sputters, looking at her, looking at the pill clock.

'What?'

'My pill. It's down there. Help me. Help me. I had it in my hands. I had it—'

Around them the green glow switches to red.

He thrashes around, and she knows the more he thrashes the less chance he has of finding it. She dives. In the blackness they bump into each other. She feels the pressure in her ears, skimming her hand on the earthen stone. Every twig, pebble or shell, she thinks it is the pill. It is hopeless. She cannot find it. The tide will have moved it. She surfaces. 6:01 a.m. She does not want to see this. She is treading water. Helpless. Whitney comes up on the far side of the room. He cannot reach the line. His face is stricken. He cannot breathe. His eyes fix on her. Light enters the room. Eerie refractions. Outside the sun will be up. 6:02 a.m. This is it for him.

'Aina! Aina, I—'

He is sinking below the surface.

She kicks over to him. His hand grips hers and she holds it tight. And she could just go on holding it until he goes limply under. She could … She waits. Considers it. He grips tighter and she feels his scar, the smooth patch of skin. And she remembers the ark. All that blood. His blood. She takes the pen from around her neck. She is treading water. He is slipping now and she grabs him by the collar and hoists him upwards. 'Take the line,' she says. 'Hold on. Do what I say, you'll be okay.'

She struggles to hold him up as she unscrews the barrel of the pen and tips the contents into her palm. The tissue floats away and she wedges the pill into his mouth and forces his jaw shut with the palm of her hand. He is losing consciousness. Veins patterning around his mouth and temple. He grabs her hand. Grabs the pen. He bites down. And his eyes fix on her as the weight goes out of him.

24

Refractions

SHE ROLLS HIM ON TO his back, slips her arm beneath his, and he is horribly pliant, as she lifts his chin from the water and lifeguards him back to the stairs. He slumps in the half-light. Then coughs, dazed, spluttering. He tries to stand and has to sit back down. His eyes are fixed on the pen that dangles uselessly about her neck.

She wants to run, to pass like a cloud over the land. All that work, she thinks. All those minutes, scraped together. Gone. For nothing.

'You had a spare?' he asks. Voice hoarse.

She stands exposed. Cold. Empty. She should not even be here. 'I found it,' she says. 'Kept it for safekeeping.'

He pouts, as if unable to pinpoint the source of something distasteful. 'Safekeeping?'

She nods. 'An emergency … such as this …' She knows that her words fail to tessellate with the particulars of the situation. Her explanation is like a piece of jigsaw that is misaligned. Not quite flush. And Whitney knows too; he is not stupid.

His face configures into disbelief. 'You're lying,' he says. 'You were planning to leave. You said it yourself.'

Light from the attic fills the stairwell. Dawn. She feels it pass right through her. The kitchen ripples with emanations of red from the pill clock. If she goes now, she might still find the pill; the one that Whitney dropped. But the water is dark, vast and deep; there is too much of it.

'Whitney … I found a way …'

'A way to what?'

She takes a breath. If she explains it right, there is a chance that he might see, that he might come around or at least understand. 'There's a lag,' she says. 'Something off-kilter.' And she explains about the pill, how it is no longer calibrated to eight-hour intervals. He listens quietly, without cross-examination or unsolicited offers of judgement. She detects something in him; it feels like admiration, or respect. He looks at her in a way he has not looked at her in years. Aware, perhaps, of his own ignorance.

'The day you were caught in the rip,' he says, sitting up now. 'The glass in your foot. That was the day?'

She nods. 'I think when you went at it that time with the speargun, maybe you altered something. Or I don't know, maybe it was always this way.'

'A design flaw?'

She tells him about the watch. The alarm. The notebook. Retracing her steps, filling in gaps. Explaining every action, every choice, or trying to at least. Because if she can get the words right, she would surely make him see.

'I wanted to tell you.'

He rubs his throat and looks at the watch. His face narrows. 'And you've been at this … how long exactly?' He coughs. Looks around. At the ceiling and the walls. The narrow confines of the stairwell.

'Two months.' She cannot read him. 'Since spring,' she adds.

'A while then …'

She goes upstairs into the attic, takes her journal from beneath her mattress, and the morning illuminates the rows, the columns. Her timings. 'Fifty-four days,' she explains. 'See for yourself.'

He studies a page, another, then raises his eyes to her.

'I can't stay here, Whitney. I just can't. I need to know one way or another if he's survived.' She considers her next words with care. 'We can go together, across the spine—'

'Ah. The spine …' He hauls himself to his feet. He appears stunned, groggy, but with each breath he seems to be regaining something of his strength. He sloshes up out of the water, into the attic. He sits on his bed, staring at the pages of her journal, turning them occasionally. He has all the little pieces of her before him, and she has no idea how he will put her back together.

He turns towards her. Eyes cold and grey, like deadened silver. He considers her for a moment.

She looks to the window, out to sea. The tips of the rocky spires rise from the bay. The needles. Spiked. 'You said there

177

was smoke,' she says. 'Out past the spine. Aren't you in the least bit curious? It might have been Max—'

'Forget it, Aina.'

She tastes iron in her mouth. Rubs a finger around her gums. The finger comes out pink and she sucks on blood. Another tooth is coming loose. One of her molars. She feels light-headed. Dizzy. She just wants to know what happened. If he is still alive. She steadies herself. 'I'm going, Whitney …' She hears indecision creeping into her voice. 'I'll go alone, if need be.'

'No.' He closes the notebook and sits straighter.

'No?'

'We have to work together on this. They're testing us, it's just like the Warden said.'

'Jesus, Whitney.' She shakes her head. 'Look around. No one's coming.'

He calls her by name, but his voice falters, and she sees a different quality in his eyes: pain, or a certain vulnerability. He blinks it away, sits straighter. 'We just wait this out,' he says. 'The flood will pass. The Warden will come.'

'This isn't some test, Whitney. The radio's dead.'

'You've just stopped listening,' he says, striving to remain composed, rational. 'They're here, Aina. I know what I saw, up on the hill. Please, be patient. For me? We're so close.'

The pen hangs empty about her neck. He is trying to make this personal and she cannot bear to look at him. She feels disgust. A cold liquid flows through her heart. The key. The matches. If it had not been for the piano … If Maxime had never ventured from the cubby …

She can feel herself running out of options. She speaks softly. 'This isn't about you, Whitney. I have to find him. If there's even a chance that he's alive, I have to try. You can understand that, can't you?'

He turns, exhales. 'It doesn't change anything. You've described a violation, Aina. The Warden won't stand for it. I'd be guilty by association.'

'This isn't about the Warden,' she says. 'It's about Max. He's out there, Whitney.'

'Yes.' He speaks coldly. 'And if he is, parole's our only hope. We need the Warden onside.'

'Trust me, Whitney. Please.'

'Trust?' His jaw tightens. 'There's no trust left, Aina. You've seen to that.'

He stands.

She backs away, uncertain.

'You really haven't thought this through,' he says. 'The ramifications, for me, for yourself. You've been bumbling around, benighted. Blind. You've no idea ... no idea. Come on.' He taps his wrist. Holds out his hand. 'The watch, hand it over. I can't leave it with you now, can I?' he adds. 'It'd be negligent.'

She has nowhere to go.

'I won't ask again.'

'Whitney—'

He grabs her wrist. Squeezes, and his fingers claw, and she tightens her hand into a fist, but she cannot pull her arm away. He grips, finding cavities between tendon and bone.

'Jesus, Whitney, get the fuck off.'

He won't look at her. She pulls, kicks, knees at him but she is unable to connect and they stumble across the room, crashing into things. His armpit is a vice and his back is too broad and she cannot see her wrist. Her foot is caught between his and they trip, momentum carrying them over. She lands. Flattened. Winded, cannot get up. He still has her wrist, and he is bending her elbow in ways it is not meant to be bent. Everything taut. Every fibre. Every sinew. She makes herself compact, grits teeth. And when he has the watch, he releases his hold and blood surges back through her arm. A hot ache. She rolls on to her side, cradles her arm and curls into a ball. Cheek in a puddle of her own drool.

Floorboards creak beside her and she hears him stand. His voice comes from above, panting. 'I won't let you fuck this up,' he says. 'Take your pills at the designated times. No more running. No more bullshit. The Warden will come.'

She looks up as he fixes the watch to his wrist. He dimples the reset button with his thumb.

His thumb—

If there is a test, this must be it.

———

The rain continues all afternoon, a low thrum. It keeps her awake past dark. Eventually, she lights a candle, takes her journal and flicks back over her entries from the last two months. Maps of various trails, records of times. Sketches of the croft. She glances at Whitney's sketch of Maxime, and the pain of failure spreads, orchestrally complex.

Long sky … Charged earth …

She sleeps fitfully, and in her dreams, the attic walls fall away, and she is floating above the croft, gazing left, gazing right, to a height at which she can no longer hear the waves. The croft becomes a speck on the landscape. There is peace. She goes higher and stars appear, unfamiliar constellations, and she can see the curvature of the Earth. A faint emanation of light away in the east, against which a column of thick smoke rises. The chimney of an old distillery. Or a refinery. Particles of dust and ash blow everywhere on the wind, clogging the night sky. The smell of toast. And she hears Whitney's voice, and the closing of drawers. *Aina, have you seen my matches? You had them for the candles, for his birthday.* She does not know where they are. And Whitney gives her a look of frustration, as he settles back into his armchair and continues reading aloud. *The olfactory bulb connects directly to the amygdala and hippocampus ...*

And she is back in the apartment. She remembers the piano. Her grandmother's piano. The smooth waxy feel of the enamel teeth. Whitney is rushing to get out of the door. He bites a triangle of toast, kisses Max on the head and kisses her on the cheek. Max sits on the stool, his back to the piano. She is late for rehearsal and he has a book open on his lap, the dictionary. He reads aloud a passage on embers. About the etymology of the word. 'From the Saxon,' he says, '*emb-ren* or *ymb-ryne*. It means a circuit. A revolution. And there were such things as Ember Days, too,' he says. 'Days that marked feasts. Or the seasons. A run around the sun.'

'Okay, Max, into the cubby, please.'

Her taxi is here. Rush hour, crosstown. She needs to leave. She tightens the lid on her coffee, whispers, 'Bye, Max' and closes the door. The lift is slow in the mornings so she takes the stairs. In her shoulder bag, she carries pages of annotated music. Through the revolving door, the noise of the day hits.

And later, after rehearsal – a new modernist opera by Delaney; she had collaborated on the libretto, and the opening is in less than a month – they go to lunch at the Arts Club, taking their old booth, a bunch of them, and she looks to the bar, the mirror. She remembers Whitney, the time they first met. His old posters still adorn the walls, framed now. The campaign work for Baumbacher. An album cover for one of Delaney's solo projects, and there, the original poster for This Rough Beast: the head of a ram on a lion's body, piano-key grin, curved horns spiralling into clefs. St Luke's Church, 7 p.m.

Lucia's there too, in a polo shirt and athletic wear. She has come from the pool.

A drummer tunes his cymbals on stage. Someone makes a joke and Aina smiles on cue, and the cymbals are like wind among tall grass. She reaches for her key, the key to the piano, and it is not there about her neck. She checks her pockets, checks her bag. Front pouch. Back zipper. Nothing. She asks vaguely, 'Has anyone seen …'

Lucia is moving glasses and bottles, politely making room for their pizza.

She must have left it in the apartment, on her bedside table, or the bathroom, or left it in the piano, and the panic is instantaneous. A flash. There is no time.

'Aina?' someone asks. 'Are you okay?'

'I have … I have to go.'

Aina, have you seen my matches?

She hears the sound of footsteps on the stairs. The stairs. Six, seven, eight, nine, ten stairs. Impossible. A door opening. The hinge yawns, discordant. Traversing into a higher pitch. And she remembers standing, the lid of the piano raised, as she takes the pliers and twists the tuning peg. Maxime stands in the doorway. Maxime. He is here in the attic. Alive. Droplets forming on his nose; they run down his cheek. He is drenched. Water, she thinks, but the smell catches in her throat, and when he strikes the match, everything erupts in a broad ball of flame.

She grapples around. Wakes. Whitney's pale hand grips her shoulder. He shushes her to stay calm.

Something in his eye compels her to be still.

'What?' she whispers.

His smile is tentative. 'The water,' he says, 'Come, look, it's draining away.'

25

Cairn

Brown grass deadens the valley. She should have left, gone when she had the chance. That blasted yacht … She walks the attic, picturing Maxime, thinking of ways she might escape. Eleven paces. Turn. Eleven paces. Turn. An even tempo. Yan tan tethera methera pip. She walks, rubbing the space on her wrist where the watch once was, massaging her forearm. Her leg cramps. Her knee is stiff. She would be lucky to run twelve-minute miles on the flat right now.

Eleven paces. Turn. Eleven paces—

Whitney is dusting off the chessboard; he sets it squarely on the bed. The board is missing pieces but he has appropriated substitutes. A salt shaker for a queen. Black buttons for pawns. Lacking a willing opponent, he must play against himself. It is farcical to watch.

How could he have been so stupid, losing his pill like that? Unless … Did he know about her spare and drop his on purpose? Maybe it was a test of her loyalty; a means to bring her back in line. It seems a stretch, but he is capable of such deception.

Her mood shifts, mezzo forte to mezzo piano. She looks at herself in the pocket mirror, and wipes the accumulation of dirt from her face. The woman staring back looks lost and drawn, like a miner who has spent too much time underground.

She wonders what would have happened if she had let him go under. It would have been relatively quick. But in that split second, faced with a choice between Whitney and Max, she chose Whitney. And nobody forced her; she gave him the pill willingly, a crime of complicity. The guilt bores into her. There must be something she can do, something she can use. She makes an itinerary, takes stock. The attic is cluttered but much has been discarded, hidden or lost. The hammer is missing, and the speargun is no longer propped at the end of Whitney's bed. He must have hidden them for safekeeping. But there are only so many places that would accommodate things of that size. The rafters. The chimney breast. Under his mattress.

Sharp and precise, a pain infuses her jawbone. Something shucks loose. She fishes around, wincing, and spits out a tooth. A molar, black at the root. Cool air whistles against her gums.

On his wrist, the watch beeps, marking the hour.

She observes him now, casually. His hands are broken and bruised. Gnarled. Calloused. White to play. He leans forward, considers the board. A rod emerging from the top of his jeans, cylindrical. One of the harpoons. She could take it from his belt and slide it into the soft gap between his ribs. It would be easy. Blood gushing up through his fingers like water between floorboards. See him stagger!

There must be something she can do.

By mid-morning the water has retreated, leaving the kitchen a mess of dirt and pieces of broken plate and chippings of jigsaw. An old marble rides between flagstones and disappears beneath the dresser, but there is no sign of the lost pill. The door to the garden hangs on its hinges. Outside, the garden is puddled. The oat field too. She looks along the beach and the scale of the devastation becomes clear. The freighter has broken up on the rocks – and several other wrecks beside *Håvsra* have vanished for good. Nine vessels now. No *Rorvik*. No tugboat. It is a disruption in chronology. Everything is off-kilter.

She goes quietly back upstairs. Whitney lies sprawled on his bed, napping. His paperback splayed upon his stomach, the Tromsø novel. His face is restful, slack and stubbled. She could wake him, but why bother. She strips her bed and hangs her sheets in the garden to dry, and instead of heading back inside, she continues through the gate and up the track. Mud oozing between her toes as she walks. Mud. Lovely black mud.

Every step is an act of defiance, taking her further up the valley. At the tor she rests. The blue sky overhead is reflected darker by the ocean. A pleasant breeze, she does not care for time. The granite slabs are warm in the sun, and she climbs up to the highest one. Atop, there is the cairn … Strange that it was not blown over in the storm. She looks out to sea, feels suddenly precarious. Something is off. Something is wrong. It takes her a moment. She counts the rocks on the cairn – thirteen, no mistaking it – one extra. Vertigo twists. She scrambles down off the tor, jumps the last few feet and lands beside a pattern of indentations in the mud. Footprints. A man's, size ten or eleven. They must be Whitney's. They must be. Except he only ever wears the flat-bottomed waders, and he has not been out in weeks. And these are an unfamiliar tread. Deep and widely distributed. A man of considerable size.

26

Shadows

S HE STEADIES HERSELF AGAINST the doorframe. Her heart is in her ears and her fingertips and the soft gaps around her eyes. Half a mile back to the croft, she has run, fast as she could muster, and for the first time in days, it is not dread or loathing she feels, but adrenaline.

Senses primed. Everything is heightened. Time constricts.

She takes the binoculars from the table and approaches the window. Hands shaking, the hillside is magnified in disparate fields. Brown, white, beige. Nothing. In the distance, the tor is a lonely point of triangulation against the cropped grey sky. Her heart judders. Someone is out there, she thinks. Whitney was right.

Steady. One breath every three seconds.

Yan tan tethera.

Yan tan tethera.

Yan tan tethera, methera pip.

Breathe.

The wind pipes gently, compelling everything to motion, and the sounds of the waves merge in a quickened hurried rush. Seconds pass, and a pageantry of shadows sweep upwards to the plateau.

The muddy tract that leads to the moor looks muddier now, as if someone has recently clambered down, slipshod through the boggy patches where the barrow's wheel would stick. The land. The grass. The denuded willows and the reeds on the backside of the marsh. Twigged stumps of oat poke through the mirror-like surface of the field. Everything pulses, rests and stirs. Aina pans across the valley, eyes skipping from thing to thing, she gleans for something foreign, an anomalous form stiffening against the wind.

Aeolus, Zephyrus, Notus … The wind enters through the back door, rattles the croft and channels the distended air. Whoever has come, they cannot have survived long out there, not without shelter. The land is too exposed and the wind is boundless, infinite.

Seen from distance, the croft would look deserted. Perhaps whoever came ashore headed inland, bound for the moor or the spine. And for all she knows, the footprints, though pristine, they could be weeks old. She raises the field glasses once more. An ocular Venn of left and right and she looks to the moor, checks the line of the hill. The valley darkens and colours leach into dank monochrome, punctuated only by strips of standing water on the lower reaches of the track. The berm has been flattened considerably, and she scans the beach. A man moves among the wrecks, cautiously, carrying a speargun with practised stealth. She recognises his stoop: Whitney. She had assumed he was still sleeping upstairs, but he must have woken while she was out and gone looking for her.

It is suddenly quiet.

For the first time since the flood, she is alone in the croft.

She looks to the stairs. There is an opportunity here, one she might not get again. She hurries swiftly up to the attic and starts checking the floorboards around his bed, one by one, to see if any are loose. She checks his mattress, checks the rafters. Taps the wall — he must have a hidey-hole some-where. She taps the skirting, hears a hollow sound, and behind a portion of board, she finds a dark recess. It extends a couple of feet, a narrow gap. There is no pill. No hammer. No filleting knife. Just a bundle of worn papers bound with string. She unfolds one. The paper is crinkled and tattered, the crease disintegrating. The page has been torn from a book. One of Giacometti's essays. Sketched lightly upon it is a face.

She takes them downstairs, where there is more room and better light, and she fans the pages. A dozen and fifty more. A portrait on each: some made in blue, others in green, a couple are violet. They might be Whitney as a boy. Or her, back when her hair was longer. The child's left ear is slightly elfin. Max — and scrawled at the bottom of each, a caption, showing his age:

Eleven years, ten months.
Eleven years, eleven months.
Twelve years.

Twelve years, one month.

Twelve years, two months.

There are so many. She spreads them on the table as she would the jigsaw, and begins arranging them in order, sixty-two in total, spiralling outwards, the same face at regular intervals. The hair is at different lengths in the pictures: cropped, becoming unruly, then shoulder length and tucked back behind the ears. A gradual morphing of features.

She finishes, stands at the sink and watches as Whitney comes stalking back up the track. The way is clear. Saltwater has killed off the brambles. There is nothing to slow him down.

'Aina! You in there?' Outside, the gate bangs against the post. 'Aina!' He appears in the doorway, breathless, and there is as much relief as there is anger in his voice. 'I told you,' he says, leaning on the architrave. 'We don't go out.' Something causes him to stand a little straighter. 'Where've you been?' he asks.

She concedes. 'You were right,' she says. 'Someone was aboard that boat.'

She tells him about the cairn and the footprints, and she searches his face for some hint of reaction but he just swallows, grips the speargun. 1:48 p.m. She rubs her wrist. Feels her empty pen against her breast bone. 'Whitney,' she says, 'did you ever think, it might be him out there?'

He squints tentatively. 'Who?'

She motions to his pictures, spiralled on the table. 'Max.'

He takes a step forward and halts when he sees them. 'Where'd you get those?' he asks.

She shrugs. It does not matter now. 'You drew them, didn't you?' she says. 'One a month ...'

192

The last one puts Max at fifteen years and two months. The paper is so delicate, and he takes it, holds it gingerly and runs a finger down the serrated edge. 'It was a way of keeping him alive.'

Fifteen years and two months—

Fifteen years—

'Why did you stop?' she asks.

He looks up and his face is unreadable. She sees his ghost: younger, faltering, less sure of his own prowess. And before he can answer, the lunchtime alarm sounds, louder than usual, and there is an odd synchronicity to the sound. The numbers on the pill clock reconfigure. 1:50 p.m. Out of habit, she reaches for her wrist. Across the room, Whitney cradles the speargun in the crook of his arm and draws back his sleeve. She sees the small black rectangle. He dimples the reset, but the beeping continues and he dimples it again, bringing the watch to his ear. His face contorts, confused by some apparent malfunction.

'Have you done something to this?' he asks.

Be-beep.

Be-beep.

Be-beep.

The sound stops and she realises it was not coming from within the room. She grips the edge of the dresser. Feels blood in her fingertips. Outside, the latch clicks. The gate squeaks. The wind, it must be the wind. Clothes rustle louder, trouser legs, else it could be her bedsheets that have blown free of the line. Let it be that. The homemade pegs have not held. They are short on wire. Short on elastic. Short on everything besides time and the wind, which whistles through the croft, stirring the thick, water-laden air.

Angels breathe on the back of her neck. The light changes in the room and a shadow sweeps the wall.

In the doorway, the wet flagstones invert the sky.

She wants for a clear view up the garden but Whitney has line of sight and he looks from her to the door and whatever he sees coming down the path sends him scrabbling. Back. Back. Back. He collides with a chair and the sharp staccato honk is the loudest sound—

The nearness of the man catches her unawares. Haggard and in tatters. A silhouette, the sky bends around him. She holds her breath. Shadows reclaim the land and she can see him: feet planted wide, braced for waves. He is broad and bearded, young, with a full head of hair cut short, and his left eye is black and clotted, the blood vessels ruptured from a recent injury. She watches him scan the room from the floor to the sink and the radio, nodding at each. His gaze rests momentarily on her and she feels herself eroding. She cannot move. His eyes seem to suck the light from the room.

The stranger's clothes are crusted from the sea and split in places. His boots look almost as old as he, caked in mud as though he has crawled from the earth. He carries a drybag on his shoulder. Finally he speaks, a soft, lilting voice, 'Do you think we might come in?'

Whitney has backed up as far as the room will allow. Sprawled against the dresser. He picks himself up, raises his weapon and struggles to keep it level.

The stranger regards the speargun. One hand grips his drybag. With the other, he begins slowly unbuttoning his slicker.

'*We?*' asks Aina.

The man nods.

He steps slightly to one side and all the wind goes out of the world. There is a child. A girl, leeward like a sapling, safe within his shade.

27

Child

THERE IS A CONSTRICTION in her throat. Dryness. She coughs fine particles of sand. There are too many faces in the room. Too many hands.

Yan tan tethera methera pip.

Yan tan—

The child peers out from behind the man. A child. Here? Her body seems so tiny. A compilation of limbs loosely bundled. She must be about ten, maybe a year either way, and Aina has the urge to kneel and draw her close, to rub warmth into those grubby little hands.

She looks from the child to the man and back again, seeking the architecture of one face in the other. Different mouth.

Different brow. The hands? No, they are different too. She tries to imagine how this girl will grow up, how her face may change, tectonically shifting, to resemble the man's, but she cannot perceive, cannot extrapolate … the future is a gap that her mind cannot bridge.

After twelve years, alone but for Whitney, the strangers' faces beguile. The last person she ever met was the Warden. She is certain he was fair-headed. And before: living in the high-rise. The city, all those interchangeable faces. All those lies, telling anyone who would listen, *This is my nephew, yes. He is staying with us for the summer. Visiting from across the river.*

Maxime.

The girl's eyes are lighter, but she is similarly slight.

On the roof, the tarpaulin catches in the wind, and Aina's heart is a balloon, pushing the breath out of her lungs. 'Your daughter?' Aina asks. The question slips out, expanding like a bubble rising from depths.

The side of the younger man's face is a yellowed bruise, and his left eye is partway bloodshot. Up by his hairline is a single clean wound, dressed with stitches. He scowls, ever so slightly, and the skin at his temple pulls tight. He has been asked the question before, she thinks. A hundred times maybe, and however he tries to disguise his anger, the question still offends. Pride awakens. There it is. The look on his face; she remembers that. Remembers how it feels, to see the doubt on people, to be the subject of their assumptions, their theorising. A neighbour heckling her on the stairs: *Poacher! Burglar! Thief!* The sullen face of the prosecutor as he made his case. The child must have been stolen, he said. There was no other explanation. No other way.

The wayfarer does not speak. He does not have to. He says it all with his eyes. And the girl makes no attempt to contradict. She stands, motionless, a hand on the man's slicker. Poised. Keen eyes and an intelligent face. She takes stock of the room, scrutinising everything, as though these are things on which she will later be tested. Unphased, unhurried, the child scans slowly, and Aina tracks her gaze. She imagines looking on the scene for the first time. The muddied floor. The chess game, stove, kettle, sideboard. The pictures of Max laid out on the rotting slab of wood that passes for a table. She wants to gather them up, hide them away.

Aina sees Whitney adjusting his grip on the speargun. His shoulders tighten. What is he doing, pointing that thing at the girl?

The father sees him too. But he does not react. He simply smiles, leans slightly towards the child and asks, 'You still think we'll be safe here?'

The child hesitates then nods, slowly. Aina catches her eye. It is like looking through time.

'And what about him?' The man gestures at Whitney. 'Should we be worried about him?'

The child hesitates. 'I'm not sure,' she says.

'But is he hostile?'

'Potentially.'

'Based on what?'

'Based on the weapon.'

'And what else?'

The child looks away. 'Various unknowns.'

Aina listens, mesmerised by this voice that is quiet but assured. A beautiful voice. An octave lower than she would expect of a child her age, as though damp has settled in her lungs.

'Such as?' asks the man.

'We don't know his temperament.'

'What about the weapon?' asks the man. 'What can you deduce?'

'It appears cared for. But not recently fired.'

'And what else? Might he be skilled in marksmanship?'

The man has a feigned sense of impatience, and the girl bites her lip. She will not be rushed. 'Not especially,' she says.

'Based on what?'

'The gun seems heavy to him. And he favours his left eye even though he's right-handed. I think his sight is waning.'

A broad grin spreads across the man's face. Aina looks at Whitney, and for a moment their eyes meet. She wills him to lower the gun, but he stands there, trapped in a threat from which he cannot retreat.

The man grows in stature. 'Anything else?' he asks.

'He likes the way the weapon feels in his hands ...'

'Yes ... he does. But?'

'I'm not sure he has ever fired it. He carries it as an accoutrement.'

'*Accoutrement?* Meaning?'

'A prop,' says the child. 'Ornamentation.'

'Very good. And what's our threshold? A table-length? The beam of the boat?'

'Six feet should suffice,' says the child.

A mix of malice and bewilderment spreads across Whitney's face. The man takes a step back. 'Very good,' he says. 'And what of his companion?'

The child pauses and looks at the floor. 'The woman is the better climber. The faster runner. She has more stamina ...'

Aina listens. It would feel awkward to be appraised so bluntly by anyone, let alone by someone so young. She feels like an eavesdropper, a ghost, and she remembers the court-room, the hard wooden bench, listening as the judge labelled her selfish, wayward, irresponsible.

The man asks, 'You think she is a threat?'

'No,' says the girl, raising her eyes to the man's.

'But will they help us?'

The girl considers Whitney, the speargun, and she looks again at Aina. 'I think she might.'

All trace of affront has been diminished and the father – she is certain that he is her father now – he smiles proudly and signals for the child to step back in line, but the girl, so little and stubborn, she remains in the doorway. Her eyes return to Whitney. Distrustful. She asks, 'Why did he turn those people to stone?'

The man shifts his weight and considers his words care-fully. 'The man is a sculptor,' he says loudly. 'An artiste. They are works of art.'

While the girl might miss his mocking tone, Aina does not, and neither will Whitney. He inhales sharply, tension running through him.

Long-drawn dimples crease about the girl's mouth. 'Are they religious? A depiction of God?'

The man furrows his brow. 'Why don't you ask him?'

Whitney clears his throat and stands a little formally. There is a small delight to be had in watching him weigh up whether to explain his work to this girl. He answers curtly,

'They're commemorative, yes, but they're not representations of any deity.'

'I … don't understand. What are they then?'

Whitney coughs. He has run out of words.

Aina watches the wayfarer scratch at his beard. Dirt is lodged under his fingernails. The man speaks softly, 'They are a testament of guilt.'

Whitney adjusts his grip.

The house creaks.

Nobody moves.

'I like them,' says the child. 'They are crude, but I like them.'

Whitney looks along the speargun, his patience waning. 'What do you want?' he asks.

Aina can only watch. The man's hands are all knuckles as he reaches for the child, grips her shoulder and compels her backwards. His other hand moves slowly down the bag-strap, towards his midriff. It disappears into his slicker, searching for a hilt or a handle or something.

'Easy, mister. Steady there,' he says. There is something familiar about him. The soft melody of his voice.

'Dad …' The child glances at the clock. She tugs on the man's slicker.

1:56 p.m.

If the stranger has any need for timeliness, he does not let it show. 'The child is too forgiving in her assessments,' he says. 'She's still learning. Still has that tendency to see the best in people. It's something she was born with.'

'She get that from you?' asks Whitney.

'No. She did not.'

'From her mother then?'

Her mother. Where is she? Aina takes half a step forward, watching the man. Has he left her somewhere? Has he … Strange that he is covered in mud, having come from the sea. Twelve days since the boat, *Håvsra*, ran aground. She pictures him, stumbling out of the waves and kneeling on the beach, digging his hands into the sand. Kneading it. Whispering to it, prayerful. Except the mud on his slicker is peaty and dark, and the sand on the beach is golden and fine. 'What were you doing up on the moor?' she asks.

The man does not answer.

Aina goes on. 'Your clothes,' she says. 'They're covered in mud. Your hands too.'

'They were watching us, Aina.' Whitney growls angrily, his face contorted. 'They were observing. Waiting like spies.'

'Surviving,' says the man. 'Forgotten. Abandoned, the same as you.'

'We have not been abandoned.' Whitney takes his hand from the barrel of the gun, lifts the receiver from its cradle and speaks in a flat mechanical voice, 'Warden, come in … Warden, this is Long Sky Croft. We have two wayfarers. Fugitives. Their motives are unknown—'

The stranger chuckles.

With one hand on the receiver, Whitney struggles to keep the speargun level. 'Warden?' he says. 'Come in, over.'

'A technical difficulty?' The younger man watches Whitney intensely, waiting for something. His chest heaves. 'What do you think?' he asks, addressing the girl over his shoulder.

The child shakes her head. 'It's more serious than that,' she says.

'Based on what?'

'I …'

'What evidence do you see?'

'Dad? The Warden …'

'No, what evidence is here. In this room. Look. Infer …
Use your eyes.'

She looks at the ceiling. Her voice is quieter than before.
'The high–water line,' she says.

'Go on.'

'The paint is peeling.'

'Meaning?'

'The entire floor was flooded.'

'What about the radio?'

'It's not properly sealed. The circuitry will be ruined.'

She knows something, thinks Aina, besides innocence and
optimism and the workings of radios. There is something
dark, hidden. A burden.

Whitney drops the receiver; it swings and nicks the wall.
He takes the speargun in both hands.

The man draws a long, deliberate breath. Sighs. His hand
still rests inside his slicker.

'What's your name?' asks Aina. 'You must have a name …'

He looks up. A trace of a smile as his crusted eye weeps.
'Kessler. I'm Kessler.'

'And this is …?'

'My daughter, Ruth.'

Aina looks at the child. 'She was born here?'

He speaks in fragments. 'A lighthouse. An island. Eleven
years west.'

'You were exiled?' she asks.

Kessler nods. 'Yes. The girl's mother and I.'

Whitney steps forward. Still with the speargun. Setting
himself. She pleads with him, tries to make him see sense,

but he just shakes his head. 'We don't know a thing about him.'

'He needs our help. They both do.'

Kessler stands motionless. 'You're making a mistake, mister. Don't do this.' In the corner of the kitchen, the dial on the pill clock turns from red to green. 1:57 p.m. He looks up. 'I'm sorry for our haste. We don't mean to intrude … We don't mean any harm. But … I'm going to use your pill clock.' Slowly his hand leaves his belt. 'We don't want trouble.'

He takes a step.

Aina watches. Waits. Ruth stands in the doorway. The harpoon is primed. Light runs the barrel length. A gleaming horizon. If he shoots and misses, he will hit the girl.

She remembers the Warden, remembers him telling them that their pill clock and all the others are calibrated centrally. 'Whitney,' she pleads. 'If your thumb is read by one, it can be read by them all. Please, Whitney. Let him pass.'

'He wants our pills. Who knows how many we've left.'

'There are more pills in that clock than there are pebbles on the beach,' she pleads.

Kessler wipes his mouth. 'She's right.'

'And how do you know that?' Whitney pulls the weapon tight into his shoulder. Water drips from the tap into the sink. Collecting. Bulging. Falling, as Whitney's finger tightens on the trigger, squeezing a quarter-inch. Kessler steps forward, arms raised, cautious, like a man stepping into water, unsure of its depth.

Aina readies for the thunk. He is going to shoot, and without thinking, she steps between them. Whitney feints one way and attempts to go the other, but she mirrors his movements, left, right, she won't let him past.

'Out of the way.'

'No.'

'Let go! Aina. Please.'

'No.'

Resistance goes out of him; she knows he will not fight her now, and with gentle fingers she lowers the barrel of the speargun to the floor. There is movement behind her. A whirr and a click; Kessler lifts his thumb from the scanner. The pill clock deposits a capsule: half red, half white. He closes his fist around it.

'Go ahead,' says Aina, addressing Ruth. 'It's okay.' But Ruth stands, quietly shifting. Watching, waiting. Alone, like Max in the doorway, clutching his blanket, woken by their shouting and the crashing of plates.

Whitney takes a step back. 'What's the matter with her?' he asks.

Kessler places his pill on his tongue. 'Like I said, she was born here.' He swallows. 'She has no need for them.'

28

Porridge

EVERY SO OFTEN, SHE glances at Whitney. He sits with the speargun across his lap, eyes on the pictures of Maxime, which she has collected and placed on the dresser. He seems content to listen as Kessler steers the conversation, prompting Aina with questions about the land and the seaweed and the oats, and she gets one or two things wrong, deliberately, so that Whitney might correct her, but he will not be drawn. It was a good idea to make porridge. She has bought them all some time. And if Whitney is concerned by her charity, he does not let it show. He shakes seaweed liberally from the canister, and, on the surface at least, the tension in the room is reset.

But how did he survive out there, on the boat, without pills?

'You both must be famished,' she says.

Kessler closes his eyes and lowers his face to the bowl. Steam rises, and his shoulders heave. He inhales slowly, and there appears something spiritual about him, as though he sees something in the bowl to be revered. She watches him, wafting the air with his hand, cupping it and lifting it to his face. It is a bizarre ritual. Ruth bows also, and they whisper quietly. The prayer is brief. Kessler picks up his spoon.

'It's been a couple of days,' says Kessler finally. He tastes the porridge, savouring its heat. He takes a skinny glass vial from his grab-bag. Inside: a thin brown bark, which he grates to powder using a special curved utensil. The smell is invigorating. Warm autumn afternoons. Spicy and sweet.

Whitney watches him. 'Is that cinnamon?' he asks.

Kessler nods. 'Have some. Here, help yourself.'

But Whitney refuses. He might interpret the offer as an insult to the provisions they have to hand. Or else he is too wise, far too wise, to place himself in another man's debt. Especially a stranger's. 'I like it just fine with seaweed,' he says.

Yes, thinks Aina. Unadulterated. Bland. *Pure.* She would like to try the cinnamon. The dry sweet heat might counter the damp that has settled inside of her. But when Kessler offers her the bark and the grater, she lowers her eyes and shakes her head. It goes against her instinct, but it is better to keep Whitney onside. At least for now.

'Oats is oats,' adds Whitney.

Kessler does not take any offence. He slips the vial back inside his bag, and the porridge loosens his tongue. He proves a willing talker, speaking between spoonfuls, holding her gaze. She looks at the gash on his forehead, and he taps it with his spoon. 'Caught it on a cupboard during the storm,' he explains. 'Wood on wood! Knocked me out clean.' He gestures at Ruth, who chews quietly. 'We'd have lost the mainsail a lot sooner if it weren't for the little one. Isn't that right, barnacle? A dab hand with the needle, she is too.'

Aina smiles, but it feels hideous on her face – a mask – and the child can tell, she thinks; she can spot suspicions a mile off. And Aina is suspicious. There is no denying it. She tillers the conversation round, probing subtly, and Kessler talks on, seeming to anticipate their questions. He talks dutifully, almost gracious for the opportunity, pausing only occasionally to add a little hot water to his porridge.

And she is no longer listening. She is thinking: they show up, fortuitously, in time for the lunchtime pill, after so many weeks at sea and a dozen days stranded on the moor? It does not makes sense.

'Excuse me,' she says, leaning forward and interrupting bluntly. 'But ... what did you do for pills?'

Kessler pauses with the spoon halfway to his mouth, eyes flitting between them, watching Ruth now, wary of her reaction. She eats. Eyes. Hard, glinting. Perceptive. And Kessler meets Aina's eye and he clearly understands the urgency of the question. But he takes another slow bite. 'I'll come to that,' he says, 'I promise.'

There is nothing for Aina to do but nod.

'Now, where were we?' And he waits for the awkwardness to pass before continuing. 'Yes, a thin wedge of rock. One mile long. All that bleakness. All that ocean. That's where we were sent.' He points west. 'Out there … The edge of Arcady …'

He tells them about a lighthouse, rising from the northernmost tip of an isle. Aina can picture it quite vividly. The faded cylindrical bands of paint. White now grey. Red now pink. He seems possessed of a certain nostalgia, inhabiting his memories, yielding to them as he talks eloquently, using words that Aina has not heard in years. It is like listening to a kind of dialect, a mode of speech from another time. *Balustrade. Promontory. Cupola.* She has a vague recollection of these words. They refer to something geometric. Architectural. Staircases perhaps. And he talks about the chores and the upkeep and the lamp. The night it went out.

'Boats passed in the darkness,' he says. 'A flotilla, adrift. They broke up on the rocks. Every last one.'

'What of their crews? Did you see anyone? Any sign.'

He shakes his head. 'Whether it was war, or famine, some mass evacuation that went wrong, I don't know. It was like they had been drifting for years.'

Aina looks out the window towards the needles.

'What are you saying?' asks Whitney.

'Come on, you know, with the permafrost. Maybe it spread …' He glances at the pill clock. 'We might be the only ones left.'

Kessler talks about their isle and its rock formations, a yachtsman mistakenly tightening a sail ahead of a squall.

'Must have really been a testing place,' says Whitney.

If Kessler senses provocation, he does not react.

Whitney thumbs the edge of the table. 'Makes me wonder,' he continues. 'What a man might have done, to be sent to such ends.'

'Touché.'

The porridge slides, heavy and glutinous, from Aina's spoon.

The room is suddenly quiet. Whitney chews slowly. Aina is embarrassed for him, for herself. If only there were wind, loud rattling gusts that would shake the entire croft. But the only sound comes from the child, rolling a marble back and forth along the tabletop. She must have found it under the dresser. It looks oversized in her fist.

Aina asks, 'What was her name, your wife?'

'She wasn't my wife. We weren't married. But her name was Tola.'

'Pretty name.'

'Yes.' He turns to Ruth. 'She joked that we'd been sent to Ithaca.'

Whitney carries his empty bowl to the sink and turns to face the room. 'Well, that doesn't make sense,' he says.

Kessler sits forward in the ladderback chair. The wood cricks. He does not seem much accustomed to sitting still, or else he is not accustomed to pettiness. Or maybe he is simply ill at ease indoors; one of those men who crave wider spaces, so they can see what approaches from a ways away. 'What's that?' he asks.

'In the stories,' says Whitney. 'Odysseus was trying to return to Ithaca.'

'So?'

Whitney turns slightly. 'Well, it seems like you were fixing to leave.'

Noisily, the girl scrapes the last of the porridge from her bowl. 'Maybe that was the joke,' she says.

Aina feels the dampness of the wood through the wetsuit, a cold, clammy unpleasantness, and she imagines Tola, alone, out there in The Limits, knowing she would give birth. Nine months, the terror she must have felt. She places her spoon in her bowl. She cannot eat. She should say something, offer condolences, but how can she comment on the nature of grief? The emotions are too complex and her language is blunt, coarse, denuded. To describe grief would require precision, nuance; things that are absent, lost. They were sealed behind doors, long ago.

She clears her throat. 'You know, I think I will try the cinnamon.'

Kessler hesitates.

'If you don't mind …'

'Of course.' He reaches into his bag and hands her the vial and the grater.

She adds some to her own bowl. The powder is fine. Sweet and incensed, a hint of orange, the porridge tacks to her spoon.

Time passes differently now, with more people in the room. The ceiling feels lower. The windows smaller.

Sensing currency in small generosities, she fills the kettle, sets it on the stove, and the walls glisten, damp to the touch as the wood burns grudgingly. It is a simple thing to make tea, and she is glad to have something practical to do, but she finds herself distracted, thinking about the lighthouse and thinking about Tola, and – what is taking so long? – she returns to the stove and pats lightly the belly of the kettle, testing for warmth, but the kettle is cold and her fingertips come away wet with condensation. The fire has died, and the scuttle is empty, and the flood has reduced the stack of peat in the yard to mush.

'Whitney,' she says. 'Maybe you could pop down to the beach. I expect there'll be some wood there.'

His eyes clench. His brow furrows. He seems to be looking for an excuse not to comply. 'I—'

'Assuming that's okay with you,' she interjects, speaking to Kessler. 'I believe the boat was yours.'

Kessler consents. And with obvious reluctance, Whitney gets to his feet. The long-standing obligations between guest and host require that he makes some concession to comfort and warmth. She knows this, exploits it, for he will not want to argue with her in front of the younger man. He rises from the table, leaning heavily on the speargun, as though the simple act of standing requires an immense effort, and he exits the croft without a word.

At last she can breathe.

Kessler waits until he is out of earshot before asking, 'Is everything all right? With you? With him?'

And what can she say? She nods. 'The air will do him good,' she says.

Kessler and Ruth exchange a glance that hints at a shared scepticism, but he does not probe. He talks on, asking her about their fields and their crops. He does not admit the precariousness of their situation.

'The soil's good here. You can grow things.'

'We could,' she corrects. 'When we had seeds and better weather.'

A short while later, she hears Whitney returning along the path. He comes into view, and he is carrying a cabin door awkwardly across his body. Due to the narrowness of the gate, he pivots and sidesteps, and the physicality of the act seems to have stirred some life in him. He props the door against the wall and stamps, inelegantly, almost losing his balance as he puts his heel through the panelling.

She winces, remembering the glass and the berm. He will do himself an injury, she thinks, or he will rip the waders. He recovers his balance. Chuckles heartily. He is fine.

'I am fine,' he says.

Kessler produces a claw hammer from his drybag. 'Here,' he says, offering the handle to Whitney. 'Use this.'

He receives the hammer, tests its weight against his palm. 'We lost ours in the flood,' he says wistfully.

'Why don't you keep it,' suggests Kessler.

The gesture carries meaning, and it is not lost on Whitney. 'Thanks,' he says. 'That's kind. Thank you.'

Aina looks to Ruth, who seems to be wary of this alignment between the men. Perhaps it is instinct. Perhaps she has seen it before. Silent, peripheral, they watch, as the men revel in their preparations.

'Is it pine?'

'Chestnut.'

Whitney remarks on the thickness of the wood and the colour. 'It'll burn well.'

'And hot.'

'Here, pass the crowbar.'

It is a noisy endeavour, reducing the door to kindling. Whitney quickly tires himself out, and Kessler takes over, making daggers of wood, six to eight inches long. He stuffs them into the brazier and the scuttle, and when he has finished, all that is left of the door is splinters and dust in the dirt. He stands back admiring his efforts. 'There's plenty more along the beach,' he says, signalling to Whitney. 'From the yacht. You're welcome to it.'

———

Smoke lends the room a blue infusion. The air thaws. She offers a second cup of tea, and though Kessler accepts, Whitney refuses, explaining that one cup is all he needs. A pettiness in the insinuation. She takes the plant from the windowsill and sets it on the counter. The nettles bristle. Black with only the murkiest hint of green. She turns and feels eyes on her.

The child is watching, closely. 'You make tea from that?' she asks.

'Uh-huh.' Aina removes her pruners from the toolbox. '*Urtica dioica*,' she explains. 'A nettle. It has the capacity to revive.' She beckons Ruth to join her at the sink but the child waits until Kessler glances up and nods permissively. 'Have you ever seen a nettle up close before?'

Ruth shakes her head. She is shorter than Aina, probably short for her age. She rests her chin on the sink.

Aina continues, 'It makes good tea. Almost sweet. It's good for the muscles and joints. As you get older … well, you appreciate things like that.' She bends back a leaf to reveal the stiff little spines. 'Careful. It's got a sting.'

'A sting?'

'Yes. Cut here.' She points with her finger. 'And here.'

She helps with the pruners, pressing the girl's fingers between the handles and her own. The stiff blades squeak, unoiled, and the clipped leaves fall. A dozen of them. Aina gathers them up and places them in the pot.

'What do we do now?' Ruth asks.

'Now, we wait.'

She remembers the book upstairs – Lionel's book on gardening – and she leaves Ruth watching the kettle while she fetches it from her bedside. She opens it at the index. The child crowds close as Aina runs her finger down the list of names.

'*Urtica … Urtica …* Here,' she says. '*Urtica dioica.*' She flips through chapters on compost and netting, and locates the page. She reads a few lines, mostly about the particular genus and the parts of the world where it is found, and the page is scribbled with marginalia. A black pen. Her own hand.

Steam rises from the kettle. She returns the oats to the shelf, wipes the countertop and the sink, and replaces Kessler's mug with a clean one, Whitney's mug, which she has just cleaned. The Danish mug. If Whitney objects he does not let on. And when she looks up, she realises that the child has lost interest in the book. She is gazing up at the shelf, a perturbed look upon her face.

'What kind of meat is that?' asks Ruth, pointing up at the sealed jars.

'That?' says Aina. 'That's mutton.'

The girl looks at Kessler but he does not reply. He seems unwilling to be drawn.

'Mutton is another word for sheep,' Aina explains.

The child's eyes narrow, almost playfully. 'Why don't we just call it sheep then? We call a fish "fish", don't we?'

'You're right,' says Whitney, leaning forward in his chair, keen to impart. He nods. 'It's an irregular convention. A confusion of etymology, so to speak. Beef for cow. Pork for pig. One derivation for the animal, another for the meat.'

Whitney adds, 'And there are further complications. For instance, the juvenile sheep is called a lamb.'

Ruth takes the pruners and with a steady hand, she clips another leaf. 'And what about people?' she asks nonchalantly.

Control drains from Whitney's face. His jaw goes slack. He swallows. 'People?'

'Yes. Humans. Is it "people-meat", or something else? Like, is man meat one thing and woman meat another?'

Aina holds her breath. She glances at Whitney. He is static. Eyes fixed ahead as if staring into a void.

He stumbles. 'I ... Well ... We ...'

The child pauses. The water is boiling now. 'And what about child meat,' she asks. 'Or juveniles. Do we call that something else too?' – and Aina turns, sensing a displacement of subject and tone. Something shimmering in the child's eyes. A mischievous delight.

Mirth.

The child's calm breaks. She smiles and makes a ghoulish noise, and she waves the pruners at Whitney for comedic effect.

Kessler's laughter is sudden and loud. Augmenting. Still Whitney does not understand.

'She's joking,' explains Kessler. 'She's pulling your leg.'

It is a disarming sound. This laughter. It feels impolite. But the faces of these two, the synchronicity of the man and his daughter, as Ruth twirls and bobs and Kessler sits, amused, seeming proud of her capacity for making jokes. Their patter is disarming, infectious.

'I'm sorry. Really. I am.' Kessler wipes his eye.

'Not at all.' Aina smiles.

'She had you pretty good, though.'

'She did,' says Aina. 'She really did.' And Aina looks at the child. The sight of her provokes all sorts of unspoken feelings: relief, wonderment and vague unnameable sensations. And she is not paying attention to her surroundings or the plant, and the kettle whistles. It catches her off guard, and she draws her hand away, brushing the inside of her wrist against the plant's stem. Zings blimp, whitening on her skin. Round little islands. Alive and bobbled to touch.

Kessler asks. 'Do you keep many sheep?'

Whitney sits straighter and draws a hand over his face. He smiles, weakly. Eyes skittish. 'We don't,' he says. 'Not any more.'

29

Kindling

THE DOOR CLICKS SHUT and Aina leans against the wall. Ahead, the stairs ascend into gloom. Yan. Tan. Tethera. It is a relief to be out of the kitchen, away from the child's gaze; it might be years since she has laid eyes on a woman, if she ever has at all.

And the mother. The wife. Whatever happened to her?

Tola—

You're an artist? Kessler's voice comes through the door, resonating warmth.

I dabble ...

It's natural for you to take sculpture as your medium. He is consoling. Patient. Probing. And Whitney answers, talking stoically about the satisfaction he gets from creating something out of disorder.

A luxury, she thinks, to make art while the world burns.

They have made a pact of sorts; an agreeable truce. The four of them sat at the table, as the wind ticked up and the afternoon darkened and the dimensions of the room appeared to blur. The deal is perfunctory: Whitney and Aina will give up a share of their mutton and provide temporary shelter and, in exchange, Kessler and Ruth will let them salvage what they like from the wreck. There was some debate about the Law of Admiralty, and who might be entitled to what, only no one could agree on what distinguished the various categories: flotsam, jetsam, lagan and the other one.

Meat for wood. It is a simple enough trade. And the castaways will stay in the barn for now – bed and board – for as long as they need. And then what? Where will they go, where *can* they go? Strange that Whitney does not seem perturbed. Maybe he has other ideas … And though the door is closed and the voices are muffled, she can gauge a level of enthusiasm from his tone. He is telling Kessler about his projects, and how, rather than use the wood to heat the croft, he will use it to make charcoal that will fire his kiln. Kessler does not interrupt.

She climbs the stairs with practised stealth. Twelve stairs, steep and narrow. The air is cooler in the attic and she is stiff from having sat for so long. From the dormer, the needles skewer the bay. Stark. Glinting. Backlit by sea.

The wetsuit is dry, rubbery and as she peels it back, the air is cold on her shoulders. She takes a crinkled shirt from a hook on the door and continues theorising, wondering how far have they travelled, and from where, and how has he coped without pills. If there was a dispensary hidden on the boat, she would have seen it. But something is not right. There are gaps in her logic, and it cannot be meat alone that Kessler seeks; it must be something else. He would not set out aimlessly, not unless he absolutely had to. This is not a man to leave things to chance; he would have set out with a destination in mind. And he must have pills, he must have, and if he does, might he be willing to share?

She just needs to be patient, remain alert and bide her time. She will wait until the child is asleep. Then she will find a way to put her questions to Kessler without unsettling him.

There is a way out of here, she thinks. There must be. Not all that is hidden is lost.

———

Late-afternoon. They have been outside in the sun for an hour discussing the fields and the peat, which is far too sodden to burn. Ruth plays about them, running circles round the croft. She is expert at finding things in the mud. Funny-shaped rocks. Fossils. The sheep's skull. Her eyes are keen. 'Dad,' she calls. 'There's a chess piece buried here. A rook I think.'

'You know,' says Kessler, lowering his voice. 'You could forget this place. Come with us.'

'Leave?' Whitney chuckles. 'Not for us. Not right now. But you go. You do your thing.'

'Really, you'll stay?'

Whitney looks at her, puffs out his chest. 'The Warden's due here any day,' he says confidently. 'We're up for parole.'

'And I suppose it was the Warden who told you that?' asks Kessler, a smile creeping.

'He did. We expect him any day now. Isn't that right, Aina?'

She is aware of some change in the atmospherics and suddenly the idea to wait seems flawed. Ruth is out of earshot, and she might not get another chance.

She asks, 'How did you ... survive, out there so long?'

Whitney looks at her.

Kessler looks at her. And before he can answer, Ruth runs up the side of the croft. 'Dad!' she shouts. 'Dad, come quick. Look at this!'

'You mean in the storm?' says Kessler, distracted. 'We pitched a tent up on the moor. We've seen worse.'

But he has misconstrued the question. She means without pills. How did he survive without pills.

'A tent?' says Whitney. 'I wouldn't have thought it would hold.'

'It was rather snug, actually. Ruth's the expert. She made the pitch against one of your peat banks. Out of the wind, a great spot ... Would you like to see?'

'Maybe after. Let's start on the wood, while we've got the tide.'

'Yes! Yes, of course.' Ruth has Kessler by the hand and he looks briefly at the needles, and says, 'She was a fine yacht, wasn't she, barnacle?'

Ruth nods, pulling his arm, until he relents and lifts her one-handed into a fireman's carry. She shrieks as he bounds up and down the garden, laughing with glee.

And while Kessler is occupied, she pulls Whitney aside. 'Aren't you in the least bit curious?' she asks. 'Where they came from?'

'It's obvious, no? This is our test. The Warden sent them.'

She watches them play, this man and his daughter, the easy camaraderie. He is giving her a piggyback and is spinning round and round at the top of the garden, stumbling, making a show of being dizzy. And she looks at Whitney, unable to follow his logic. 'I really don't think this is a test,' she says. 'I think you're coming at this all wrong.'

Whitney squints down the beach. 'Well, we'll find out soon enough.' He turns away and shrugs and slips the crowbar into his belt. 'Come on, lad,' he calls. 'We should get going while we've got the tide.'

And Kessler comes down the garden, breathing heavily, seeming a little embarrassed at how much fun he was having. He sets Ruth on the ground, and stands for a moment to catch his breath. 'You be good for Aina, now.'

Aina watches as they collect their ropes and nets. There are things to be done. Wood to be salvaged. Men's work, apparently. She watches them head off down the path. And beside her Ruth just smiles. A good little girl.

30

Shell

AINA SWEEPS THE CROFT. There is so much dust. So much dirt. She mops the floors twice using an old jumper of Whitney's fastened to the broom. She hangs the sheep's skull above the back door. Creamy and stitched, the eye sockets are sunken voids, like boreholes whirled by glaciers. Occasionally, she watches the men through the binoculars, striding purposefully across the tidal flats, crouching every once in a while to inspect a piece of the wreck. As the older man, Whitney seems to cling to some assumed seniority. He points and instructs, and Kessler hauls, setting the wood to dry in broad pyramidal forms along the berm.

She should question Ruth. But if she is too direct, the girl might clam up. Better to wait and let Ruth come to her.

Air bubbles from the spout of the teapot. She rinses, scrubs and rinses again, and she cannot tell if the stains are new or if they are old. She stands at the sink. Scrubs. Then she just stands, watching the clouds blow down from the moor, and it is a curious thing to behold, the way they start, fat and bulbous, and as they descend, they wisp out and down and thread into vapours. Silken and cold. The wind has changed … She hears a soft rustling outside. It cannot be the washing; she has taken it down and folded it crisply. But there … again … a haw.

A bleat …?

Impossible.

She looks towards the door. It will just be something rusted moving in the wind. The vane turning on top of the barn, calling out for oil, or one of Whitney's mobiles, made of axles and cogs, left tangled and racked by the flood, now creaking in the wind. Time slows down and she exhales. The water begins to drain. Circling indefinitely. Smells. Sounds. Fragmentations. Everything stops.

She is alone in the croft.

She tries to slow her breathing.

She is here. Alive. Now. And she is certain that if she were to take the binoculars and look to the needles, she will see herself there, scaling the boat. Or instead she will be swimming out past the rocks. Or there will be a figure on foot, running laps. Two miles along the cliffs before cutting inland. Hobbling back across country with protrusions of glass from her foot. Round and round these versions of her run, chasing and chasing, overtaking her. Yan tan tethera methera pip. The sky turns white and the world carousels and at the centre is a spindle, winding yarn. She pulls on the thread, yanks, and over the spine comes the sheep. It is followed by an animal with amber eyes. A beast, loping up the path. It waits. Watching the croft. Nose to the dirt. Circling the spot where she put the sheep under the spade.

Bless us, O Lord, for these Thy gifts, for the doors You have opened and the doors You have closed …

The bleat comes again, closer now.

She turns to the doorway. Ruth stands smiling, holding something in her hands. Beautiful and pink. Buffed by waves. A conch shell, perfectly intact.

'Sorry,' says Ruth. 'Couldn't resist.'

Aina rinses the sink, and looks again at the shell. 'Did you find that here?' she asks.

Ruth shakes her head. 'We brought it with us. It belonged to my mum.'

Aina nods. 'It's very beautiful.'

'Here. You can hold it, if you like.'

Aina dries her hands and together they sit on the back step. Raising the shell to her ear, she listens for the sound of the waves. The weight of the shell surprises her, and she turns it over, inspecting the speckled brown spots and fronds.

'Sometimes I think my mother is inside there,' says Ruth. 'I think she crawled in and got lost. I know it's silly.'

'Do you remember her, your mother?'

She looks at Aina. 'I never met her. Well, I did, but I don't remember it. I was too young. So it's not so much memories I have. But, I can sometimes picture a face, only when I'm not really trying though, and each time it's a different face, you know? Other times it's just a feeling. Shapes, colours.'

Aina hands back the shell.

'You have a son, don't you?' says Ruth. 'The boy in the pictures?'

Aina glances at Whitney's pile of sketches on the dresser. Something flutters through her. The child is as bold as she is perceptive.

'Sorry,' says the child. 'Is it rude to ask?'

'No, it's not that. Ask away. It's just …' She rolls her hand through the air, then stops.

Ruth traces the shell's flared edge with her fingers. She is quiet, contemplating, and when enough time has passed, she says, 'He's the reason you're here, isn't he?'

Aina wrings her hands together and she remembers the tiled room. The superintendent barking, *One minute*. And whispering into Max's ear.

She picks a spot on the hillside. Hears the waves. 'For someone so young, you don't miss much.'

The child shrugs. She won't be won with compliments. She is patient, strategic and at ease in the silence. And, in a way, Aina is glad for the child's curiosity; it bears rewarding. 'But you're right,' she says. 'We weren't supposed to have children; we weren't allowed. A doctor friend helped us.'

'My mum and dad, they weren't allowed to marry. But they loved each other anyway.'

'You know the word for that?' asks Aina.

'Stubborn?'

'I was going to say "defiant".'

'Yeah, I guess.' Ruth scratches her cheek. 'What's his name, your son?'

'Maxime,' she says. 'He was about your age, when I last saw him. I never wanted to leave him. I expect it was the same for your mum.'

'Do you think?'

Aina shrugs.

Ruth holds the shell closer. 'Maybe they're trapped in here together.'

'Maybe. It looks pretty roomy in there, doesn't it.'

Ruth takes a moment to consider this. 'My dad says that I came from my mum's tummy. That I grew inside her. Is that true?'

'You don't believe him?'

The girl wrinkles her nose. 'It's just sometimes I can't tell if he's making something up for fun, or if there's some other reason, like an indulgence. The stuff he tells me about cities, buildings, people, those stories I don't mind. They don't always make sense, but … they have no bearing on anything.' Ruth looks around. 'It's the other things.'

'What does he say?'

'Like when my mum gave birth to me, sometimes he'll say that it hurt her a lot, and other times that she didn't feel a thing.'

Aina suppresses a smile. 'Men often say that. Most of the time it's because they don't know.'

'I think it must have hurt.'

She elbows Ruth gently in the ribs. 'I'd say you're probably right.'

'Did Maxime hurt you?'

She looks at the shell in the girl's hands, and remembers the night of Max's birth. Those hours, filled with as much pain as all the years that preceded them. But the pain, to describe it as an abstract thing does not seem fair to Max or the girl. She takes a breath. 'What I'm going to tell you,' she says, 'it's not to scare you. I just think that one day, you might be glad to know.' She stares ahead, up the garden at the dry-stone wall, and finds a rock to focus on. 'They cut Maxime out of me. So, yes, it hurt, but I've never once doubted if it was worth it. I don't regret the years we had together, how he had to live, or how it started. What you were describing before, giving birth, I'll be honest with you, I've never been in so much pain, before or since. When the contractions started—'

Ruth looks up, head tilted quizzically.

'Did your dad tell you about those? No, I suppose not. It's a muscular pain, every few minutes. The body trying to turn itself inside out.'

'Like vomiting?'

'Sort of. Only the pain starts lower down and it gets a lot worse.' She continues, 'By the time Whitney returned with the doctor, it was the middle of the night, and I was set up in this tiny hidden room inside our apartment, a small window-less cubby where I could scream to the top of my lungs without waking the other people who lived in the building. You know what a panic room is?'

The child's frown deepens, and Aina explains, 'It was where Maxime was going to live, a place no one would find him. And I remember the contractions, my God … they went on for hours, and I was exhausted. And Whitney, you might not think it to look at him now, but he made himself useful, and if it wasn't for him, neither Maxime or I would have lived.' She pauses, checks that Ruth is following, then continues. 'Towards the end, I remember, Nangelis – that was our doctor's name – he told me to lie on my side, and I felt his needle going in, cold fluid running down my spine. After a few minutes, I couldn't feel my legs. And I felt something on my belly. The tickle of a black marker pen. And that's when the good doctor began instructing Whitney, his own hands not being steady enough. Nangelis, looking for redemption, and Max was his one good deed to make amends for all the shit he'd done. He took a scalpel from a glass of boiling water. Gave it to Whitney and said, pointing, *You're going to cut: from here … to here.'*

She remembers the silence as Nangelis lifted something from her. The candle bobbing low as shapes moved in her periphery. A prolonged wait, everything uncertain and then the doctor laid a bloody and smeared thing on her stomach. A boy. Unable to support its head. Fingers bunched tight; grip coming reflexively. It felt absurd to be tethered to something so small. The power of the thing. And Whitney cutting the cord. He glanced at her. Tired-eyed, almost smiling, cradling the pliers in his hand as the cord bulged, and he clipped, and the blood pulsed out. The child's face curled into a ball. Riven by fury and lines, and she held her breath, counting, as though waiting for thunder. And his mouth opened up and a soft sound purged from his tiny chest. She held him and tried to get him to latch on to her breast. To quiet him as much as anything, and his mouth gaped around for something to fill it.

A speck flies down the valley, it must be the magpie, but it is too far off and she cannot be sure. She looks at Ruth beside her, and the girl is waiting patiently, unphased, holding the shell loosely in her lap.

'Can I see it?' she asks. 'Your scar?'

Aina lifts her shirt and shows. 'The bottom one, the smile, that's Whitney's handiwork.'

Ruth peers closer. 'What's the other one?'

'That's what they did to me later, after we'd been arrested, and they'd taken Max away.' She tucks her shirt back into her jeans. 'To make sure I couldn't have any more. But like I said, it was worth it, all the pain. Least it was for me … Pain will be blunted by time in ways that love cannot.'

Ruth looks sceptical. 'Is that why you left Maxime? Out of love?'

She hears the wind in the reeds on the backside of the marsh. Hears cymbals. Sees Whitney coming back up the track. 'No,' she says. 'No, it's not because of that at all.'

31

Seconds

SHE CAN SEE THE room, long and narrow. The walls are curved, tiled, cold. Footsteps echo and somewhere a door slams. The superintendent's eyes. Grey, the colour of the sea. His mouth barely moves as he speaks. And suddenly he yells: *One minute!*

Beside her, Ruth waits expectantly.

'There was an analogue clock on the wall over the door,' says Aina. 'You know the type I mean?'

Dash. Dash. Dash. Dash. Five.

Dash. Dash. Dash. Dash. Ten.

She mimics the second hand's slow unstoppable arc. A tree falling. She continues, 'We only had a minute. And Maxime.

I wish I could remember his face but it's blurred. I can see the way he moves though, loping like his father, not really ready for Whitney's embrace. And to begin, I'm standing outside of their arms. Whitney turns and gathers me in as well. And there are tears on his cheeks and in his hair. And Max asks, *What's going on?* And I tell him it's okay, and he asks, *What's happening?* And I tell him that I love him, I love them both, but I have to go. And he asks me, *Where you going?* And I whisper into his ear, his ear's a shell, and I tell him, *I'll come back for you. I'll find you. I'll always love you.* And Whitney cannot look at him. He's looking at me, and his hand goes to his Adam's apple, like this … and he pulls on the skin. And I tell Max, *Be good for your dad.* I tell him that none of this is his fault, that I have to go away. And Max's face is distraught. He says that he wants to go with me, and I tell him that's not possible, but I wish it were, and he asks me what's going to happen, and I tell him, *You're to go with your father.* I look at Whitney and he buries his face deeper into Max's shoulder. And I don't know what to say. I try to tell him that we've been told to choose. That I'd nominated myself to go, because that was our plan, if something ever happened and they found out about him. I'd be the one to face atonement. It was the deal I struck with Whitney, when Nangelis first agreed to help. And Whitney looks at me. And he looks away. And his eyes glaze over as he looks at the boy. Not at me. The boy. He hugs Max tighter. That's when I knew.'

She looks to the sky. To the beach. Whitney is almost at the gate.

'I remember Max was confused, he's asking me, *What's happening, Mama,* and there's the sound of footsteps, growing louder on tile. The superintendent is breaking us apart. I'm kicking, clinging to my son. And Whitney is clinging to me. To me. Not to Max. And I'm yelling, *Get off him. Get off! Don't take my boy—! Take me! Take me! Stop—* And I can feel the screams at the back of my throat. His face is lost. He's held round the neck by uniformed guards; I'm prised off. And Whitney holds me by the elbow, as they carry him away.'

32

Contraband

DOLLOPS OF COLD MUTTON land in the pan. Sizzling. Congealing. The meat browns, and Ruth and Kessler are drawn by the activity. Occasionally Aina prods the meat, and they talk about food. About the things they used to eat, and various methods of cooking.

'How long does it need?' asks Kessler, hovering.

'A few minutes is all,' she says.

'You can't really overcook it,' adds Whitney.

She is not sure about that. Anything will turn to mush if left bubbling on a stove for long enough. She adds a pinch of cumin and turmeric – part of her bounty from *Håvsra*'s stores – places a lid on the pan, and once the two men have laid the table they sit, fidgeting with the cutlery in anticipation of the meal. Whitney considers himself in the back of the spoon, scratches his stubble. Kessler pauses, then takes from his drybag a small bottle. Sea green, vaguely medicinal. Its label has washed off long ago. 'Aperitif?' he asks, as he chooks the cork and adds a drop to his mug.

She watches the drink being passed. Whitney gives it a sniff. 'Go on then,' he says. 'Pass me a mug.'

When the bottle arrives at her, she holds it under her nose. It smells like pure paraffin. 'Did you brew this yourself?' she asks.

'I found it,' replies Kessler. 'I think it's from barley.'

Ruth sits quietly in the doorway, making a bouncy ball from dozens of tiny rubber bands. She draws them, one at a time, from a small cardboard box that she carries in her knapsack. She holds the ball like a slingshot as she hooks the band, stretches it around, again and again.

The child eyes the bottle. She looks hopeful. 'Can I have some?' she asks.

Kessler shakes his head.

'But you said—'

'I said: *When you're older.*'

'How old?'

Kessler thinks about this. 'Fifteen,' he says. 'Not before.'

Ruth bounces the rubber ball off the floor and the wall. 'How about when I'm twelve?' she asks hopefully.

Kessler ignores her.

'Thirteen?'

'Fifteen or not at all.'

She catches the ball one-handed and frowns. 'By the time I'm fifteen there won't be any left.'

He shrugs. 'That is a risk, I guess.'

The child's eyes narrow. 'But I've been eleven for ages,' she says. 'I want to be twelve. You said I'm due a birthday.'

Kessler looks doubtful. 'I did?'

She bounces the ball and nods.

Aina knows the look. She remembers Maxime pleading for an extra hour before bed. How difficult it was to deny him. *But you promised* ...

Kessler eyes Ruth directly. 'And when exactly was that?'

'On the boat. Right before you hit your head.'

He smiles, doubtfully, and considers his options. 'Barnacle. If you can get all dozen jacks, you can have a birthday. We'll split the difference.' He thumbs a chip on his mug. 'Deal?'

'Meaning what?'

'Meaning you can be twelve ... and you can have a swig of that when you're fourteen. How about that?'

The girl haggles. 'I want to be twelve. And I want the wine when I'm thirteen.'

'Ruthie, you're not offering anything in return. Remember our lessons on negotiation.'

'I'm offering you peace.'

Kessler looks at Aina. She smiles by way of support.

'Ruth, know a deal when you see it. Twelve and fourteen. Final. That's all you're getting.'

The child takes an old set of jacks from her pocket and sets them on the floor. A clay-like archipelago. 'Okay, well. Here goes.' She bounces the ball, catches it and bounces it again, and this time while the ball is in the air, she claps twice and scoops up one jack before catching the ball. Her moves are practised. Swift and precise. She bounces the ball again, claps twice and scoops up two jacks this time. On she goes. Counting to six, counting to seven. Counting to eight. Scooping up the jacks.

When she collects the dozen, Kessler raises his mug. 'Happy birthday,' he beams, watching her carefully. 'A toast. To my daughter, on her twelfth birthday.'

The men clink mugs and Aina clinks the bottle and Whitney winces as he imbibes the wine. She drinks it neat and it burns her throat. She takes a second gulp, quickly, before the heat can subside.

———

The mutton disseminates the smell of worn shoes. Grease. She will make a rich broth from the juices. Nothing will be wasted.

As they eat, Kessler talks about the lighthouse, and he talks about horseshoe crabs, which is all they had to eat on the island. 'I'd forgotten the taste of meat,' he says, looking at Ruth. 'Real meat. You should savour it.'

Aina smiles. And Whitney does too. The meat is creamy, salted, and it disintegrates against the roof of her mouth. She does not need to chew. She traps it with her tongue. Fibres in her mouth. Succulent threads of yarn. Splinters of wood.

'Won't you have some, Ruth?' she asks. And Ruth shakes her head. She is trying for thirteen jacks now. Determined, but the ceiling in the kitchen is not sufficiently high and her hand is not sufficiently quick, and twelve appears to be her limit.

'Come on, barnacle,' says Kessler. 'You might not get another chance to try mutton.'

'Dad, it's sheep,' she says. 'Just call it sheep.'

The child turns her back on them, bounces her rubber ball, claps and scoops up jacks. Yan tan tethera. And Kessler talks on about horseshoe crabs, and they are not like any crabs that Aina has heard of before, with pincers and claws. These sound more like an insect.

'They'd come out once a year to mate, and Tola would be waiting for them. She wasn't squeamish about it.'

And Aina remembers taking Maxime to the Southside Market and watching him take it all in. Scorpions. Locusts. The vendors' oversized woks would sizzle. She remembers the taste. Seasoned with so much chilli that they only tasted of spice. They could have been prawns.

A thick, clotted smell occupies the kitchen. Meat in a pan. And she looks up and imagines the walls of the croft as a shell that breaks and peels away. And there is nothing to contain her. She eats. The meat is on her tongue. And the croft is inside out. Maxime. Maxime, he was part of her. Is part of her still. She can almost feel him, caught in the under-tow of time. The inversion of her body as Maxime was born, a capsule of her own making ejected into the world. And ever since, she has been split in two. A tangent of truth and fiction. A broken link. A worn skin.

Whitney sits back, sips his wine. He is a little drunk. 'They grow up fast, don't they?'

She stares down at the table, circling a dark knot with her finger. And beside it, Kessler's bottle stands with letters embossed upon its neck.

She looks at Kessler. He grips something beneath his shirt. She cannot see what it is. A kind of talisman.

'Dates matter,' she says. 'Especially to a child.'

'Evidently.' Kessler stares at her with a priestly calm. 'But how should I have gone about keeping track?'

The wine's potency hits her. 'There are ways,' she says.

Whitney's face stiffens.

Kessler looks daunted, weary, perhaps older than she first surmised. A vein throbs at his temple. 'We left there with a week's worth of food,' he says. 'Ruth, me, and that was it. Nothing else. Ruth was six months old … I didn't know … I didn't know what to do.'

'Did you have paper?'

He nods. 'I had paper, it wasn't that.'

'What then?'

His eyes are drawn towards her neckline. 'I didn't have a pen.'

Electricity fills the room. The ball bounces, skips and rolls into Aina's foot. The jacks are scattered across the floor. A trail of islands. Knuckles made of bone.

33

Ithaca

A PALE MOON RISES behind dark thin twists of elongated cloud. She ploughs her thumb through the soft pond of wax, flecked with tallow, that has burned down from the candle and slowly hardens in the base of the dish. The white sheen crinkles. A furrow. Almost luminous.

The waft of something, once tobacco, comes from across the yard. Outside, a tangerine nib flares, uplighting Kessler's nose, his cheeks and brow. A man on vigil, deferring sleep, framed by the wider doorway of the studio. His features recede into shadow as he exhales slowly. He appears relaxed, but underneath that calm exterior, he remains watchful, cautious, and rightly so.

Whitney sits quietly, facing away from her. There is a rigidity to his back, a stillness, that suggests contemplation. She can sense his fear, suspects that it has been intensified by the wine. Where is the speargun, she wonders? It must be upstairs. At least that is something.

Kessler draws hard on the cigarette one final time and the orange arcs away, tossed into the night. And though she can no longer see him, she is sure he is there, watching from the doorway. His eyes crystalline and black, as he waits for Ruth to settle.

The juices of mutton slick her hands and she scrubs between her knuckles. The water in the sink is the colour of foul milk, and the taps have a silver edge to them. Their chipped bowls dry, stacked upside down haphazardly, like the basilica of an abandoned city. The barn door creaks gently with the wind, affording her a brief glimpse of warm, citrusy light. Ruth lies couched in a banana-coloured sling, which Kessler has strung from the rafters. A makeshift hammock. He goes to her, places a hand on her cheek, and he leans forward and grazes her forehead with his own. His lips move. Whispering. Maybe he speaks to the child about her mother, of some quality that she possessed, which he sees now in her.

Some call it stubbornness. Others call it grit.

She remembers Whitney telling Maxime of the night he was born, as a way to get him to sleep. He honed in on the rosy aftermath, avoiding the slow, complicated specifics of the night, delivering a neatly abridged eulogy that became neater and more abridged with each telling, and the more she listened, the more uncertain she became, until she was not sure whether her version had ever happened at all. He dresses the scene in warm tones, a dangerous confluence of nostalgia and euphoria; the picture is one of bliss. There is no mention of PTC, the years of anguish, of Dr Nangelis, the terrible extraction, or his part in it. Details that are important to her are extraneous to him. She remembers a lingering panic. Holding him, newborn, in her arms all through the night, jerking awake, fearful that sleep would overcome her, lulling her until her grip would loosen and the child would fall to the floor.

Your mother's a lioness, Whitney would say. *You know that, lad?* And Maxime would gawk at her with incredulous eyes. *Really?* She would snarl playfully and claw the air. And Whitney would say, *You see? She belongs on your ark.*

And Tola … It would have been worse for her, not knowing if Ruth would be immune. How on earth would she legislate for that? At least Aina had anaesthetics, and though the numbness did not last, it was better than nothing. She remembers Nangelis holding her hand. Telling her to look away and then Whitney taking the scalpel and gently tracing the line across her belly. Soft, like the end of a feather. A feeling of being unpacked. And something considerable was lifted from her. A stony face in a bundle. Granite. Its head attempting to turn one way then the other. Nangelis placed him on her chest. Bloody. Hands in fists. A hot coal.

She wipes the table, wipes around Whitney, who sits silently, alone until Kessler returns, closing the back door behind him.

'Did she go down okay?' asks Whitney.

Kessler nods. 'She did, yes. Eventually.'

'It'll be strange for her, I imagine. Waking up in an odd place with curious things on the wall. She won't be frightened?'

'Frightened? Oh, no. No, don't be silly. We're accustomed to worse.' He produces a second bottle, which he stands upon the table. 'Have a drop more. Please. It's not often we get to share with company.'

Whitney receives a measure gratefully. 'You travelled then? All this way.'

Kessler nods.

'How's that?'

'How did we travel?' He settles into the chair. 'On foot to begin. Do you remember the ice? Did that ever make it as far as here? It used to come every winter …'

And he starts telling them about walking out on to ice. How hard it was to judge distances. And Aina glances at Whitney, but he only stares at Kessler.

'But how?' she says, quietly sliding on to a chair.

Kessler stops.

'I mean, what did you do for pills?'

Kessler sets himself. He seems prepared for this. Slowly, he draws breath and his voice drops to a whisper. 'Something woke me,' he says. 'Ruth was asleep; she was only six months old, but she slept well, packed tight in a crate, and I knew – it was a kind of premonition – even before I stretched out my hand, that the bed on Tola's side was empty. I felt a cold expanse, like it hadn't been slept in for days.' He takes a sip of his wine and he is a little drunk in the eyes. 'I stood on the landing, listening for the sounds of the house. Of movement downstairs. The padding of feet on softly scalloped stone. There was silence. An awful stillness. I could feel it overtake me; a grey light on whitewashed walls; and the roped banister was heavy and tacked with salt. I came down the staircase into the room, a wide octagonal entrance hall;

there was this wooden bench about the perimeter.' He pauses. 'You know, all this was land before. You know that right?'

'Kessler?' she asks. 'What happened to Tola?'

'I can see her.' Kessler smiles politely, and it might be that he smiles at some memory, or else it is a way to buy himself time. A few seconds. Enough to compose himself. He wipes at his eyes. 'She used to love horses.' He laughs, and she recognises the laugh as a means to disguise hurt.

He goes on. 'She had been a vet, before. Too good for the likes of me. And she could tell you from the angle of a horse's head or the bracing of their legs, she could tell if they were feeling anxious or trapped or in season. And ... she talked sometimes ... about this mythical island, way out at sea. A treeless place, she would say. Overrun with horses that roamed the hillsides. And left unchecked the herd grew and grew. Fillies and colts began to be born out of season. And somehow the horses knew the strain this placed on the island. Maybe it was evident in the impact on food, on space; Tola, she thought it was instinctual. And the way she told it, whenever a new foal was born, the weakest member of the herd — be it mare, stallion, nag or the one that was most infirm — they'd leave the herd and trot off into the waves.' His voice is thinner, like air at a high altitude. 'A sacrifice you see?' He stops, as though he is not sure how to proceed. Colour has drained from his face. He takes a sip of the barley wine, and it seems to lend structure to his mind, and he is back in the room, the octagonal entrance hall at the base of the lighthouse. 'She is there,' he says. 'On the far side of the room, sitting on the bench. She looks at me. And I remember the look in her eye; she was looking on things for the last time. You must have thought about it.' A wry smile. He looks straight at Aina and his gaze rests a moment before shifting. He continues, 'I pleaded with her: go and hold our child a last time. I thought: if I can just get her in the room, get her to lay eyes on Ruthie, then she would stay. She stood, and for a moment I thought she was about to go back upstairs. But she stopped short. She shook her head. She must have known she would falter. She let go of the banister and that was it. There was no way to stop her.'

'There's always a way,' splutters Whitney.

Kessler ignores the interruption. 'She started undressing,' he says. 'I didn't understand at first. She stood there, in the centre of the freezing room, deprived of sleep. Off went the coat. The jumper. Her gloves. Boots. She made a neat pile, and she looked at me. I asked her what she was thinking and she just said, *You'll have more need for these than I.*'

He takes something from the drybag. Aina closes her eyes. She feels faint. Nauseous. And she cannot quite grasp all that he is saying. These sights and scenes, the possibilities, they do not correlate to her familiar vistas. Her imagination is a dead, unresponsive thing, like a muscle grown slack from underuse.

When she opens her eyes, Kessler is holding an old pair of pliers. The handles are sheathed in blue plastic. He places his thumb between the jaws, a little way above the knuckle, and mimics the application of pressure.

'She stood naked, holding these, here, like this—'

He makes a clucking sound.

Aina spreads her palms upon the table. The wood is warm, rotted, warped. Kessler begins unbuttoning his shirt; he lifts something over his head. A cord of leather, threaded with something old, preserved. It looks like a rune.

'I think I just sat down. And that was it. She set the thumb in a bowl of ice, and we sat there looking at it: this strange protrusion of stump and bone where her thumb should be. And there was so much blood. More than you'd imagine.'

Aina glances at Whitney and his face is twisted, unrecognisable, a tree struck by drought. His mouth is slack. 'She walked out on to the ice, barefoot, in barely a stitch. And you didn't even try to stop her?'

'When we talked about it, I just assumed I'd be the one to make the sacrifice. That I'd ...' He looks at his thumb. 'She never told me what she was planning. Her mind was made up, I don't know when, days or weeks before. What does it matter? What could I do? I ran the thumb under the sink, washed off the grit, and then Ruth awoke. And she started crying and wailing, hungry, or maybe she knew. She'd been a good sleeper until then. I went and I held her and I tried to shush her; I didn't want that sound to reach Tola. I just held Ruth tight, as close to my ear as I could, so the sound might expel all thoughts from my head. My ears ringing. And she cried and cried. But that kind of fury, a hungry baby can't sustain it. She went quiet. Hot and exhausted. And we sat there waiting for the pill clock. The silence was the worst thing. At 6 a.m. I placed my thumb on the sensor. I placed Tola's thumb on the sensor. Nothing happened. And I thought, it must somehow check for a pulse, some kind of sensory — not just the thumbprint, but, I don't know, proof of life. And I knew, at that moment, somewhere out on the ice, Tola was kneeling, holding her bloodied hand to her chest. I pressed the thumb harder. Wiped the bloody mess and tried again and the pill clock clicked ...' He loosens a notch on the watchstrap.

'You felt relieved?' asks Whitney.

Kessler rubs the stitches on his forehead, a light caress. 'Of course, in a way. I'm not proud … But it was vindication that what she did wasn't in vain. Possibilities opened up. A vast new plane. Hope.'

Aina sees the disgust on Whitney's face. 'Hope for what?' he says. 'She left you. Abandoned you. What's there to be hopeful for?'

'Whitney—'

'It's okay.' There is a softer element in Kessler's eyes. Lead instead of steel. 'It's all right,' he says. 'You're right. I felt so much anger. I thought it'd never leave me. But … Time. That's all it ever takes. Love comes back. And I know, children are supposed to outlive their parents. I tell myself, over and over, that it was natural. That she was sick. Post-partum, or something. But the reality is, her reasons don't matter now. They can't change anything. You under-stand? I'm here. Ruth's here. And that wouldn't be if it wasn't for Tola.'

Whitney's face scrunches up. 'She left. She took the easy way out.'

'Look, mister, my anger died a long time ago. My guilt died too.'

'But she abandoned you. And the child. The selfishness. How could she—'

'Whitney, she did it so that they might leave.'

Kessler's eyes flicker to her, and the skin around them is puckered and wrinkled, as though he has been too long in the wind, but there is a light within his eyes. A shining reci-procity. He rubs his chest as if to emphasise his ribs and he says, 'Hunger is a hard thing to overcome. The reality is we keep going. Ithaca's out there still, eleven years that way. But we won't be going back.' He hangs the cord around his neck and buttons his shirt.

'And you left her? You didn't bury her? You just …'

'Does Ruth know?'

'She knows … bits.' He slows, suddenly, like a runner approaching a cliff. He looks at Whitney. 'Most of what I've told her is true.'

'You tell her that guff about the horses?'

Kessler does not respond. He sits staring at the pliers.

Finally Aina speaks. 'How many pills do you have?'

Kessler nods slowly. 'It's been a while since I counted them.'

Her voice is hurried and rushed. 'Enough for a year?'

He nods. 'Maybe two.'

'You buried them?'

'On the moor. The thumbs too. Stored them in brine.'

Aina's chair cricks as she leans across the table. 'There are others, out there, like us?'

Kessler grips the rune about his neck. His bloodied eye seems to darken. 'A few,' he says.

'Were they alive?'

'For a time.'

'Did you kill them?'

'When I had to.' He sets his empty glass on the table. 'Not everyone was as welcoming as you both.'

The back door shakes. The lock is broken and Aina goes and ties it shut. The rope is tacked. Heavy. And the wood is rotting. A thin divide, keeping out the dark.

She can tell he wants to talk. And Kessler refills their glasses, outdrinks them both, and soon he only fills his own. Sipping. Talking. Flushed as he reaches for the bottle again.

He tells them how he waited three days before heading south with nine spare pills. He carried only things that had some practical use. He did not bend to sentiment. He stepped out on to the ice with Ruth bundled tight; a journey into the unknown. The terrain: jagged and unexpected. Without logic. Without order. A white expanse, through which he would clamber, rest and set off again, breath frosting his muffler. And above him, the sky opened up and light mottled the clouds. In the afternoon, the ice became slick, magnificent in its brightness. The sun his only foe.

Nine pills spare. Three days. Seventy-two hours.

The wind blew deliriously. Insisting upon things. Loud enough that he cannot hear Ruth's cries. The way he describes it, Aina can feel the cold sting of the wind. He hunkers on. The next day, the sun staggers a little higher into the sky. He has good weather. But he knows the ice will not last. He heads south, picking his way as best he can, into spring.

Aina is lost in his words. There is too much here.

During the crossing, he sees shapes, blurred smudges of light, a phenomenon of gaseous forms that cloud the way. Or it might just be the weather. He sees a line of grey stanchions rising on the horizon. With no sense of scale, they could be fence posts, or the towering spires of a distant ruined city. He hurries on, through another night. Sweat gathers. Cold. It feels warmer. And the ice cracks and gurns, and feels increasing unstable. At times he must backtrack, working southwards in a series of detours. And when daylight finally comes and the sky lifts in a haze, he sees the stamens of huge turbines. Pillars of steel, rising in a field from the splintered ice. Hundreds of them. But only a handful have their propellers intact. The rest are scattered about on the ice, bent and frozen like beached tetrapods.

His eyes water in the wind.

It is getting harder to see.

And Aina has so many questions, about the baby, about nappies, about food, and it does not help that Kessler avoids telling his story linearly. He makes a riddle of geography and time, jumping forward and back, skipping chunks, and one minute, Ruth is a child, burbling words. Waddling along. Unscripted. And then she is in the sling once more, carried on his back, a baby again. And Aina cannot tell if her scepticism is the product of this scattergun approach, or whether there is something fundamentally wrong.

On he goes, skipping ahead. They stay for a year in an old deserted village. Three streets. A post office, a pub. A bus stop. The timetable is still pinned to the noticeboard. It is a place of shanty. He finds half a barrel of barley wine in the cellar of one of the fisherman's cottages, which he decants into bottles. The bottles on the table. Green. Familiar. She cannot think. Kessler is talking. He does not let up. On he goes, speculating about the residents who would have been evacuated, or left for dead. Up on the hill, behind the village hall, there is a berm or a burial ground. And their only company is a forgotten housecat named Sax, who they find walking along the harbour wall. The last inhabitant of this demarcated outpost.

'Sax.' Kessler smiles. 'Ruth loved that cat. She'd forever try and corner him. A half-wild thing, with a bell and a collar, picked on by crows. He'd sit, waiting for us each morning.

Licking his paws among the broken lobster pots. But he'd never let us near enough to pet him. Maybe he was sick. Else he wasn't ready to live with people again.'

He tells stories of other places, other times, about how he swam out to sea, gambling on the tide to recover the yacht. His story comes in fragments, splintered like light on the face of a diamond, and sometimes Whitney interrupts, asking about the different pill clocks, and whether they were all alike, and what kind of footwear he had, and on and on, and Kessler has an answer for everything, and after a while Whitney just sits there, an accommodative drunk.

And Aina thinks about the cat. The muddled ratio for transposing cat years into their human equivalent. And she remembers a cat was fifteen after the first year, twenty-four after the second year, and each human year after that was equivalent to four cat years. She never understood it. Time is a measure. A fix. It cannot be elastic in that way.

But it does change, she thinks. It always changes. And as if to emphasise the point, Kessler returns to the story of his first crossing, time and time again. It seems to hold a pull for him. And she wonders for how long were they out there. Kessler does not say, he focuses on certain specifics, talking at length, and she begins to see things a little more clearly. The ice feels warm, smooth, like glass left out in the sun. His eyes hurt. He is going blind. And the baby is no longer crying. They need shelter, warmth, and he needs pills. He has four remaining, when he sees a red light, blinking atop one of the turbines. He approaches the base. Metal rungs fixed to the shaft. He straps Ruth to his back and climbs. Ten. Fifteen. Twenty rungs. He cannot feel his fingers, can hardly see. He navigates by feel, and at the top of the ladder, he finds rivets and the raised imprint of a curved door. The frozen handle is round, like a ship's wheel, and he takes it in both hands, holding this now instead of the ladder, and he twists clockwise and counter, until something yields in the stiff, unoiled metal and the door swings inward, and he falls forward out of the wind. Darkness. It is a relief. He is in the belly of a turbine, but he feels safe. He finds a light and fluorescence plinks on until he switches it off. His eyes cope better in the gloom. Outlines in the dark. He has a sense of the shape of things. The room is a cabin, ten feet long and four feet wide. A bunk is fitted against the far wall. Someone lived here once. An engineer or a caretaker, sent out to sea to manage the upkeep of the windfarm. It would have been cheaper for them to stay in the vicinity. There is a rota of names. Some magazines. An old camping stove that is empty of gas. Cupboards. A sink. And in the corner of the room, the light of a pill clock turns green.

Whitney stirs. 'You know what model those turbines were?'

Kessler shakes his head, and Aina explains that back on the mainland he had worked for the DER.

Whitney gazes up at the wall. 'Probably be the TR-30s if they're still standing. Tell me, did they have two blades on the propeller, or four?'

'Is this a test?'

'Answer the question, Kessler, and you'll find out.'

He smiles, wearily. 'The propellers all had three blades as well you know.'

'Very good. But here's the thing …' Whitney leans forward, elbows on the table. 'How did you feed Ruth, when she was so little, I mean?'

'We foraged. We were lucky—'

'But out there on the ice?'

Kessler strokes his beard. 'There was an auger, a couple of hand-drills stashed in the turbine. I used those to bore holes in the ice, and we fished that way. There was the odd seal, too. You ever had seal meat?'

Whitney shakes his head.

'Yeah, I don't expect you ever will now. But to your question, I honestly don't know how we managed. It was easier once we made land.'

'Bit convenient, though, wouldn't you say, finding that auger?'

'Is it?' Kessler pours the last of the bottle and stirs his tea. The spoon goes round. He holds it by the tip. Nothing can be gained from stirring it any more, but he stirs it all the same, eyes fixed on Whitney.

Whitney is the one to look away. 'What do you think, Aina,' he says. 'Are you buying this?'

She thumbs the side of the table. 'I am, yes. None of this sounds in the least bit convenient to me.'

'A split decision then.' Whitney snorts lightly. 'Well, go on then, lad, humour us. On with the story.'

Kessler settles himself, sips his drink, then continues. 'We stayed three days in the first turbine. Stashed another nine pills using Tola's thumb, and then we left again. I brushed Tola's thumb free from grit and lint, bound it carefully, and it was a relief to be back out on the ice. In the cabin, there was too much time to think and not enough things to do. The days passed, and in time the ice became increasingly solid. Thicker. Harder to drill, but by then we had some surplus fish, and on par it was less dangerous. Three days on, three days off. I followed the line of turbines. Until I saw a smudge of something ahead. A squall perhaps. It carried density. Some kind of abutment. A vast triangular cliff rising like the prow of a ship.'

'Land?'

He nods.

Land she thinks, and glances at the window, the door. The night is still. Quiet, except for the occasional ushering of the waves. The tide must be on the way out. Given the moon. Given the season … the weather will soon be on the turn.

Whitney's scowl deepens.

Kessler talks on, covering a broad expanse of time and place. And she wonders how it would feel to wander blindly like that. Unless … Except … She goes to the front window, stares out at the blackness. Somewhere in the bay the needles rise. Something is not right. It does not make sense that Kessler has just happened upon them. They have a purpose, she thinks. She turns, on the table the bottle glints. Something sets the nerves in her foot jangling. A ricochet of memory. The colour: green. Emerald. Lineal. Familiar. She remembers the day she went swimming and was caught in the rip. Something is not right. Of all the places to shelter, the bay at Long Sky Croft is one of the least appealing, and with the wind from the south, it would be treacherous. Exposed. And that is before accounting for the rocks. An experienced sailor would only risk an anchorage if they knew the channels. Or if there was some other reason that made the risks worthwhile. *They knew we were here,* she thinks. And they knew a pill clock was here as well.

'Can I see it?' she asks.

Kessler sits straighter. 'See what?'

Whitney looks doltishly at her, confused. But Kessler knows. A smile crosses his face. He places his hands flat upon the table.

'Your map.'

34

Census

KESSLER REACHES DOWN INSIDE his slicker, past the hilt of something protruding from his belt. And he takes a well-worn laminated map from his pocket. Concertinas of land and sea unfold on the table. Contours of summit, cliff and channel. It takes her a moment to understand. The scale is all wrong; the distances too great. It is too big, too vast, and all the detail is lost. She follows Kessler's finger to a strip of land and the coastline is familiar. There is the headland, the moor, the northern cliffs and the spine. She sees a chain of islands leading off into the west, from the place they call Whit's End. Beyond that, scatterings of islands and little archipelagos, the field of turbines, a spectacular grid, each one marked with a Y. Thousands of square miles. And a winding dotted line that marks the route they must have come from the lighthouse, heading east. Her eyes trace Kessler's journey. All that way, travelling with Ruth. Eleven years, he said. And now the present. Here, Long Sky Croft, and finally she has context. A sense of what lies beyond the spine. To the east, land. They are on the westernmost tip of a large peninsula, dotted with hundreds of cabins, crofts and shielings. Many like her own. A map to all these pill clocks. Each one marked by a dot. And a number.

1387 – Long Sky Croft.

'You made this?' she asks.

'No,' says Kessler. 'I found it.' He goes again to the bag, riffling through, eventually tipping the contents on to the table. Glasses. Gloves. A paper folder. 'I found other things too.' He spreads the documents around. Plastic wallets. Profiles. Dockets. Ledgers. And there it is. A book of names. Page after page. She runs her finger down the columns. An index of incarceration. Who and where:

1200

1220

1230

And running beside the numbers, a list of respective names. People called Karim, Anatoly. Gloria. So many of them scratched out by hand.

Into the 1300s, and on to the next page—

1387, Long Sky Croft. Abigail. Oko. There is Lionel. They all have crosses through their names. And there they are, at the bottom. Whitney O. Aina O.

'You said your son's name was Max?' asks Kessler.

Aina nods.

He turns the page. Croft 1388, another list:

~~Antonia H.~~
~~Calvin J-P.~~
Maxime O.

She cannot even begin to understand. The world halts. 'Max,' she whispers. He has been there all this time. 'Are you sure? This is him?'

Kessler shrugs. 'It's been right all the way so far.'

There is a light scampering movement from the roof. A bird. It will be pilfering twigs and sodden grass from the gutters. Whitney hears it too; his shadow flickers on the wall as the candle draws down. The flame becomes static and tight. A dot, shrinking in on the wick until there is no more wick to burn and the light goes out. Smoke rushes upwards like separate strands of thread unwound. The smell, more intense than while it burned, why is that? There is no point in lighting another candle now. The dawn is almost here, and there is comfort in the half-light. Blue. Black. Silver. A breeze carries the sharp tang of the ocean. She cannot hear the waves. The tide will be out, revealing a plane of mud, sand and silt, left bare in a wet glaze.

She thinks Whitney is about to speak, and he looks up, almost wraithlike, at the ceiling, the sink, the wall, anywhere but the table and this map.

Her son. He has been there, all this time. Can it be?

Reality shifts as a cold current, and she has a sense of something coming up from the deep. The weight of truth, a sudden fear. There was a simplicity in not knowing, an easy regularity in keeping everything aligned. Undisturbed. Balanced. Stagnant.

She gazes at this representation of the land. Maxime's land. East of the estuary. It looks to be forested, hilly in places. Criss-crossed by rivers. She imagines scenes: Max felling trees, herding sheep, fishing; Max sanding the hull of a canoe. Max – he will be in his twenties now. And she is certain he is alive. She can feel it. She pictures him listening to the Warden as he explains the pill clock. And he would have obeyed, he has some of Whitney in him after all. When she looks up, Kessler is looking at her. He is waiting for a response.

'I'm coming with you,' she says.

35

Parole

A FTER ALL THESE YEARS, there is hope, a great light upon her. She looks to Whitney, expecting that he will share her elation. But Whitney pulls on his Adam's apple. Clenches. And there is an incongruency about his mouth. Displeasure. 'This is a trick,' he says. 'A ploy. They want us to run.'

How can he be so dismissive?

'Please,' says Kessler; his face is kind, imploring. 'This is no trick. If this is your son, please, come with us.'

'How?' Whitney gestures towards the pill clock. 'We can't leave.'

Kessler leans forward. He takes a moment to respond. 'I wasn't lying about the pills. I've enough for you both.' He pauses to let this sink in.

'You expect us to believe this?' says Whitney. 'That you've a cache, buried up on the hill? That you've been collecting the thumbs of the dead all these years, keeping them in brine?'

But Aina is thinking: a trove of pills equates to a repository of time. A form of freedom.

'This is your plan?' Whitney has his head in his hands. He pushes back his chair. 'This is a set-up. *He's* setting us up. We can't be a part of this.'

'Whitney—'

'You trust this man?'

'What choice do we have but to trust him?'

'Come on, Aina, don't be so naïve.' He turns to Kessler, indicates the spread of dockets and maps. 'Where did you get these?' he asks.

'I found them.'

Something does not makes sense. Aina reaches across the table to take Whitney's hand, but he flinches at her touch. There is fear in his eyes. He seems tired. A man too afraid of the sun to step into the light. 'Please, Whitney—'

'Where?' asks Whitney. 'Where'd you find them?'

But Kessler does not respond.

She leafs through the documents. 'Whitney, it's him,' she says. 'All this time. He's been there … at the neighbouring croft.'

But Whitney refuses to look. He stands, approaches the sink, and, gripping the taps, he lowers his head in benediction. Aina sees him in profile. He might rip the tap clean from the wall.

'We could go with them,' she says. 'Whitney? We could—'

'Stop.'

'We could—'

'Enough!'

'But ...' She will not be cowed. 'He's out there. Waiting for us. We can go. Unless ...'

Something tessellates. The only way she can make sense of Whitney's reluctance. She goes to the dresser, and sifts through his sketches. Max. Max. Max. Max. Max. The pictures fall from her hand. Green. Yellow. Red. Blue. Violet. She has seen this colour-coded chronology some place before. It takes her a moment. The map, she retrieves it from atop the dresser. Unrolls it. There was always something in the geography that never felt right. The way the eastern seaboard tapers into a long straight spit. The violet point. She holds up the last of Whitney's pictures: Maxime, aged fifteen and two months. She feels an implosion. A black hole in her stomach. The pictures follow the same chronology. The last face, drawn in the same shade of violet.

Seven years—

The floor bends.

'You knew ...' she says. 'That's why you stopped going for your runs.'

'Oh, please. For once, can't you see this for what it is?' Tension fixes his face. 'The Warden's coming,' he says. 'This is what they meant by parole. It's a chance to redeem ourselves.'

She cannot breathe, cannot get enough air into her lungs. 'Seven years ... You knew, and you kept it to yourself. For what? For something to hold over me? Jesus, Whitney, all those times I've wondered if he's dead, and you could have said something. And you didn't. You let me suffer alone, and you talk about redemption?'

'I stood by you, Aina, every step of the way. Remember that. It would've been so easy to blame you. Your box of matches, your piano, the ideas you put in his head. Aina, that's on you, and I forgave it then. I chose you, and I choose you still, every day for however many years it is.'

She looks down at her hands and she is making fists. He is trying to stir her guilt.

'Look,' he continues. 'If we do the right thing here, we've a chance to all go back. Me, you, Max. This needn't be in vain.'

'And what about them?' she asks. 'Kessler and Ruth?'

Kessler sits straighter in his chair like he is about to speak, and Whitney darts forward to interject. 'Think, Aina, what's he doing here? Really? Because since the moment he showed, he's been playing us. Trying to make us think there's no parole, to act out, to leave the croft. But if we're caught, what then? What happens to Max? Have you thought about that? And what do you stand to gain, huh?' He points at Kessler. 'What did the Warden promise? Safe passage back for you and Ruth. Clean records. Am I getting close?'

'I swear,' says Kessler, pleading for calm. 'Aina, I'm telling the truth—'

'Don't talk to her,' barks Whitney.

But Kessler will not be stayed. 'Aina. I swear, I'm just trying to help.'

She cannot think, she needs to get her bearings. She studies the wayfarer, trying to comprehend the logic of it. If he had been sent by the Warden, he would not have all these thumbs, all these pills. He would not have landed in the middle of the storm, wrecking the boat on the needles like that. And the girl, she is proof too. It cannot be staged, it would be too elaborate. She tries to explain this to Whitney, but it is like stepping out in front of a train.

'Oh, Aina,' he says. 'There's no win-win. It's always been a zero-sum game with them.'

Kessler stiffens.

'And his daughter turning twelve. And we've been here twelve years. You don't think that's a little suspect, a little too convenient? Come on, Aina. Not to mention the nonsense about a trove: he's just telling you what you want to hear. It doesn't exist. There's no escaping. The system's perfect. There's no getting around it.'

'They said the same about PTC, didn't they, but we found a way.'

She lets him stew on this a minute.

'Nangelis told me once,' she continues. 'I asked him why he wanted to help us. You know what he said? He said: *Given time anything can be corrupted.* And he was testament to it. He'd lived inside that system, become a part of it, and then at the end, he couldn't go on.'

'What's your point, Aina?'

'Whitney, every system's got a flaw. In the perfect ones, they just aren't known yet.'

He shakes his head. 'We only leave here with the Warden's blessing. Not before. He knows that. Ask him.'

'Whitney.' There is sorrow in Kessler's voice. 'Friend, no one else is coming.'

'No?' Whitney points at the radio. 'But the Warden's listening, isn't he. I've spoken with him. A few weeks back, before the storm.'

Kessler looks away, reluctant. Hesitating. Something is about to happen. He bows his head as Whitney's accusations gather pace. He starts arranging the chess pieces on the board in front of him. He sets the pawns in staggered banks; it appears random at first. But then it becomes clear. The familiarity strikes like light from a distant star. Black to play. Checkmate in three. Kessler's fingers close around the black knight. He looks at Whitney, and she does too, and Whitney's face shifts. A tick. Confusion. He frowns. Deeper, as Kessler slides the knight slowly across the board. 'Knight to B7,' he says. 'Check.'

The air is still.

Kessler speaks. 'I'm really sorry. The Warden's dead. He's been dead for years.'

Whitney laughs, dismissively.

'The voice you heard was mine,' says Kessler simply. 'I was just trying to find out who was still alive.'

Whitney shakes his head. 'Doesn't prove a thing. All it proves is you were at the Warden's … which, like I say, makes sense, if this is parole.'

'Stop it, Whitney,' says Aina. 'Please.'

Her words go unheard. Kessler stands and steps away from the table. At the other end of the room, Whitney reaches down into the sink – eyes on Kessler – and his hand rests on something. Aina cannot see what; she has her back to the dresser, caught between them. And opposite her, propped half hidden in the hallway, the speargun. The geometry is rhombic. She cannot move.

Yan tan tethera.

Yan tan—

Kessler moves first. He lunges for the speargun and Whitney moves to intercept but he is slower, and Kessler gets to the speargun before him, and he spins round, intending to kneel and aim in one single action, but Whitney has something in his hand. A bowl. He swings. Connects the base with the side of Kessler's head. A clopping sound as the bowl fragments. And he swings again, with his fist this time, but Kessler is already going down. The speargun is loose in his hands. Whitney skitters it across the floor, out of reach.

Aina stands, screams at him to stop, but he straddles Kessler, grabs a pointed wedge of ceramic and jams the shard into Kessler's neck.

Kessler tries to breathe. Gurgling. An airway punctured. Blood bubbling. Fear in his terrified eyes.

Ruth—

Something clicks. A mechanism. A flywheel. The child, asleep in the barn. She must not see this. She must not. Aina must get her out. She runs, out of the kitchen and into the yard.

36

Magpie

I N THE STUDIO, THE hammock is slung, grey in the light. She approaches, past the domed kiln, a kind of igloo, half expecting the hammock to be empty, but Ruth is there, nestled beneath blankets in a deep, satisfying sleep. She wishes she did not have to wake her, wants anything but that. She places a hand gently upon her shoulder. The bones are birdlike. She whispers. 'Ruth? Ruth, we have to go.'

One for sorrow.

Two for joy.

Three for—

The girl's cheek is cold against the back of her hand. The child blinks awake. Startled. She looks left and right and all round. She slips from the hammock, fully clothed. Her breath in plumes. 'What is it?' she whispers, keeping the hammock between them.

'Get your things. We need to go.'

The girl edges away. 'We're leaving?'

She knows how this must seem. Knows that the girl will be alert to urgency. She must stay calm. 'It's okay,' says Aina, placating, limiting the details. 'We're leaving,' she says. 'I'll explain on the way.'

Ruth looks to the barn door. Eyes flickering. 'Where's my dad?'

'He …'

She could tell the girl that he has gone on ahead. A vast lie, but one which could be explained by any number of reasons. It might buy Aina time, the one thing she lacks. But another step and the girl will be out of her reach. Aina reaches for her, grabs her collar and pulls her close. The girl fights and struggles. Her voice is loud and there is steel in it. 'Get off me,' she says. 'Dad!' she shouts. 'I want my dad.'

'We have to go. Now.'

'Dad!'

'It's not safe.'

Somehow the girl knows. She stops kicking, and Aina lets her go. 'Is he dead?' she asks.

The question catches her off guard. There is no time for this. She can still see the wedge of ceramic being slipped into Kessler's neck, beneath his chin. 'I'm sorry,' she says. 'I'm sorry … to be the one … Your dad must have spoken about this. That there might be a time when you need to hide, or a time when you need to run. This is a time when you need to run.'

The girl looks about, fraught, dazed. In shock. And then with an understanding beyond her years, she says, 'Contingency D.'

Aina squeezes her arm. 'Contingency D, right. Quick, get your things.'

But the child shakes her head. 'I've everything I'll need.'

Aina nods. And she tells Ruth how they are going to run low and fast until they are out of the yard. She hears herself. She sounds decisive. 'We're going to take the path past the oat field. See those willows? And we're going to run, okay? Fast as we can. Up past the creek, all the way to the moor.'

The girl is smart. She turns to Aina and she asks, 'You need me to show you where we buried the pills?'

'Is that okay?'

Ruth nods.

Shum-shum-shum. Aina's heart pounds. 'Ready?' she asks.

Ruth pushes the door open on to the yard.

'Come on. Good girl. Stay with me.'

Outside, dawn is coming. She feels the wind at her back. The washing line blows taut, and the gate bangs, peels back and bangs again. They are halfway across the yard when Whitney's voice splits the air. 'Aina?' he shouts. 'Aina, wait.'

Hope retracts. There is no time. She cannot move, she cannot even turn. Beside her, the girl looks up, poised, and she looks past Aina. And Aina turns and she sees Whitney emerging, bloodied, from the croft. The sun is coming up. Lighting the headland. A silver-cracked dawn. He staggers towards them, long-legged, wiping his hands on his trousers. He stops, gestures the length of the garden. To her. To them both. A curt wave, an instruction. *Come.*

Ruth grips her hand. Tighter.

He waits on the step, holding the speargun against his hip. Thirty feet away. She feels the mud beneath her feet, between her toes. It is a mile up to the moor. She might beat him there by two minutes, maybe three – even with Ruth in tow – but it would not be enough. They still have to find the trove and dig it out, and Whitney is not that unfit. He would catch them there and that would be it. There would be no escape.

He gestures again.

Aina shields Ruth. Her hand feels so tiny. 'Did your dad mark the trove?' she asks quietly.

'He did.'

'With what?'

'A white pebble.'

'Do you remember where it is?'

She glances up the track. 'You leave the path at the first boulder after the shieling. Find the peat bank – our tent should still be there – and follow it a hundred yards on to the moor. You'll see it. You won't miss it.'

'Aina!' calls Whitney. 'What's going on over there? What are you doing? You bring her to me!'

'Left or right?' she whispers.

Ruth looks confused.

'At the boulder, when I leave the path, is it left or right?'

'Right.'

'You're sure?'

The girl nods vigorously.

'Okay. You go on ahead. You go east,' she whispers. 'Take the cliffs, past the cairn. Up the spine. There's an estuary. A wide river. On the other side, at the next croft, you'll find my son. Max. Tell him I'm coming. I'll meet you there.'

The girl hesitates. 'What about you?' she asks.

'I'll be right behind,' whispers Aina. 'A day, no more. Now run!'

————

Whitney raises the speargun and aims, but there is no way he could hit her from there. Aina walks over to him. Places her hand on the barrel. Ruth is through the gate and away.

'You let her go?' he says.

'She goes. I stay. That's my choice.'

'You had no right.'

'She isn't our problem. We stay.'

His watch sounds for their morning pill and she leads him inside. He has no choice but to follow. And she scans the ground looking for something she might use. Something blunt. A thing half buried in mud. She should have grabbed something from the barn. A poker from the kiln, anything.

They place their thumbs on the sensor in turn. The mechanism whirs and clicks. Her pill appears in the dispensary and she places it on her tongue. Bites.

She is aware of a form on the far side of the room. Kessler. Lifeless, his limbs wide and irregular, the toes of his feet point inward. Around his head are fragments of the bowl.

Whitney stands awkwardly. 'I had to do it,' he says. 'It was him or me, you understand? I had no choice. You saw, he went for the gun.'

She cannot speak. She disdains his blunt mathematical reasoning, and he goes on, telling her that they have proven their worth, that they have been tested. Tempted. He offers no hint of remorse; excitement underpins his words. 'Now the Warden will come. We'll be received back. We've passed, Aina, we've proved loyal.'

She wants to object, to say, *But what about Max?* All this time he has been there, and Whitney has known, and he did nothing. Nothing. She does not know this man. He sounds biblical. She dare not object. Not yet. She is waiting for the moment. Then she will strike.

'Do you think he will come today?' she asks.

'Maybe. Maybe tomorrow. But he'll come. Any day. We should be ready.'

He leans the speargun against the wall. By design or by chance, it is too far away for her to reach. He crouches by the fire, head bowed, giving thanks, or bidding for mercy. Moments pass. The clock blinks. Each second tips her closer. She can act now or wait. Act now or wait. Act now or … She sets herself a countdown. Removes the choice. She will act in five, four, three, two, one.

The clock blinks.

'We should bury him,' she says.

He looks up from the fire. 'Bury him?'

She nods, knowing Whitney will not volunteer himself. The mud. The digging. There is no art to it. 'Where did you put the spade?' she asks.

He stares back into the fire. 'By the dresser,' he says.

She sees it, propped in the alcove where the dresser meets the wall. And she has permission now. Justification for walking further into the room. She takes the spade, and continues round the table, taking the long way back to the door. She grips the handle. Smoothed ash. A grey wood, stained with dust from the years of peat. Feels the grain. She nears Whitney. Feels the pocket of heat from the fire. A few feet to where he hunches. His hand on the speargun casually, to help him stand. She holds the spade across her body, one hand on the handle, the other on the shaft. A firm grip. She pauses. She can count the hairs on the back of his neck. The clock blinks. She draws the spade back over her shoulder. A quiet whoop; an innocuous sound in a croft full of wind. And when he stands, he turns. A corkscrew. Pre-emptively aware of her closeness, or some measure of her intent. The second, quicker whoop. She arcs the spade down and round with deft precision, holding firm to the handle and the shaft, and he reacts to the danger. First in his eyes. Then by raising his arm in front of his face, deflecting the blow. She catches him somewhere on the head. She is not sure where. He stumbles, off balance. Takes a step. Stands at the sink. His hand goes to his ear. A line opens up on his face, a seam across his nose and his cheek from the spade's edge.

'Aina—'

He slumps. He cannot stand up. He sits on the floor. Eyes wide. Blood fills the gash.

On the moor, the mist plays tricks with sound. An odd incubation of acoustics that keeps her breath and her footsteps close. And there is something else. She is not alone. Something caws, clicks and rattles nearby.

It is 10:30 a.m. Mid-morning. She has the watch now. Whitney did not fuss. He did not plead. She left him there, shackled to the sink without a word. And his shouts were lost on the wind as she hurried past the willows and the creek. She has the watch and the speargun now, but she will only let him go once she has found Kessler's pills. She fastens the watchstrap about her wrist.

Ahead, the shieling emerges from the white-out. Fuzzed shades of grey, condensing into black. Angles slanted. Something once rectangular on the verge of collapse. She goes on. She could walk this path with her eyes closed. Picking her way through the pockmarked mud. Scraw. Cloven tufts of grass. Everything dank. She comes upon the boulder, an embedded hunk of limestone, which the path skirts around. She leaves the path to her right, and her footsteps are more considered, more deliberate as she attempts to stay perpendicular to the moor. She drops down a small decline, walking parallel to an old turbary, a cutting bank that has grassed over and sunk. The mist has a dense quality, as though it has been resting here, undisturbed through ages. She sees a triangular abutment adjacent to the peat bank. Kessler's tent. Her heart quickens as she walks on, searching the ground for the white pebble. One hundred yards. One hundred yards. How far is a hundred yards?

The peat bank ends, and beyond is the open moor. She walks out, cautiously, no waymarkers here. The ground seems close, indistinct. The rich fibrous smell. Vertiginous. Treacle. Puddled. She sees nothing but black. She must have gone too far. She turns, what she thinks is 180 degrees, and starts to go back. Ahead there is only mist. The land is unfamiliar. She has no compass. And she feels suddenly vulnerable. Disorientation here could be fatal. She does her best to return the way she came, until she spies a groove in the moor, the turbary, and the tent brings rising relief. Her panic quickly subsides. She starts again. Counting her steps, studying the mud and the edge of the pools, looking again for a patch of flattened grass or a footprint, some sign that someone has passed. But there is none. And there is no pebble. The girl must have been wrong, or else Aina has been tricked. She returns a third time to the tent, and checks the camp just in case. But the child is too smart for that. It is not the instructions that are wrong. It is something else.

She has mud up to her knees when she heads back to the shieling. There is nothing more to do now. She will wait until the mist clears and then she will walk concentric circles, spiralling outwards from the camp. She will be thorough. It will take a while, but there is nothing she can do about that. If only the mist would clear.

The caw comes again. A flash of black and white. A flutter of wings. Blue trim. The magpie settles on the roof, struggles for balance, claws on tin as it eyes her. The bird pecks at something under a talon. An egg? Aina cannot see. Peck. Chip. Peck. The magpie shifts and Aina sees the bird's treasure, a small pebble, white and round.

She kneels, sinks her hands into the mud. There is no noise.

A kaleidoscope of moments shift in and out of focus. Kessler. Ruth. The Warden. Maxime. The burning sensation on the back of her neck starts to cool. She thinks of his face at the apartment window, seen from the street below. He has been out there, all this time. But without the trove, distance and time become elastic once more. She will never see him again, she thinks. She will remain at Long Sky Croft, sinking into the mud along with everything else. The waters will continue to rise, and hope will be lost, as bubbles seeping through wood.

Maybe Whitney is right. Maybe this is parole … It is a tempting thought. A way to make sense of the situation. But when she comes down off the moor, she emerges from the mist, looks down the valley, and the croft is so tiny, a coffin of the past. She sees all the versions of herself – child, wife, mother – and all those who inhabited The Limits before her – Lionel, Tola, Grandma Kithi – her kin nest within her, whispering:

Yan tan tethera methera pip.

Da-da-dum. Da-da-dum. Da-da-da-da-da-da-dum.

She remembers the piano in the corner of the room. Whitney sharing her stool as the two of them played: him the bassline, she the melody. Different hands, the same tune. Different hands, she thinks. Different hands. She rubs the knuckle on her forefinger. Looks closer at her thumbprint and sees the whorls as a clef. She has dominion over distance and time, if she wants it.

Long sky.

Charged earth.

Warm fire.

She looks back down the valley to the croft. One choice left to make.

37

Brine

THIS IS HER, WALKING calmly down the path. This is her, leaving the moor for a final time. No more peat. No more earth. No more digging. She passes the creek, the willows. White shelves of fungus upon the bark. He will not hear her coming. She will not let him speak. She has made this choice alone. As Tola did. As Whitney did before. It is her decision. Retribution wound with love. Love for the boy. That reliable tether. And for Whitney, too, in a way. She has done all she can. She has kept her side of the bargain, but they are on divergent paths now. They have been for years.

The gate bangs softly against the post. The wood will not align. She sets the spade against the wall and she half expects

Whitney to have worked himself free but he is still there, chained to the sink. He looks up, smiles a little. Self-satisfied. Not unsurprised. He humphs out of his nose. But when she takes the speargun and loads the rod, he begins to shift, uneasy. The chain rattles as he yanks and pulls against the sink.

'You're deluded,' he says. 'You've lost your mind.'

'Enough, Whitney, please.'

'Someone's got to tell you. Someone's got to—'

She lays the speargun on the table, takes a brown vat of bog water from beneath the sink and begins arranging a makeshift brining station.

1:37 p.m.

'Aina?'

She checks the acidity of the solution and sets water to boil. She lays the pliers beside the speargun. Looks at Whitney. 'Which will it be?'

'What?'

She gestures at the pliers then the speargun. 'Which will it be?'

She thinks he might laugh, but he coughs, and as he draws his hand away, cables of blood and spit taper in suspensions from his mouth.

'You're serious?'

She tries to answer him. But whatever she says it does not change things. She has made up her mind. 'I'm leaving, Whitney. This is my choice. The pliers or the rod: you choose.'

'Please. Aina. The Warden, he's coming—'

'Stop it, Whitney. No one's coming.' She shakes her head.

'Aina—'

'You think saying my name changes anything? Won't you ever say *his* name.'

He smears the trickle of blood on his chin and rolls it between thumb and forefinger. 'You'll die out there, Aina. Alone. You'll die – think about that. You're risking this all for a lie.'

'Not a lie. Not a memory either,' she says. 'He's out there.' She points at Kessler's copy of the Census. 'This is proof. I'm going to find him.'

'And the trove? Did you find that while you were gone? Hmm? You didn't, did you. And I'll tell you why, Aina, because it doesn't exist.'

'Whitney, please ...' She weighs the evidence. She thinks of Max. She thinks of Max and she thinks of Tola. And she looks at Whitney. Sees only a man afraid, trapped on the wrong side of a river. 'Enough Whitney, please. Stop lying.'

'You were lucky,' he says. 'Be grateful they didn't ask you.'

'*Grateful?*'

'What I did took courage.'

She halts, looks at him directly. 'Did you ...?' Something clicks. 'Oh.'

'Did I ... what?'

'That day, when they came. Did you take my key? Did you leave him the matches?'

'I swear—'

'Did you want him found?'

'No,' he says. 'I swear it wasn't like that. I couldn't live with myself. I swear. Aina, believe me.'

'Then why abandon him now?'

His eyes rise to meet her own, and they look different. A calm sea under grey light. He props himself up against the sideboard and tries to stand, but he is barefoot and shackled and Kessler's blood slicks the floor. 'I was trying to protect you. From this. From … having to choose …' His breathing is pained, shallow. He sits back down. 'I wanted to tell you. You don't understand. But parole is the only way we all go home. The three of us. You, me, Maxime.'

She says, 'You've seen him though, haven't you? He's out there. And you knew?'

He nods, his eyes swell with a hint of regret. 'Once. Years ago. Across the spine.' He tries to sit up, but the movement causes him to wince. 'He was across the river, and it was through the binoculars … I had no inkling until then. I was shocked. I didn't know whether to call out and I just watched him. He looked well, healthy, and he walked down the bank, carrying wood, and he didn't even know I was there. It was just pure dumb luck that brought us both to the river that day. He on one side. Me on the other. And before I knew it, it was too late. He had gone off into the wood, and I had no flare or way to signal to him. But I went back, several times, trying to find a way to cross. I tried to send him messages, notes sent in bottles. I thought there had to be a way. But it was just a few seconds, and I began to doubt I'd even seen him at all.'

His confession pierces her like ice. 'He's alive. You're sure?'

'I don't know, Aina, it was seven years ago,' says Whitney. 'I never saw him again.'

'Why didn't you say anything? What were you thinking, Whitney? So many times, I've wondered if he was dead. Do you know how that feels?'

He tells her he knows exactly how it feels, that he wanted to tell her so badly, so many times. He shakes his head. 'You don't know how close I came. But I had to be sure. And then … I started to doubt, and deep down, I knew you'd choose him. You see? If you knew he was alive and knew how close he was, that you'd find a way, you'd go to him. And …' Whitney holds up his thumb. 'I knew this is where you'd end up. The closer we got to parole, the less it seemed worthwhile.'

'There is no parole, Whitney, you understand?'

'How can you be sure?'

'Kessler's list, his testimony, that's proof. They confirm everything. It's been twelve years and no one's coming. Max is out there alone.'

His eyes rise to the table. The gun. Beside it the pliers. He draws breath and holds it. 'Won't you wait? Sleep on it. Give it a day. Just to be sure.'

She glances at the pill clock. 'You've got twenty minutes.'

He looks at the ground. For the first time his fear seems undiluted by hostility or malice. 'Please, Aina. You're making a mistake. This is parole; it has to be. It's the only way we get to be together. We can all walk out of here …'

'Whitney. Stop.' She cannot listen to this any more. She takes the speargun; he lays sprawled before her.

'Aina … I never meant for this to happen. You know that?'

'I know.'

'Okay,' he nods. 'Okay.'

He does not fuss. He is done pleading. He seems a little relieved that she has made the decision for him. She points, and he closes his eyes, holds his breath, making a larger target of his chest.

38

Metronome

THE CROFT BELONGS to the wind now. It will come and rummage, popping tiles from the roof. A complicit wind, mining grit to bore holes in the stone walls. The guttering will creak and overflow, dampening the moss on the shaded northern walls. And the water will seep between cracks, freezing at night. The days will shorten. And each day the thaw will arrive later and later. 1 p.m. 2 p.m. Late afternoon. And before long, the sun will barely rise at all.

Freeze. Thaw. An accumulation of variance. Up-down, in-out, fast-slow. Days and months and years and hours, minutes, seconds, while things contract and protract, and the wind – Ana then Kata – inhales and exhales, chipping pneumatically at the rock, flattening the valley and the spine, and dissolving Whitney's body into the earth. He will leave a strange indent on the flagstone. And through it all, the pill clock will blink green at eight-hour intervals. Eternal, a meek glow in the fog.

Some semblance of her will remain too, walking among the complex algebra of chipped mugs and broken ceramics, the stumps of trees preserved in the peat and the contours of glass within the berm. A residue. An imprint. A stain. Evident in the close reading of particular flora. Evident, too, in certain oils trapped within ice.

The blood will dry between flagstones.

The world will breathe.

And the metronome ticks, clacks, back.

Yan tan tethera.

Yan tan tethera.

Yan tan tethera methera pip.

———

A black dot spreads across Whitney's chest. The harpoon is embedded below his collarbone, a rivet, pinning the fabric of his shirt to his flesh. The arrowhead protrudes from his back, scraping the wood, and his shoulder slumps lower. His eyes open wider, a glimmer. She lays the discharged speargun on the table beside the brace of spare harpoons, crouches beside him and takes his hand.

'You have enough of everything?'

She nods.

'Which way will you head?' he asks. 'East?'

She smiles, weakly, and rubs the back of his hand.

He closes his eyes. The pain must be excruciating. 'You'll run,' he says. 'Up the valley. Along the cliffs.'

He squeezes her hand and something seizes in his eyes. Love or regret. They no longer see distance, or time. A dulled sentimental aspect: it could be innocence, or the profusion of fallacy. His face assumes brittleness and cricks forward as the last of his breath empties away. She looks, not at his face, but at his hand. His thumb. She takes the pliers. And when she has finished, his hand falls limply upon his lap.

Rain overflows the gutter in coded dashes. She has the drybag almost packed. Oats. The patched-up inflatable raft and a slosh of kerosene, which she finds in the studio among Kessler's things. She takes also a long Yakutian knife from his belt. There are a few more things that she needs. Vital things.

She rolls Whitney's body on his side, uses the pliers to remove the harpoon and washes his blood off in the sink. Up the valley, the wind's dropping. Where will Ruth be now? It is almost eight hours since she left, a significant head start, but Aina knows the terrain and the child will be easy to track. She will be along the spine by now, halfway to the estuary. Beyond, the neighbouring croft. Maxime's croft. He is there, she thinks. Waiting for them both. She rubs her feet. Stretches. Massages her calves.

She takes Kessler's compass and holds it flat. The needle will not settle and she returns it to the bag; it may still be of some use. She rolls her colour-coded maps together with

Kessler's copy of the Census, and the sketches of Maxime. She collects fresh socks, some warm clothes and makes clogs of the waders. There is a little room left in the bag. She tests its weight. It will slow her down, but she is in good shape. She will manage.

The pill clock blinks. She has her pen and a semblance of a plan. It is almost time.

She draws the tie on the bag closed, and she stands, thinking of all the times she has approached the pill clock and presented her thumb. The whirr and the click. Three times a day for so many years. So many renderings of her, walking the beach and the moor and the oat field. She looks up at the sculptures. The back of the marsh. The beach. The boats dotted along the berm.

Kessler's body lies sprawled on the flagstones. His head among the ceramic fragments of bowl. A portrait of violence, the shard protruding from his neck. She closes his eyes. Places the pliers above the knuckle, whispers a short prayer and cuts.

Green, the sensor waits.

She places Whitney's thumb and then her own, and the pill clock releases two pills into the dispensary. She places one on her tongue, the other she places on the sideboard. Next, she places Kessler's thumb and a third pill is released. Finally she takes Tola's thumb, the rune on leather; she holds it up, but the sensor refuses. The thumb is too long decayed and any print is barely visible. Still, she has two pills. She clasps them in her hand, takes her pen from around her neck and stows them safely inside.

The pill clock turns from green to red, and she cleans the pliers on her shirt and seals the jar. Kessler's and Whitney's thumbs swirl and bump against the glass. She double-checks that she has screwed the barrel of her pen on tight and places it around her neck. Everything else goes in the drybag.

Outside, the sculpture on the back side of the marsh stands, unreadable, conveying anger or pride, she cannot tell. She has three harpoons, two pills, one speargun. The drybag clinks on her shoulder. It is 2:05 p.m. – she has a day to reach the neighbouring croft. She will find Maxime, Ruth and whatever else waits for her there. She will explain everything to them, and she prays that they will understand. She looks through the doorway, to the garden and the gate beyond. In the distance, the dark slopes of scree rise against anvils of cloud.

39

Pathways

AFTER EIGHT MILES THE rain lets up. Her feet in the clogs are bruised and nicked, but she is warm and moving freely. Her knees feel loose; the ground is soft from the rain, and the crosswinds are merciful coming off the headland. She is making good time.

She shelters briefly beside an abutment of rock on the lower reaches of the spine and sips water from a flask as she scans for signs of recent passage. Broken twigs, flattened grass. Glimpses of Ruth. The ground has been compacted by some kind of animal. A sheep maybe ... Except there are bones in the dirt. Feathers. The ribcage of a bird. And the tracks are not cloven as they would be from a trotter or a hoof, but petalled. A four-toed paw the size of her hand. A wolf, perhaps, or some other large beast. It might have been there for years.

She pauses, and she looks back – she cannot help herself. Hairlines of smoke rise from the croft, either from the chimney or the kiln. Whitney will still be up, she thinks, keeping the fire stoked. The thought breaks the logic of time. He will always be there, tied to the physical objects in space.

The wind blows and the broad table of moor glints with reflections of sky. She picks up the bag and goes on, whispering now to the children, Ruth and Maxime, telling them to wait, to stay put, that she is coming.

Yan tan tethera.

Yan tan tethera methera pip.

She breathes, and the air feels fresh. Washed.

On and up. Late afternoon, her shadow lengthens and she travels slower, buffeted by gusts, checking her progress against familiar landmarks. Three miles an hour. Then two. She is not as fit as she once was. She stumbles on, guided by the slope and the cairns that mark the way. Hands on wet rock, and as she climbs, the vegetation limpens, becoming infrequent on the scree. Snow lies undisturbed in sheltered crags. It is a tricky ascent. Her socks and the clogs offer protection from the rocks and the cold, but she cannot recall what it feels like to be dry, and the weather finds a way between everything. Legs chafe. Sweat chills in the small of her back, coarsening the fabric against her skin. Water collects on the end of her nose, to be carried off on gusts.

Up switchbacks, night comes late, and the wind billows holes in the cloud as she clambers slowly. The single track follows the ridge, becoming narrower and narrower, tapering to the width of her shoe. She has to go slower. On either side the rock drops away into darkness. Everything grey and black. A sense of precipice: one misstep and she will fall. Three miles of this; it is exhausting to be so exposed, but she is almost at the col.

The watch sends its pulse. 10 p.m. She unscrews the pen and takes the first pill. Sixteen hours to find them. She adjusts the straps on the headtorch, fitting it snugly to her head. The beam is white, flecked with mist, and she goes on, leeward, and it is easier now that she is out of the wind. Down through cloud, the ground is rocky and steep, and then the rocks give way to soil and the ground is soft with ferns. Forgotten fragrances: sandalwood, wet bark, detritus. She removes her socks and her shoes, and the slope carries her along, and she settles into a rhythm. Long sky. Charged earth. Warm fire.

The eastern flank is hidden in the dark, but she has an impression of a vast swathe of land. A gentle breeze moves through the grass. She tries to imagine how it would appear in daylight. A widening field of view, becoming wider as the shadow of the Earth comes down off the spine and the light gives definition to the vast expanse. Pale green and yellow. Verdant pockets. Across the marsh, to the estuary. A wide tidal river.

Descending, the land warms and the air warms also. And the headtorch picks out footprints half the size of her own. The sound of a river grows louder. She sees where Ruth's footprints enter the river, flat and sleek and wide. Half a mile of blackness. On the bank, she takes the raft from the drybag and pulls the toggle. Yellow rubber inflates. She should have given it to Ruth. She should have ... What was she thinking?

She wades out, clambers on to the raft and pushes off, using a piece of driftwood as a paddle. It is a relief to use her arms, a different kind of exertion, and it takes her ten, twenty, thirty minutes to cross. She hauls herself on to the bank. This is it. The furthest either she or Whitney has been from the croft. The point of no return. But her elation is short-lived. She scans the shore for footprints, some sign of Ruth, but the mudflats are pristine. Unbroken. Silver by the light of the torch. She looks back up the estuary, sees the dark silhouette of the distillery breaking the treeline. She must be a mile downstream from where she entered.

Her only hope is that Ruth crossed at the point of maximum low tide, when the currents would be at their weakest. She runs back up to the ruined distillery; there is no time to explore it now. She cuts into the forest. She cannot risk sleep. Not even for an hour. She must go on. Maxime is out there. And Ruth too. She will be sheltering in a nook of tree roots, or an abandoned backwoods cabin. Aina can see her sleeping, pictures herself standing over her and waking her with a gentle hand. *Ruth.* She will be cold from a night in the open, but there will be dried bannocks for breakfast and tea from the Thermos. And Ruth will ask about the Thermos, about how it works. And she will explain to her about insulation, and how it is possible to preserve heat. 'Certain materials are better conductors,' she will say. 'Some stay warmer for longer.'

Dawn approaches. Shades of sky from black to cerulean blue. She is hungry. Exhausted. Her throat … She slows to a jog and then a walk. The forest is vast. Here are the trees, the great pines, and she knows it cannot be far.

But the trees are different to those that she remembers in the park behind the high-rise. Here the bark is cracked: rectangular plates, peeling like old wallpaper. Nothing seeps. Nothing flows. The wood is a desert. And there is a fineness to the soil as though it has been sifted and drained and sifted again. Devoid of water. Becoming sand. No give. No spring. The pathway is a dark canyon in the wood, and this side of the river, the land is dry. No sign of people or sheep. Everything is brown and golden. And the air is thick with spores or pollen. Musk − like a shed where wood has been cut. It is thick. Bronchial.

In the distance, three or four miles away, she sees lights. A cabin. Not far. An hour, tops.

5:27 a.m. She has plenty of time.

She walks on, imagining hopeful little scenarios. She will find Ruth, any minute now, sleeping in a hammock, strung up between trees. Except, wait, no, she left the hammock behind. It does not matter. She will find her. She is almost there. She picks up a path. And she pictures the two of them emerging from the forest into a felled tract of land where a bird circles overhead, riding thermals higher and higher. A meadow of long grass where they will breakfast. And when the child asks her about the trees, she will tell her that they are a special type of pine, and they are in rows because that's how someone planted them, years ago.

Stay close, she will say. *Come on.*

The sound of wind, or waves. There will be cumulative signs of habitation. A ploughed field. An orchard. Soft fruit growing under nets. Everything indicative of tending, measuring and mending. The marks of an ordered mind. And when they come upon a gate, she will halt, and beyond, they will see a ram tethered in the garden.

What's that? Ruth will ask. A strand of hair blows across her face. *Should we go around?*

And if she is to look at Aina then, the child might intuit some sense of her disquiet. But before either of them can speak, the watch on Aina's wrist beeps. The morning alarm. Kinetic. She fumbles it quiet and the wind chuckles away through the trees. Trouser legs flap and cavort on the washing line. They have been fastened with homemade pegs.

A man appears at the door to the shed. He removes a pair of woodsman's gloves. The man steps closer, ducking between the washing. He looks like Whitney. Oh God he looks like Whitney, except younger. His arms are flecked with sawdust and he carries an axe or a mattock. He holds it loosely by the handle, and now he sees Aina and he sees that she carries a speargun, and he adjusts his grip, bringing the axe or the mattock up across his body. Knuckles whitening.

Maxime? Maxime, wait.

The young man stops.

In the corner of the garden, the ram chews on grass. It looks up. Snorts and resettles. The breeze tickles the bones of a windchime on the porch.

I'm your mother.

To be able to say that. For it to be true. She takes the speargun from her shoulder, leans it against the fence, and she says aloud, 'I am your mother.'

Maxime's eyes narrow. His elbows drop. The mattock is lowered.

Mama?

The tops of the pines bend and release and the washing flaps louder in gusts. She steps forward, curious, uncertain. The ground is soft and then it is solid, metal.

CLACK.

The sound is something mechanical. And it is followed by a secondary click and the whistle of something being loosed.

The impact is noiseless. Breath. Vision. Sound. Sensations cease, obliterated by a white space that engulfs her. And it is impossible to immediately discern the cause. Aina has fallen. She is on the ground and she must have tripped over a root, or stood upon glass, and something is very wrong indeed. Her leg, her leg. The flood of everything pours up from between her shin and her knee. An aftershock as raw as the first incision. And she looks down and there is some kind of contraption fixed on her leg and she cannot make sense of anything; the pain is too great and she must look skyward. And she glimpses Maxime, by the gate, and she longs to return to the dream. And the pain becomes absolute, eradicating in its breadth, and she can only transpose it into something audible. Not a scream. But the inhalation of a scream. Swallowed. Gulped. She grits her teeth. *GNNNNNNNNNNNNN.* A mess of taut spittle. Fibres. Frayed. Hands like talons clawing at the dry earth. Dirt beneath her nails. White sky above treetops. She gathers herself. Musters the will to look.

Oh God

Oh God

The sunlight picks out motes and it picks out the rusted manacle that bites her leg. The blunt serrated jaws of the thing. It has closed on her leg beneath the knee. It bites sideways, and there is no way she can stand now, let alone walk.

40

Tree

THERE IS NO CROFT. No Maxime. No Ruth. She is alone. The path is clear. A wide, straight path. Overgrown, but used. An old track used initially by loggers or sheep, until something drove them out. She is alone and she was not looking where she put her feet. And she is trapped now. She scrapes away at the dirt.

Yan tan tethera.

Yan tan tethera methera pip.

Breathe.

She fills her lungs and she screams and it all comes riding out. The pain. The effort.

'RUUUUUUUUTH!'

She calls until her voice is hoarse. Nothing – but the cabin cannot be far. Ruth will have known better than to stay on the path. Wind rustles the foliage. A hot dry forest. Breathe. Stay calm. The watch on her wrist. 5:31 a.m.

She scrabbles in the dirt for the drybag. Tries to prise open the jaws of the trap using sticks and harpoons, but she only succeeds in bending the shafts of the spears and making kindling of the wood. Blood seeps through her jeans. Puddles with the soil, turning it a sticky, rich caramel. She is pincered. The contraption is iron or steel, a sizeable piece, part-buried in the earth. Not so heavy that she cannot move, but it must be spring-loaded, and when she shifts her weight, it threatens to ratchet another notch closed. If she could just wriggle free, or move her foot, but it is hopeless. So she digs and digs. Gradually, the trap comes free of the earth and she keeps pulling and pulling and then tugging. And something is caught. And she sees the chain leading from the trap, noosed around the trunk of a mature pine. She yanks and pulls and gathers her breath. The trunk is three feet wide, sixty tall.

The pain in her leg subsides under numbness or shock. She unwraps her binding and her ankle is shattered. The foot is indigo, swollen and disjointed. If she lives she will lose it. That is the best she can hope for now.

She hears Whitney admonishing her. Taking her to task for all her risks. *Look at you now*, he says. *I warned you, didn't I.*

She yanks again. Checks the chain for weak spots. Nothing.

Think.

Kessler's knife. She takes it from the drybag and draws it from the sheath. It is a considerable task, but he has looked after the blade, and if she could just … the bark comes away with ease. And the only other option is to amputate her leg, but if she did that she might pass out, and there surely is not time. She starts cutting at the trunk. Sawing. Splintering. Making a smiling groove in the wood. She runs calculations, projections. An inch every five minutes, at this rate she will be through the trunk in three hours. The cabin cannot be far. A quarter of a mile? She checks Kessler's map, and goes on chipping ferociously, using the knife in one hand and a harpoon in the other. If she can topple the tree, she could carry the trap with her.

At 6 a.m., she takes the second and final pill. There is no ceremony to it. She puts it between her molars and bites down. There will be another, she thinks. There has to be. This will not be her last. She stabs at the wood. Saws. And she does not care for her leg now. The pain is no more. The wood is soft in places and it splinters easily. She cuts, making wider the cut, and she goes on for an hour, two, on her knees, and her progress slows. Ten minutes for every inch now. Fifteen. Back and forth, her hands are bloody and blistered and the air is warmer. Sun shines through the trees. The smells of dawn. Ancient plants. A fragrant stirring of moss. Her arm aches. Her elbow, if she could only stretch out and lie down. It is so peaceful here. The soil, so inviting. She could just take a minute. Eat something …

No.

She discards her coat and jumper. The sun warms her face. Energising warmth. She finishes her water, rips her jeans to the knee. The air soothes. She goes again. And she talks to herself as she works. 'Long sky. Charged earth. Warm fire.' The sun rises above the trees, illuminating the spine in the west. The sky is so blue. She has not seen one like it in years.

Her heart is racing.

Her leg is black.

Long sky. Charged earth. Warm fire.

Warm fire.

11:45 a.m. The cut is a wide gash. She sharpens the knife, eats a handful of oats. If only she could stop time, find some form of stasis where she could track back and forth, perpetually, like a metronome or light rebounding between mirrors. She could live in hope, knowing Ruth is out there, somewhere, with Maxime. Maxime … 11:46 a.m. She harries on. Filings pile at the base of the ravaged trunk. Soft, pale against the dirt. She tries pulling on the trunk, the chain, it is no use. Her arm is lead. Her fingers cramp, knuckles seize. She rubs them. Tries to get the blood flowing, but she cannot get warm. She stands, hops awkwardly. She no longer cares about keeping the weight off her leg. Cold, shivering despite the sun, she digs on, convinced there is time, though two of the harpoons are nubs and useless now. She goes again with the third, stabbing at the wood. Sawdust sticks to her arm, to her face. There is progress. She tries a new grip. Switches the knife and the harpoon between hands. The harpoon is blunted and the handle snaps off the knife and she just has the blade now. Cutting into her palms. And the sun beats down on her, filtering through the trees, casting her shadow shorter and shorter.

She has until 2 p.m.

This is it.

Less than an hour remains.

She takes the kerosene and empties it against the trunk. One match. The smoke will carry across the sky, and Ruth will be watching for her. She will have found Maxime, and together they will be watching for a sign. There is time. She must hurry. The fire will burn the tree to cinder, and she will topple the trunk and drag herself free.

She pulls the chain taut. Backs up as far as the chain permits. Yan tan tethera methera— She sparks the match and the kerosene whumps, sending flames up the trunk. The heat is something else.

1:33 p.m. Maxime will be making lunch. Please, let him look from the window, see the smoke, smell carbon on the wind. Come on, come on! The wind arrows up the track, a westerly, feeding the flame, and the wood, the forest, everything it touches is kindling. The sawdust withers and the bark pops, and the next tree over is alight. The pale white core of the flame will turn the sand to glass. She tugs and hoiks and pulls but the chain is a cold anchor and the trunk steadfast. Flames hiss and whisper, and she cannot get too close. It is unbearable. The tree burns, a flaming pinnacle, the centre point for all the shadow in the world. Oh, God. This will be her imprint. And the wind is coming too. The flames have crossed the track. Stinging, sweat and blisters. Let them see this beacon. Let them see it, else the whole forest will burn and the cabin too, and – God, what has she done? She will become an effigy. A witch among elm, ash and oak. A ghost of time, waiting—

The wind blows the candle and the trunk sways, a flaming hour hand, counting back from midday:

Twelve.

Eleven.

Ten.

Toppling faster, the timber splinters and cracks. And the ground shakes on impact. Sparks scatter. She coughs. Spores of pollen and dust sear her lungs; another branch falls.

She holds her breath, exhales.

A voice whispers in her ear. A voice? She squints down the track. Shadows dance across light. Movement. The voice is louder. A clattering melody, shouting:

Aina, we're coming!

Mama! Hang on!

Her heart surges. An instantaneous expanse of possibility opens. They are coming. Ruth steps forward, aged eleven. Aged twelve. Orange as everything else. Her little hand reaches out, silhouetted against flame. She can almost reach her. And behind Ruth, Maxime. Taller, a man now. Maxime – his hand is warm, firm. His fingers clasp. Maxime. Maxime … She tightens her grip. Maxime. He has come. The child is alive. She is home.

ACKNOWLEDGEMENTS

Thank you to Karolina Sutton, Caitlyn Leydon and everyone at Curtis Brown. To my wonderful editor, Emma Herdman, and Greg Heinimann, Lauren Whybrow, Lilidh Kendrick, Ros Ellis, Ella Harold, Amy Donegan, Lindeth Vasey, Joe Hall and the whole Bloomsbury team who made this possible.

To my writing buddies, Gemma Reeves, Keith John Lewis, Megan Davis, Naomi Ishiguro, Kelleigh Greenberg-Jephcott, Campaspe Lloyd-Jacob, Sophie Kirkwood, Richard O'Halloran, Elizabeth Macneal, Emily Ruth Ford, and to Senica Maltese, Tim MacGabhann and Yeo Wei Wei who read early drafts. To the lovely people at Brixton Book Jam, the Bridport Prize, the Bristol Short Story Prize and the Seán O'Faoláin Prize, and everyone at UEA for their support and generosity, particularly Philip Langeskov, Jean McNeil, Giles Foden, Henry Sutton, Laura Joyce, Andrew Cowan and Joe Dunthorne.

Special thanks to the following friends: Ciarán, Gwen, Dori, Andrew, Eleni, Pete, Chris H, Tan, Rob M, Zara, Dave, Tim H, Gaika, Jamie, Rich, Steve, Mike & Em. Kwhame, Tonya, Harry, Alan, Simo, Deak, Ruby and Tobes, Olivia, Matt C, Daniel, John & Chris. Tim V, Dylan, Susan, Matt M, Nick & Eri, Brian S, Keala, Claudia, Rob B, Sean and Paul.

And to the Kanetskys: Setsuko & Al, Mike & Cheryl, Cathy & Eric, Tanya & Tom, Nancy & Brian, and the Satos, Omuras and Kobayashis. To my dad. To the Baileys, Overhills and Jacksons, especially my grandma, Eithne, and my grandad, Ron. And to Jim, Helen, Lewis & Louise, Olly & Kate, Margaux, Naomi, my mum, Christina, and to Jen, for your love and support every step of the way, thank you.

ABOUT THE AUTHOR

TOM WATSON is a graduate of the Creative Writing MA at the University of East Anglia, where he was the recipient of the Curtis Brown Prize in memory of Giles Gordon. His debut novel, *Metronome*, was shortlisted for the Bridport Prize, and his short fiction has been shortlisted for the Bristol Short Story Prize and awarded runner-up for the Seán Ó Faoláin Prize. He lives in London.

A NOTE ON THE TYPE

The text of this book is set in Bell. Originally cut for John Bell in 1788, this typeface was used in Bell's newspaper, *The Oracle*. It was regarded as the first English Modern typeface. This version was designed by Monotype in 1932.